ON A DIME

A Novel: Senseless in Lewes

ON
A DIME
Senseless in Lewes

REVERE REED

The events and characters in this book are fictitious. Some real locations are mentioned for authenticity, but even then the details are imaginary.

ISBN-13: 978-1475009927
ISBN-10: 1475009925

Additional copies can be purchased via:
(1) CreateSpace.com/3820807
(2) Amazon.com
(3) Select stores in Delaware

For Carolyn,
who encouraged and supported me
every step of the way.
We're an awesome team!

Acknowledgments

To the Rehoboth Art League Writers' Group for providing a forum for making better writers out of all who are fortunate enough to attend their meetings. I am especially grateful to the four who have been at the core of the group during my years there: Liz Dolan, Sherry Chappelle, Gary Hanna, and Linda Blaskey. Their knowledge, literary accomplishments, and enthusiasm for writing are inspirational.

To my early readers - Amy Jane Reed Parker, Sharon Markle, and Charlie Siegmann - thank you for your help, interest, and most of all your encouragement.

To Bonnie Hudson for her help with the escheatment process.

To Ashlee Reed Hidell and Tim Hidell for their feedback on my cover.

To novelist Ed Dee who generously agreed to lend his expertise to a stranger's efforts. His insights helped me improve my story in many ways, and his kind words persuaded me to keep working on telling it.

To Maribeth Fischer author and founder of the Rehoboth Beach Writers' Guild. Her Pure Sea Glass Festivals and classes helped me through a major rewrite and enabled me to pop my novel out of my laptop and onto some bookshelves and e-readers.

To Sue Frederick who helped me with "final" line-editing. Any remaining errors are due to my last minute tinkering.

To the readers who have gotten this far. Please keep reading, and do not blame any of my friends above for shortcomings found herein, they are mine alone.

Part 1 - August 2

1 – Tuesday 5:58 a.m.

Unable to sleep, Mars sat at his computer in the corner of the bedroom searching his project records for something out of whack, for some thread that he could follow back to the embezzler. Anxiety had forced him from his bed hours ago. He needed to find a lead that he could give to the Secret Service when he met with them later in the morning.

He had been called into work for an emergency meeting early on Sunday, less than forty-eight hours ago. When he entered Lightship Bank and Trust's parking lot and spotted their CEO's limousine, he had known that it was something big – maybe a merger or another dreaded acquisition.

It had been neither. Instead Mars, and the handful of other attendees, had been informed that money had disappeared from his accounts - not his personal ones, but from dormant ones in the Deposit Account System that he managed. Nearly a half million dollars had been stolen by someone who understood the checks and balances of the system. It definitely looked like an inside job.

Anxious to clear his eleven team members - and himself - he had been on edge ever since. So far nothing suspicious had popped up. Based on dormant account reports that had been reviewed at that Sunday meeting, Mars knew that the funds had still been intact at the end of June.

He had scoured all of the processes that had run since then. Mars had also scanned each of the changes his team had made to his DAS system in the past month. Nothing out of the ordinary had popped up.

On a hunch, he went back to his folder from the big conversion project that his team had completed over the Fourth of July three-day weekend. Ten minutes later an e-mail had his full attention. It caught his eye because it was from him, but he had no memory of the subject, "Emergency Override Needed!" It had been sent at 22:38 on Friday, July first.

Mars's heart beat wildly knowing that the mail had been forged. He knew exactly where he had been then; he had not been working. With his crab cake dinner churning sourly in his stomach, and trembling fingers, he clicked the mail open. A groan escaped as he read.

He turned to make sure that he had not woken his wife. Only a dozen feet away, Sally was still snoozing under a light cotton blanket with one leg partially exposed.

His eyes flew back to his laptop. He read on.

Even as a cool salty sea breeze wafted through the front windows, Mars felt his skin flush. Sweat dampened his tee shirt.

The mail requested a last minute modification to read an unfamiliar test file into a job that had been used to reformat their master file of customer accounts. Mars massaged his temples, as he tried to come up with an alternate conclusion to what seemed obvious; his team had converted almost a million of the bank's checking and savings accounts using bogus data. There was no doubt in his mind that the input data had been manipulated to move the money, and worse yet, he had been framed for it.

He leaned back in his ergonomic chair feeling anything but comfortable. Staring blindly at his screen, the offending mail blurred as he thought about the only person that could have accessed his logon at that time - Sofia.

Clammy and nauseous, Mars wiped a bead of sweat from his forehead. He raked his hands through his already rumpled hair. His heart flip-flopped as crab rose with acid in his throat. Afraid that he was about to vomit, he eyed the trash can beside his desk. He recalled the heart attack that his grandfather had barely survived and the bypass surgery that had saved his father. He wondered if he would be as lucky, or if he would die sitting here at his desk with the incriminating request still on his monitor.

Mars closed the mail, slumped forward in his chair, and dropped his head between his knees. He ticked off the symptoms of a heart attack. He wasn't sure if his left arm actually ached or if he was imagining it. *Maybe it's just a panic attack.* He considered calling 911, but before he removed the phone from its holster his thoughts rushed back to Sofia and what she had done.

He assumed that she had simply edited the file to transfer the money between dormant accounts such that the conversion totals would still reconcile. Then, after that conversion weekend, she would have withdrawn it. The $492,374 was probably safely sitting in a numbered account on some tropical island and if she was smart - and it appeared that she was - she was sitting there too sipping a Piña Colada or a nice rum punch.

She had suckered him with a low blow - *literally,* he thought without amusement. Her tidy audit trail pointed directly at him. It appeared to be the perfect frame job. Any attempt to prove his innocence, to save himself from jail, would jeopardize his family, and, even then, it would be a classic case of he said, she said.

She was playing you the whole time. You idiot! She stole the money and left you on the hook.

2   - 6:03 a.m.

Mars sat at his desk with his head and his life spinning out of control like a top in the process of keeling over. Shivering from the breeze on his damp skin, he stood on unsteady legs to shut the window. The sun peeked over the bay. The sight of it drew him out to the beachfront deck.

He continued onto the wooden walkway that hovered over his sandy backyard, out towards the orange ball peeking over the horizon. He stopped at the dune line and watched as it painted the fluffy gray clouds in amazing shades of pink and purple. Pastel reflections danced on the distant waves as they rolled silently towards the beach spreading the first light of morning on the dark, damp sand.

Growing up, Mars had spent his summers here in Lewes with his paternal grandparents in their cottage - now his home - overlooking the Delaware Bay. As he sat on the weathered bench, his mind drifted back to those simpler days. He ran his hand over the old copper box that still housed the telescope that he and his "Gramps" had used on most clear nights.

He smiled as he remembered the morning after his grandfather introduced him to astronomy. It had been his first full summer there. His grandmother had fixed eggs and fried the fish "her boys" had caught only hours before in the rain that still dripped off the roof as they ate on the screened porch. Eight-year-old Mars was tired from staying up half the night viewing constellations. Falling asleep at the table, he was awakened by his grandmother reprimanding his grandfather for not letting Mars get the rest that growing boys need. His grandfather had, uncharacteristically, not responded.

"Marshall," she had repeated more sternly this time.

"Sorry, dear, I thought you were talking to your grandson," his granddad had said with a wink.

Determined to eliminate the confusion and aware that her boys now shared a fascination with the night sky, she had decided that Marshall Hamilton Stewart III would, from that point forth, be known as Mars.

There had been a second wink, for his grandson's eyes only, when neither of them confessed that they had not viewed the red planet. The nickname stuck.

Mars had thought that the next decade of Gramps's life lessons had also stuck. Now he knew that they had not. He had not learned the main one. He had been reckless. If he had only stopped to look at all he was risking for the people he loved most. Even without knowing that his job and his freedom would be on the line, surely he would have stopped Sofia - stopped himself.

A month had passed since that steamy night. He had thought that he had miraculously gotten away with it. Like the time in his senior year of high school when he and some classmates had stolen a couple of two-by-fours that they needed for their homecoming float. Mars had barely slept for weeks and was waiting for the police to arrive for months, but nothing had changed.

Obviously, this time would be different.

A line of brown pelicans flew parallel to the row of houses, almost skimming the cresting waves, searching for their breakfast. It was tempting to sit there watching them, contemplating how many ways he had screwed up, but Mars knew he needed to do something.

Once when he and Sally had seen a "What would Jesus do?" bracelet, she had suggested that Mars get a "What Would Gramps Do?" one, but they had agreed it was not necessary. Mars did not need a rubber wristband to remind him to make his deceased grandfather proud.

He remembered his mentor beside him on the golf course in his signature tan Kangol cap - Payne Stewart Ivy style - studying a ball nestled deep in the leaves, right between two twigs. There was no way to get a clean shot. "There are no mulligans in life, Mars. No do-overs. Rule thirteen is you have to play the ball as it lies. Forget how you got here. Focus on how to get yourself back in position. One shot at a time."

Mars desperately wanted to do just that, but he had no idea how - or even if - he could. He shut his eyes and let the rising sun calm his mind. He and his grandfather had risen early each summer morning, and whether they were on the beach fishing or heading to the golf course, no dawn went unnoticed. He visualized his grandfather making the first cast of the day, his line zinging off the reel as a flying sinker pulled it out beyond the swells. He could see him turn and declare, "It's a new day, Mars. Anything is possible."

Back then it had meant that they might catch a huge fish or maybe make a hole-in-one. Mars had grown up believing it was true.

He opened his eyes. The sun emerged from a thin

gray cloud. A golden wedge of water rippled towards the shorebirds that ran stiff-legged in the wet sand, playing tag with the waves.

It's a new day.

Mars forced himself to concentrate, to formulate a plan. His first instinct was to rush back in and delete the mail, but he knew that was pointless, and may incriminate him further. His torso broke into a sweat again as he thought of the phony file-override request already securely stored in the bank's archives. Even if the Secret Service agents didn't look there, Sofia had copied several co-workers, and the agents had backed up his team's hard drives on Sunday. It was definitely just a matter of time before someone would find it. When they did, they would come for him.

Suddenly Mars knew that he had to go to Wilmington. He had to confront Sofia. He prayed that she was still there, not enjoying some sunny paradise as he feared. He didn't know how he was going to pull it off, but he resolved not to let her destroy his world - and Sally's, Peter's and Beck's.

He rushed back into the house. In the hallway closet he found a small backpack. He took it into the master bath, stealthily shut the door, and turned on the light. He was instantly mesmerized by the fool in the mirror.

He watched as his blue eyes morphed into a vision of Sofia's brown eyes coaxing him into her arms. It was one of many smoldering memories from that night that he had enjoyed - and had been haunted by - a hundred times in the past month.

He saw his own tired eyes again. "Anything's possible," he whispered willing himself to believe it as he threw blood pressure pills and a toothbrush into his backpack.

At his dresser, he slid the top drawer open. Feeling

the scrape of wood on wood echo in his brain, he looked again to see if Sally was still sleeping. She was. He pulled boxers out and shut the drawer. He picked up his wallet, and silenced the jingle of his keys as he stuffed them in his pocket. He grabbed some clothes from the closet then knelt on the cool wood floor, rolled them up, and slid them into the backpack. He returned to his desk.

Five minutes later Mars logged off and packed up his laptop. He was ready to go except for one thing - Sally. She had tucked her leg back under the covers which rose and fell with each of her deep breaths. Her blond hair fanned over her pillow and softly caressed her tanned shapely shoulder.

Mars knew that if she ever found out that he had betrayed her and their vows, he might never see her as peaceful again. He wanted to reach out to her, to feel her warm embrace, and hear her comforting words. He wanted to assure her that - somehow - he would make things right again, but he knew his emotions were too raw. He could not risk saying anything for fear that he would tell all.

He jotted a note explaining that he had uncovered a plot to frame him for the embezzlement and that he had gone to find and confront whoever had done it. He let her know that he was going to call work and say that his aunt had died. He would take the four death-benefit days and would return on Monday. Mars suggested that Sally tell the kids the same thing. They could straighten it all out later.

As he wrote the last word, Mars wondered if there would be a "later" for them. If Sofia refused to confess, he would go to jail. The e-mail had been written under his logon; he would be held responsible. He had no idea how much time he could get for felony embezzlement. He wondered if Sally would be waiting for him when he got out, if she and the kids could ever forgive him.

Mars placed the note on the bedside table. Tears welled up as he silently apologized. He brushed them away then leaned down and kissed his wife's warm soft cheek. He lingered and inhaled her scent deep into his lungs, as if he could store it there for the hard times.

3 - 6:42 a.m.

As he pulled away in his silver Ford Edge, he stopped in the driveway and looked at his house in the rear view mirror. He and Sally had been careful to retain the vintage charm when they remodeled his grandparents' cottage. It was a great house and the only home he had ever really known. Mars wondered if he would be welcome there again.

He was more disappointed in himself than he had ever been. This was a much bigger breach of the rules than stealing a few boards. He wouldn't blame Sally if she threw him out. He didn't deserve her. Maybe because his own family had been so dysfunctional in his childhood, Mars had never wavered in his commitment to make a safe and happy life for his family.

The insane night with Sofia a month ago had scared Mars into being even more certain than ever that he wanted until-death-do-us-part with Sally. He wanted them to nurture their children and later their grandchildren together. He wanted forever.

Now his dream - their dream - lay in shambles. He

had ruined everything.

As he turned left on Cedar Avenue, he opened his moonroof, letting the morning light along with the distinctive smells of marsh mud infiltrate his car. He hardly noticed. His mind was on Sally. He worried what this was going to do to her and the kids.

Nightmarish thoughts of what he might be asked under oath, of him on the stand squirming - like Bill Clinton had years ago - flashed in his mind. Hillary Rodham stood by her man.

Mars was pretty sure Sally would be more like Elin Woods. He could easily be headed for a freefall like Tiger's. Maybe he'd be able to employ Clinton's it-depends-on-what-is-is argument, but - if what happened with Sofia ever came out - it was easier to visualize some misused golf clubs in his future.

He was not a womanizer, but it looked like his one misstep was going to do him in. Guilt, fear and acid rose in his throat.

If it would make things better he would confess it all to his wife. In some ways it seemed the honorable thing to do, but he was just self-assured enough to believe that the truth would destroy her. Maybe Sally deserved to know and maybe someday he would tell her, but he could never let it become public knowledge. Mars had to find a way to keep his secret.

He turned right on Savannah Road. There were a few four-wheel-drive trucks and SUV's heading east. Fishing rods were mounted vertically on their front bumpers. Ordinarily, Mars would have had pangs of jealousy - they were going surf-fishing, and he was not - but today he was busy recalling one of his and Sally's routines.

"How much do you love me?" was his line.

"More than," she would say pausing dramatically before adding "dark chocolate." Her eyes would dance with happiness. She had what she always wanted; she had Mars.

Sally was the kid sister of his childhood friend, and from the time she had developed an interest in boys, she was only interested in one - Mars. She made no secret about it, but he did not take her seriously then. He was fifteen and a half - only minutes it seemed from having his driver's license - and she was barely a teenager. Besides, everyone knew that Mars had a crush of his own.

Mars had been crazy about one girl from the first time he saw her in her father's delicatessen. He had been fourteen then. It took him a year and at least a hundred of Ignazio's Italian subs to get up the nerve to ask her out. When he finally did - with her father watching over her shoulder - she told Mars that she couldn't go. She told him she already had a boyfriend.

Mars had been dejected, maybe even depressed, but he had not given up. When Mars was twenty, just before she had disappeared from his life, they had one night together. It had been more fantastic than Mars's best fantasies, but in the end it hadn't mattered. She married the boyfriend.

End of story, except it broke Mars's heart. It had taken a decade for his wounds to fully heal. He had dated, always searching for the woman that would make him feel what he had felt for the girl that got away - that innate, gut-wrenching, soulful kind of love. He never found it.

Instead, in his late twenties, desperately wanting to start a family - Mars had convinced himself that the girl he still longed for was just a crush gone wild. He decided that all-consuming love like that did not really exist; he concluded that it was - as Davy Jones and the Monkees sang - a fairy tale. He was not a believer.

He made a decision to move on with his life. He and Sally had been steadily dating for years. He knew that she loved him, and once he gave up on the fairy tale he realized that he had grown to love her. She was a beautiful, compassionate woman. They were good together, and he began to see that she was perfect for him.

When he was twenty-eight he proposed. Six months later they had a huge wedding.

Their twenty-plus-year marriage had been - fairy tales aside - everything that Mars wanted. It was not raw all-consuming, earth-shattering love. Instead, the love and life he shared with Sally was soothing and wonderfully fulfilling. Mars knew he was blessed to have Sally and their two children, Peter and Rebecca.

As he drove out of Lewes headed north, Mars wondered how in the world he had let Sofia get to him. How could he have been so reckless?

He felt his grandfather's disappointed eyes.

Part 2 – One Month Earlier

4 – Sunday 7:15 a.m.

Mars loaded the last of the suitcases in the back of the Suburban. The Boogie Boards, Windsurfer, and beach chairs were strapped on the roof racks. The other gear needed for a week in Corolla, North Carolina was stowed inside.

They were packed for the annual Morgan family vacation. Sally's parents had taken her and her brother to the Outer Banks each summer during their high school years. The tradition had continued through college and each year since with the group now expanded to include spouses and grandchildren.

Unfortunately, this year Mars would not be joining them. It would be his first absence since marrying into Sally's family. He regretted it, but he had no choice. The conversion of his Deposit Account System was scheduled for the following Friday, the Fourth of July.

It seemed like horrible planning, but the bank scheduled most high-risk-project installations on holiday weekends in order to have an extra day to recover in case there were any critical problems. The changes could not wait until the next long weekend - Labor Day - so Mars was stuck at home alone.

The schedule had been set since the beginning of the year, so his family had gotten used to the idea that he was not able to go with them. But now that the time had come, it was difficult. His daughter Rebecca was particularly sad.

She was a "fish" and so was he; they body surfed, boogie boarded, played wreck-a-shore, and just hung out in the ocean for hours every day. His son Peter and Sally joined them sometimes, but it was Beck that liked to play in the ocean like he did. At twelve, she was at an age where he knew that he was missing some precious father-daughter bonding time.

Beck gave him one last clingy hug. A solitary tear rolled down her cheeks. "I wish you were coming, Dad." Her pathetic plea caused her dad's heart to ache.

"You know I wish I could too, Beck, but I have to stay home and make some money. You'll have fun with your cousins." He gave her an extra squeeze, "Remember to help your mom."

"I will." She released her hold on him and scrambled into the front passenger seat calling "Shotgun!" to her brother.

"Cool, I've got the whole back to myself," Peter replied as if that was where he really wanted to sit. "See ya," he mumbled as he offered his father a half-hearted hug.

Mars had made hugs mandatory with his children; his own parents had given him too few. At fifteen Peter seemed to think they were child like, not manly, but he complied before climbing into the back, where he was already inserting the MP3 headphones in his ears. He was in a mood. He had wanted to stay home with his dad and work the busy weekend at his lifeguarding job at Cape Henlopen, but Sally and Mars had been in agreement; family time had priority.

Mars motioned for Peter to remove his headphones. When he did, Mars instructed him, "Watch your sister and your cousins in the ocean, and nobody swims if there are rip currents." No reply. "Understood?"

"Yeah, no problem," his son said making brief eye contact as he reinserted his ear pieces.

Mars met Sally at the front door and walked her to the driver's door. They embraced, and she gave him an unexpectedly long kiss before getting behind the wheel. "I'll miss you," he said through the open window.

This was going to be the longest separation of their marriage. Neither of them was looking forward to it. They had awoken before dawn, and had enjoyed Sunday-only-sex. SOS had started as a joke between them over a decade ago when they had been the tired parents of two toddlers. It had become a cherished routine.

"We'll miss you, too. I'll call you when we get in." Sally put the car in gear, looked up and added, "Good luck with your project. I love you."

"Love you too, babe."

Mars waved until they were out of sight then went inside, got a cup of coffee, and the bag with the last of the pastries. He had made an early morning Lewes Bake Shoppe run to ease the pain of the goodbyes. Peter and Beck had eaten all of the "Ooey Gooeys" as if they were their last meal, but there were two pastries left: a yeast doughnut covered in granulated sugar that had him salivating, and a filled one that seemed to have Beck's fingerprint in the blackberry jam.

He took the coffee and bag out to the beach and sat in one of the yellow Adirondack style chairs on a small platform deck on the dune line. It was a beautiful morning; the sky was blue, and the humidity was unusually low. The sun had not yet begun to overheat the strong breeze that was blowing off of the bay. It was cool enough that Mars was still comfortable in the thin sweatshirt that he had thrown on before sunrise. It felt more like Memorial Day weekend than the end of June.

Mars leaned back and thought how unusual the week was going to be. He had not been home alone for a single night since they had gotten married. He had been on business trips and on an occasional golf trip with the boys, but he had never been here without his family.

He had a whole week to himself. Unfortunately, it was not going to be very relaxing due to the big project, but that would not start in earnest until Friday, five full days from now. He would be working all week, but he was free today and would be on his own in the evenings. He was definitely going to miss his Sally and the kids, but there was something appealing about having some alone time.

What to do, what to do? Mars let the airy dough melt in his mouth as he contemplated his many options. Most of the choices that came to mind involved some of his favorite pastimes: surfing, sailing, bike riding, or swimming.

Or he could visit with some of his buddies that still lived in Lewes, but once they found out that he was home alone, they were likely to try to convince Mars to hook up for some nightlife in Dewey Beach. The bars would be teeming with college kids – lots of girls – and Mars really was not up for that scene. Some of his friends acted like they were still frat boys even though they too were married with children. Most of their shenanigans were harmless, but Mars had no interest in joining them.

The more he thought about it, the more attractive just hanging out at home became. He had been working some overtime getting the conversion process ready to install - the normal crunch time before the end of a project. He was tired.

He tilted his face up to absorb the sunrays, and thought about the project. It was in good shape. He had a few loose ends to tie up during the week. Then Friday morning they would meet to review and finalize the official implementation, and of course he would have to be on-site Friday night into the wee hours of Saturday morning when the actual conversion was going to take place.

It should be smooth sailing until then.

5   - Friday 8:58 a.m.

Mars waited in the windowless room for the team to assemble to review the installation task list one last time. It was a conference call meeting; most of the participants were at other locations. Banksall Software Inc., the vendor for the Deposit Account System that was undergoing a conversion, was sending a representative to be on-site to monitor the process and to mitigate the risks. Mars was expecting him any minute.

Truth be known, the Banksall manager was coming down from Wilmington largely to pacify upper management. Mars and his team had the project well under control, but he was perfectly content to let the vendor share the responsibility; they were paid handsomely to do so.

Mars dialed into the conference call, and was waiting patiently when Sofia Pitasi breezed in and introduced herself.

"Sorry we weren't able to give you any notice, Marshall, but we had a last minute scheduling conflict. My boss couldn't make it." Her eyes probed his as she added, "Not to worry, you're in good hands."

When her words registered, Mars realized that he was still holding her warm soft hand in his. His face flushed like a school boy as he quickly let go. He had not met Sofia Pitasi before, but he knew that she was one of Banksall's systems analysts. They had spoken by phone many times.

Her throaty, sultry voice had always conjured up an image of Susanne Pleshette, and now that he met her she wasn't far off, but there was some Loren in this Sofia. She was probably close to his age – fifty – fairly tall, fit, and good looking. Her dark-hair was cut short, which accentuated her high olive-skinned cheekbones.

When her brown eyes lingered on his, he felt as if he had just dropped over the edge of the highest climb of the Jolly Roger roller coaster. He was still in a free-fall when the meeting began.

Sofia reported the status of Banksall's assigned tasks. Mars studied her between glances at his paperwork. Even when his head was down, her spicy perfume filled the sterile conference room, distracting him further from the conversion project's plans.

Everything was on track. The most recent DAS system upgrade was being installed. It required that the master file - containing all of the Lightship Bank and Trust's checking and savings accounts - be converted to add some new fields. They had been through many similar projects; it had become routine, but they all understood that Fourth of July weekend was no time to screw up. Customers would be hitting the ATMs hard all weekend, and any disruption in access to funds would not go unnoticed.

The conversion of the master file would begin after the last of the branches closed. The changes to the DAS computer program would be installed and then they would kick-off the daily batch processing of all of the debits and credits around their usual time, midnight. That's when Mars was due to come back to work, just in case they ran into any snags. If everything went well, they would complete the process by seven a.m., and then the verification tasks would begin. With luck he would be able to head home before nine.

As each of the other participants discussed the status of their tasks, Mars had uncontrollable urges to glance at Sofia. Each time he did, he found her watching him. They were the only two at the table, and the stark, cave like conference room began to feel like an intimate setting.

Mars was flattered by her attention. He should have been suspicious.

6 – 12:30 p.m.

After a long swim, Mars settled into the hammock, in the shade of an umbrella, with James Patterson's book *Now You See Her*. It was a typical hot and humid July day on the Delmarva Peninsula, but the breeze off the bay raised goose bumps on his sweat dampened skin.

He thought about his project. One of his team members, Liz, was monitoring the conversion tasks from home. She was very competent. He knew that she would call him on his cell phone if there were any problems.

Mars was free until midnight. He planned to relax and enjoy his new book. It was supposed to be another Patterson and Ledwidge page-turner, but he could not make any progress; his mind kept drifting back to the meeting and Sofia.

Mars had been, and was still, unnerved by her. He knew it was nuts, but he felt drawn to the woman. He had seen something in her eyes, something deeply compelling. Lying in the hammock, Mars realized just how attracted he was to her. It was absurd.

"Marshall?" Mars heard through his fog. "Marshall, is

that you?"

He raised his head and saw Sofia walking towards him. His gut lurched as he appreciated her looks; she was in remarkable shape for her age - as was Sally, he reminded himself. His eyes traveled up from Sofia's feet to the black-and-white sarong that was draped over the shapely hips in her one-piece black bathing suit, and finally up to her shaded face and wide-brimmed hat.

Suddenly aware that he was staring inappropriately, Mars practically jumped out of the hammock to greet her. "Sofia, wow," he stammered. "Where are you coming from?"

"From the condo. I was just going down to sit by the water, but when I got there I decided that I could use some exercise. It's going to be a long night." Like Mars, she was going back in at midnight to monitor the conversion at LB&T. "It was so pleasant out, I just kept walking." She stood there looking gorgeous; her tropical sunscreen scent lingered deliciously on the breeze.

Mars knew that she was staying in one of the bank's condos in Port Lewes well over a mile away. Belatedly, it occurred to him how far she had walked. "You look like you could use a cold drink," Mars managed noticing that her face was indeed flushed.

"Ah, you are very perceptive Mr. Stewart," she replied. Her fashionable sunglasses concealed her intense eyes that he felt gazing at him, just as he had felt them in the meeting. "I am dying of thirst," she said dramatically, then added, "Just some water would be great."

She looked anything but near-death, and as Mars turned away from her towards his house he knew that he was very much alive. "Have a seat. I'll be right back," he said over his shoulder. He glanced down at the front of his shorts and hoped that Patterson had had him covered. Now it was his face that flushed. *How embarrassing.* He hoped that she had not noticed his very unprofessional feelings.

Minutes later, a calmed-down Mars returned with a glass of ice water and two bottles which he put on the table between their chairs. Mars swigged on his bottle. He felt another twinge in his shorts as he watched her lips and her long neck work as she guzzled.

She refilled her glass then looked east. "Wow! Great view!"

"Thanks," Mars said taking in the 180 degrees of beach and bay... and her. Small dunes covered in clumps of tall grasses gave way to a gently sloping beach. There were pebbles, shells, and an occasional horseshoe crab on the curvy line that marked the last high tide. Locals and tourists were on the sand and in the water swimming and sailing. The Cape May – Lewes Ferry was just inside the outer breakwater.

It was an ordinary summer day in Lewes, but Mars never took the beauty for granted.

"This was my grandparents' place. We're very fortunate to have it." Mars could never afford it in today's market. Even with the recession it would easily bring a million and a half dollars.

"Definitely," Sofia agreed, her eyes panning the scene. Mars could sense that she appreciated the setting and was startled when she sprang up saying, "I have got to go get some lunch. I saw one of your recommendations, Striper Bites, on my way through town. Would you," she nodded towards the house, "or you and your wife, care to join me?"

"My wife Sally is out of town," Mars said, hoping he sounded more nonchalant than he felt. "Now that you mention it, I'm starved too." He stood. "Come on up to the house, and I'll grab a shirt and my car keys."

Sofia followed him into the cool living room. "Is this

your wife and your children?" she asked, referring to the photos displayed on the mantle. She was looking at a family picture from last year's trip to the Outer Banks. It had been taken on the beach on an overcast day with huge waves rolling in behind them. Mars wondered what kind of weather his family was enjoying there today.

"Yep, that's Peter," Mars pointed at the young man clad in surfer trunks with a mop of sun-bleached brown hair. "He's fifteen and growing like a weed. That was last year; he's a few inches taller now. That's Rebecca." Mars pointed to his daughter, who, like her father, was tethered to a Boogie Board. "She's twelve, and that's my wife, Sally."

"Your wife is beautiful, and your daughter is a spitting image."

"Thanks," Mars said knowing that it was true. They were both blond with hazel eyes, tan, and they smiled the same enchanting smile. Mars felt his wife's eyes on him and began to feel like it was risky business being alone in their house with Sofia.

He excused himself and went into his bedroom where he put on his favorite chambray shirt. He left the tails out just in case his body had a mind of its own again. Mars had always thought that women had an advantage in that department - their interests were not so obvious; they communicated their desires on a need-to-know basis.

He buttoned most of the buttons leaving two opened at the neck, rearranged his hair, and brushed his teeth. Uncomfortable with his irrational attraction to a woman he barely knew, Mars was anxious to get away from the house.

When they stopped at Sofia's condo so she could get a top to throw over her bathing suit, Mars declined her offer to "come in to see the place." He waited in the car and took the opportunity to call Liz to check on his project. He had just hung up when Sofia reappeared.

Mars was impressed that she had done a complete change in less than ten minutes, a feat that he could not help noting his wife could never accomplish. Sofia's new outfit was form-fitting black Bermuda shorts, and a sleeveless shirt with matching sandals. Somehow she had even managed to change her scent from the tropical sunscreen back to that spicy perfume that had rendered him senseless in their morning meeting.

Looking at her in her pink polo, Mars recalled his grandfather's warning about the infinite number of alluring shades of pinks that could derail his life if he was not ever vigilant. Mars found it somewhat amusing that this woman that sent shockwaves through his body was coincidentally dressed in pink. Mostly it was scary.

Thanks for the warning, Gramps.

7 - 1:14 p.m.

They were lucky and got seated right away. Mars chose his favorite booth in the back corner of Striper Bites' bar area. Even with the ceiling fans he had decided it might be too hot on the porch.

"Nice place," Sofia commented as she eyed the decor. There were small boats suspended from the high ceilings, fish mounted on the walls, and a bunch of other nautical touches making it feel like it was a converted life-saving station. "The menu looks great. Too many good choices. I can see why you like it."

Mars already knew what he was having so he watched her as she perused the menu.

She looked up and caught his eye. "You look like you've decided. Any suggestions?"

"I'm going with the Striper Bites Salad topped with a Crab Cake and a bottle of Dogfish Head IPA. Everything here is good." Her eyes were on him, studying him in a way that made him flush again. Trying to be the good host he added, "What looks interesting?"

She held his gaze as she closed the menu. "I think I'll

have what you are having." Mars broke their eye contact. He looked up at the television that was tuned into CNBC. He did not notice if the markets were down or up.

"So, hopefully the conversion will go well tonight," she commented starting a discussion of the timeline and how everything was in good shape. By the time their food arrived they had moved on to other subjects.

Mars was surprised at how at ease they were with each other. They had just met earlier in the day, but Sofia seemed like a friend. They found that they had many common interests, not the least of which was golf.

It turned out that Sofia was almost as addicted to the game as Mars was. She had not started playing until just a few years ago, after her son was grown, but she was committed to improving.

"I even stopped at that club just north of here..." she paused unable to remember its name.

"The Rookery?"

"Yep, that's it. I hit a bucket there last night." Her eyes narrowed, and her brow furrowed as she added, "Golf keeps my mind off of other stuff."

"I hope you're not worried about the project." Mars said thinking that she might be stressed over being sent to cover for her boss. "It'll be fine."

"I agree," she said, but she looked worried.

Mars wondered what was troubling her. He didn't want to pry, but he felt compelled to try to make her feel better. "I belong to The Rookery. We can play nine after we eat."

Sofia stopped mid-bite and her eyes lit up. "Seriously?"

Mars glanced at his watch. "The South is hosting an Independence Day Weekend tournament this afternoon, but I'm sure we can get on Rookery North. We're not scheduled to be back at the bank until midnight. It'll take a half hour each way and two hours to play." His eyes were back on hers. "We have plenty of time. Our cell numbers are on the contact lists; the Command Center will call if they need us. We can take our work stuff with us in case either of us gets called in."

"Well, this is an unexpected bonus," Sofia said with a big smile. It was to Mars, too - the golf and the woman. His wife had been fine with his playing a game with the guys, but it occurred to him that she would probably not like him hanging out with this particular banker.

Mars wasn't even sure about spending time with Sofia, but he assured himself it was just lunch and golf with one of his banking associates - nothing more. It could even be construed as part of his job, so *no worries*.

8   – 3:10 p.m.

They talked mostly about golf as Mars drove north on Route 1 to Milford. When they arrived at The Rookery North, they carried their bags up the sidewalk lined with pink and purple-and-white impatiens to the pro shop where Mars got a cart and a bag of balls.

At the driving range, Sofia wasted no time getting started. She pulled a wedge out of her bag and fell into a practiced routine of stretching her neck, shoulders, legs, arms and even her hands. Mars was behind her doing a few cursory stretches of his own, but mostly he was gawking at her like a hormone-challenged teenager.

He reprimanded himself for noticing how limber she was. They had stopped at her condo again to get her clubs – he kept his in his car. She had left on her lunch outfit but had traded the sandals for some stylish black-and-white golf shoes and had added a pink baseball cap.

The way she moved mesmerized Mars.

He made a conscious effort to stop watching her. He watched some guys that he knew as they finished the eighteenth hole. One of them gave him a thumbs-up sign as he left the green. He had apparently noticed, even from that distance, that Sofia was looking good.

Mars ignored him and went to his bag where he pulled out his sand wedge. He tried to land some at the hundred-yard flag. He quit after three in a row flew high and landed softly within ten feet of his target. He hit some seven irons, then his five iron, and then finished up with the club he liked best - his driver. His swing felt good.

He busied himself at the cart cleaning his clubs while Sofia finished hitting balls. She had a nice swing – a bit mechanical, but she hit the ball well, at least the ones that he saw. He was having a difficult time following their flight since he could hardly take his eyes off of her.

She was indeed the quintessential "alluring shade of pink" that his grandfather had lectured about, but he knew that there was no harm in looking.

On the way to the first tee they decided to play "skins". Her handicap was twenty-three point something so he figured she would have a twenty-five course handicap. His was fourteen, so he had to give her five strokes on the front nine, including one on each of the first three holes.

Mars played from the white tees and hit a truly pathetic drive. He pulled it so far left that he was almost in the eighteenth fairway. It was definitely not the impressive start that he had hoped for. He was not surprised; more often than not, when he was foolish enough to want to impress someone with his game, he played terribly.

He definitely wanted to impress Sofia, but he was far from focused so he knew that this was bound to be one of those off days. Oh well, the game had humbled him a long time ago.

He managed to punch his second shot low out from

under the trees that separated the two fairways, and was back in position. Meanwhile, Sofia had hit a drive right down the middle followed by a nice straight second shot. She was not a real long-ball hitter, but she easily got on the green in three and two putted for a bogey. Mars followed suit, but since he was giving her a stroke he lost the hole.

Walking off the green she put her hand on his shoulder, and said, "So what are we playing for?"

"How about honor," Mars managed to answer as the heat of her hand penetrated his shirt.

"Better yet, how about drinks tomorrow night after we recover from our successful conversion?" she countered looking deadly serious.

Either something was really bothering her or she was a fearsome competitor. He couldn't read her, but decided to play along. "Fine by me, but fair warning, I can be an expensive date." As soon as the words were out, Mars regretted calling it a date, but at the same time he felt excited by the prospect.

She did not seem to notice his faux pas.

Mars managed to get his game somewhat back together, but it was a tight match. Sofia demonstrated a lot of skill for her handicap. She played with determination, but as it turned out the sand was her nemesis – and unfortunately for her, it was a magnet for her ball. She was in at least a half-dozen traps. It cost her the match.

She was a gracious loser. She even thanked Mars for not letting her win as if he had ever considered it.

When he dropped her at her condo, she gave him a brotherly punch in the shoulder before getting out of the car. She leaned back in the open passenger window. "Thanks, Mars, I needed that." She hesitated as if she had something to say then added, "See you at the bank around midnight."

"Okay, and don't forget to hit the ATM while you're there. You'll need some cash for tomorrow night. It's right by the east entrance," Mars kidded, trying to keep things light.

He watched intently until she had disappeared into her front door. *Until tomorrow night,* he thought as he drove out of the parking lot. He wondered what was bothering her as he tried to concentrate on remembering to call Sally when he got home.

9 – 8:26 p.m.

Mars showered and threw on his favorite shorts – threadbare nylon-mesh ones from the Olympic Training Center in Lake Placid. The logo had mostly disappeared years ago. Worn commando style, they were nice and cool on this hot evening.

He stopped at his desk and powered on his laptop en route to the kitchen. He grabbed a glass of water and returned. The computer had booted up so he inserted his Secure-Away fob in the USB port. It authenticated his identity when away from the office allowing him to dial into the bank's network.

Once online, he checked the status of the conversion project then reviewed his in-box in LB&T's e-mail system. Everything was going smoothly with the conversion so Mars had a few hours to kill before heading to work.

Mars flopped on his bed and picked up the book he was still starting. He was hoping to get absorbed in Patterson's fiction, but just like earlier in the day it was not happening. Instead, visions of Sofia played with his head. He had turned the page before he realized that he had no idea what was happening in the story.

He gave up, closed the book, laid it on his chest, and nestled his head into the pillow. In no time he was enjoying a tantalizing scenario that he had conjured up for tomorrow night when he collected on the golf bet. He knew it was insane to be thinking about Sofia in that way, but there was something about how she looked at him, and about how he felt when he looked at her, that he could not ignore.

The doorbell jolted him back to reality.

Mars had the book in his hand when he opened the door. He was stunned to see Sofia. She looked and smelled fresh out of the shower. She had on a pair of flattering beige Capri pants and a lime colored silky blouse.

His body flushed at the sight of her at his door. Her eyes were locked on his.

"I meant to ask you something," she said as she moved into the open doorway.

A slight gasp escaped from Mars when her hips grazed the front of his shorts as she slid between him and the jamb. This time Mars was certain that she had noticed the effect she had on him.

If there was any doubt at all, it was quickly erased. Before she was through the doorway, she turned to him. Mars barely heard *Now You See Her* hit the floor. He kicked the door shut as their lips met. Their mouths and hands were hungrily exploring each other. Like in a bad B-movie, they left a trail of clothes as they moved silently through the living room.

With the blood gone from his brain, Mars foolishly navigated them into the master bedroom. He managed to flip the light switch off as they bumped past. The only illumination as they fell onto the bed was from the screen on his laptop.

His daughter Beck had saved a picture of the rental house in Corolla as his desktop background; she wanted to remind him of what he was missing there. The photograph had been shot on a clear day with a brilliant sky. The blue light danced in Sofia's hair and off her bare skin. It made her appear as electric as she felt.

Forty minutes later they were spent, but were still entwined when the phone rang. Mars instinctively reached for it, but found that he was at the foot of the bed. As he regained his bearings, he crawled across Sofia's legs to grab the phone before the machine picked up.

"Hello," he answered groggily.

"Hi, Daddy." Mars remembered that Sally had said that she would get Rebecca to call. She had been out playing miniature golf when he had talked to his wife earlier that evening.

"Hey, Becky Bear. Did you have fun?" Mars croaked as he watched Sofia slip out of the room. He tried desperately to concentrate on what his daughter was saying.

"Dad, you should have seen me putting. I was awesome," she said immodestly. Mars smiled. His daughter was not short on self-confidence. "And Da-ad, they were real grass greens just like at the club."

Ten minutes later, Mars got off the phone he went to find Sofia. He nearly tripped over his shorts in the dark living room. As he stepped into them, he noticed that her clothes were gone. A wave of disappointment flooded through him before he thought that he should be relieved.

Then he caught a glimpse of her on the deck just outside the living room. She was dressed and was standing gazing out over the bay. Without a word, he went to her.

He stood behind her, and wrapped his arms around her waist. His chin rested on the top of her head as he pulled her against him.

"I'm sorry, Mars."

He knew he should be too. He inhaled the bay breeze mingled with their musky scent. "Don't be." He kissed the top of her head. "It's my fault too."

He was shocked at what he had done. He didn't know what to think or to say. His eyes moved up from the water to the sky. There was only a sliver of a moon. The stars were shining brightly. Mars located some of the constellations as he tried to summon the strength to let Sofia go.

He waited too long. The heat building between them was palpable. He heard himself moan as he tipped her face up to meet his. His other hand slipped under the front of her waistband.

Within minutes they were back in bed.

10   – 10:44 p.m.

Mars was awakened in a most pleasant way. He did not know how long he had been asleep or how long it had taken him to realize that he was not dreaming. When the reality hit him, his eyes shot open and immediately locked onto hers through that same blue haze from the computer screen.

Sofia stopped, smiled and whispered, "It's time to get up." She amused herself and laughed as her lips moved up to his. She kissed him lightly then abruptly stood up. "I'm heading back to the condo. You better get up and hit the showers, it's going on eleven."

Mars rolled over, looked at the clock, groaned and watched her leave the room. By the time he heard the front door shut his eyes were closed too. His brain was swirling with admonishments. He wondered why in the world he had let it happen. He loved Sally and the kids.

What had he been thinking?

Maybe if he went back to sleep, he would wake up and this would all have been an over-the-top yummy dream. He would have his sane life back.

He did not have time for sleep, or to sort it all out. He had thirty minutes to get ready for work. He extricated himself from the sheets, grabbed his towel, and went out on the deck to shower.

It rejuvenated him.

Once dressed, he got back on his computer and checked the conversion status online. Everything was on schedule. He logged off and packed up his laptop.

He was still feeling discombobulated as he went through the security gates of Lightship Bank and Trust. The large digital clock over the entrance told him it was eleven-fifty-four.

He had tried to focus on the project during the half hour drive, but instead he had engaged in an internal battle with himself. It was still underway. On the one hand, he was shocked at what he had let transpire in the last few hours. It was surreal. He couldn't have committed adultery. Not him, the guy his friends called Choir Boy. He was devoted to his wife and their family. It seemed impossible.

But then he remembered Sofia, the effect she had on him, and how she had her way with him like nobody ever had.

Mars had taken his grandfather's advice seriously. He had always appreciated beautiful women, but he had never ever been tempted to do more than look. He took his vows very seriously. And he wanted to be the best father that he could be. It was a priority for him as it had never been for his parents.

For thirty years there had only ever been one other woman; back in the recesses of his mind was the girl that he had never totally gotten over. She had disappeared from his life decades ago, before he and Sally had been married. She had never reappeared, except in the memories that he held sacred. She had been his first love and always would be even though he had barely known her.

Now there was Sofia.

There had been something about her from the get-go that had gotten to Mars. He could not understand it, but from the moment they had met, he had felt a powerful connection. Even as he thought it he knew it was a cliché, but it was true. It was more than a physical attraction and he knew, in a sense, that made it worse.

Memories of the past couple hours flowed through his mind, intoxicating him, rendering him incapable of sensible thought. He marveled at how they had seemed to intuitively know each other. He felt free with her.

He was not free. He was married, yet fantasies about what tomorrow night might bring flashed through his mind. They had a non-date set up for her to pay off her golf debts.

What a dumb fuck!

Mars knew that he may have just altered the course of his life, screwed it up forever. He knew that he needed to get back in position.

He would not go for drinks tomorrow. He would stay home to do the laundry. Maybe he would even clean out the garage as he had intended to do while his family was away. He needed to chalk the evening up to stupidity. It had been nothing more than the quintessential one-night stand. He needed to get over it. He needed to get over her.

With his thoughts vacillating between rational fears and the incredible memories of her skin on his, he made his way down the long dimly-lit hallway to his office.

Thoughts of his project were a million miles away.

11 - 11:58 p.m.

Right on time, Mars entered the conference room where members of his team were monitoring the conversion. Liz and Jason were holding down the fort.

As soon as Liz saw him, she handed him the installation task list that his team had prepared. She had kept it up to date with the status and notes for each of the active tasks. She looked tired and a bit bored.

Mars wondered if she noticed that something was different with him. He felt like she should be able to see the neon sign flashing "Cheater" across his forehead.

Apparently she did not. She sounded fine when she said, "Everything was going smooth until about an hour ago - the Loan system blew up." Her chair squeaked as she swiveled it back to the screen long enough to check on something. She swiveled back to him. "I don't think it's a big deal, but our conversion is on hold until they get done accessing our file. The Command Center knows that as long as we kick off by 1:30 we'll be fine, but they are throwing their weight around so I would stay away from there for a while."

Mars could just imagine the scene in the Command Center. The Modifications Management and Control team would be scrambling, tracking down who was doing what to rectify the problem, and reporting back to upper management. Sometimes they seemed to just get in the way, but having the quality control team around made his life easier when things weren't going exactly according to plan – like now. They would track things down with the loan team. He wouldn't have to.

Liz was right, it would be nice to steer clear of them, but he couldn't. "No. I better go check in."

"Actually, you should go get some food, Mars," Jason said as he raised a huge fork-full to his mouth. The bank put a high priority on making sure that no one starved during these off-hour installations; many a diet was foiled by an installation feast. "It's right outside the Command Center and it's disappearing fast."

Mars had not thought about eating since lunch, but now that he was seeing and smelling the food he realized that he was famished. "I guess I'll go make an appearance and get something to eat. Anything else I need to know?"

Jason grinned as he answered, "Just that our team is the best."

"But, of course, you already knew that," Liz added.

"Yeah," Mars said returning their smiles, "and we are the most humble."

He stood up. "Okay, either of you want any more food or something to drink?"

"No thanks," said Liz as her chair squeaked back to face her monitor.

"Diet Coke, a cold one from the bottom," Jason managed as he chewed.

Smiling at the fact that it was business as usual - no one had noticed how his world had shifted - Mars walked down the corridor to the large conference room that was functioning as the Command Center. When their Chief Information Officer, Nick Collins, looked up and saw Mars he was his usual tactful, charming self. "Mars, how nice of you to make an appearance."

"Nick, good to see you," he lied, noting that it was no small wonder that his boss's boss had earned the nickname Nick the Prick. Mars and other managers realized how irreverent that name was. They gave him the respect he deserved; he was their Most Valuable Prick and was known unaffectionately as their MVP.

Unfortunately, the guy controlled his purse strings so Mars had to mollify him. "According to our installation plan, I'm right on schedule. Did I miss anything other than the pepperoni pizza?" Mars asked as he flipped open the lid of an empty pepperoni-oil stained box on his way into the conference room.

He found that Liz had been right, his team's tasks were on schedule and they were on hold waiting for the Loan team's fix. He navigated his way around the room saying his hellos and checking in.

His team's representative from the Modifications Management group, George Mumford, mentioned that he had completed the requested override to one of the conversion jobs. Mars wasn't sure what override he was referring to, but last minute changes were a common occurrence. He knew that if Liz had requested it, it was needed. He made a mental note to check with her about it as he fixed a plate then headed back to the sanctuary of his team room thinking about Sofia, worrying about his marriage.

12 – Saturday 12:25 a.m.

Mars turned the knob and pushed open the door to his team's conference room while precariously balancing his plate on top of a glass of water and holding Jason's Diet Coke in his other hand. He was still in a bit of a fog.

"Looks like you have quite an appetite," a familiar voice commented.

Mars almost lost his dinner as he looked up and saw Sofia setting up her laptop in the far corner. He tried to catch her eye, but she quickly averted his and looked back at her task at hand.

Mars noted that she was showered yet again. Her attire for this phase of the evening was some linen-looking jeans with a fuchsia blouse. *Geez, how many outfits did she bring?*

Her face had a glow that had not been there earlier in the day. Mars wasn't sure if it was a reflection off her blouse, too much sun, or maybe their activities earlier in the evening. Whatever the cause, she looked ravishing.

He had to fight to appear professional. "Hey, Sofia," he managed. "Did Liz and Jason fill you in on our status?" He was certain that the Cheater sign was flashing again for all to see.

"They did. Sounds like we are right on track as long as the Loan team gets their fix in soon." Her laptop had booted up, and she began clicking away as she said, "Hope that you don't mind me camping out here, but my only other choice seems to be the Command Center."

Mars knew that he would be hopelessly distracted with her in the same room but responded, "No problem, the more the merrier."

He tried to relax. The project was not that complex in the first place, plus the conversion software and the reconciliation process had been well planned and tested. He had total faith in Liz and Jason. They had successfully completed dozens of projects much more challenging than this one.

Tension crept up his back into his neck as he worried that, with Sofia in the room, he would exhibit some telltale signs of his infidelity.

Nonetheless, there was something wonderful about having her near.

"Sofia, I hate to eat in front of you, but..." he said tasting the first forkful while thinking about her salty skin. She did not look up at him. He tried to maintain his composure as he continued, "The food is just outside the Command Center. You should go get some before it's gone."

"No thanks," she answered this time catching his eye before getting right to work. She looked worried about something again.

If anyone should be worried, it was him. They had been in his and Sally's bedroom. *God what was I thinking?*

Mars felt the now familiar flush return to his cheeks. He looked nervously at Liz and Jason to see if they had noticed what was going on. He was glad to find that they were engrossed in monitoring the project and did not seem to be paying the least bit of attention to Sofia and him - thank goodness.

He returned his attention to the food, but it quickly drifted back to the woman sitting a mere ten feet away. Worried about his instant obsession with her, he almost wished that he had never laid eyes on her - almost, but not quite. He hoped that he could enjoy those memories forever and never regret those hours.

Watching her, he noted that she too seemed stressed; she was probably having the same kind of second thoughts that he was having.

Rational thoughts gave way to fantasies about collecting on their bet, about having her in his arms again. Mars could almost feel her warm full lips.

13   - 8:55 a.m.

Mars never really regained his focus. Liz ran the show for him. He was just a figurehead whose thoughts were elsewhere. Fortunately, after the Loan team fixed their problem, his team's tasks were completed as planned. Once the conversion process was verified, they had all left for home bleary-eyed, but grateful there had been no disasters.

In the clear light of day, and returning to the scene of his indiscretions, he got very nervous. He feared that maybe Sofia had inadvertently left something behind – an earring, perhaps. He had been so out of it when she left that he hadn't noticed.

God, did she have them both on? He reasoned that if she had lost one, she would have noticed and alerted him.

Maybe.

He walked through the living room, and crawled around the bedroom and the bathroom before going out onto the deck. He found nothing amiss. He knew that he had to strip the bed, but first he inspected every inch of it looking for any evidence that would not wash away. Her perfume seemed to be lingering in every fold, or was she still in his nostrils? She was definitely in his head.

It had been so strange to be in that conference room with her all night, to have to act professional while visions of her, of them, replayed in his head. Against his better judgment, he and Sofia had affirmed their plans to meet for drinks that evening. He was supposed to pick her up at the condo at seven. He had decided that there would definitely be no repeat of last night's escapades, but she owed him drinks, and they definitely needed to talk.

He was going to insure that they were on the same wavelength. Obviously, he was wildly attracted to her, but he was married. He could not have an ongoing affair with her. He had momentarily lost his head. It had been a wonderful crazy night that he would never forget, but he prayed that he had not ruined his life.

Sally and the kids were due home the next day – Sunday. Mars's highest priority was making absolutely sure that there would be no trace of Sofia's ever having been in their house. He was not worried if the neighbors had seen her; the houses on both sides were rentals. He figured that as long as he got everything cleaned up, he should be back in position – hopefully.

He opened all of the windows, and even put the pillows out in the sun. He was growing confident that he had rid the house of her, but he knew that his mental state was another matter. He did not understand why he had been so captivated by her. He felt like a school boy again.

He had convinced himself that what he had felt all those years ago with the girl from the deli was just hormone induced lust, that what he felt for Sally was the real thing. It was a love that could endure, not the wild misdirected passion of his youth.

Now here it was again. He had felt it as soon as he had met Sofia. Yet in hindsight Mars knew, or thought that he knew, that he would never have made the first move. He had been determined to be faithful to his wife. He had blown it. For that he was sorry. And he was scared; scared of getting caught; terrified of what he felt.

It worried him that he did not fully regret the time with Sofia. He knew he should, but part of him was thrilled. The situation was so wrong, but something about her felt so natural.

He knew that he was rationalizing. There were plenty of songs testifying to the fact that lots of people had felt what he was feeling. Intellectually, he had to admit that it was probably just lust, but emotionally it was hard for him to believe that it was something commonplace.

He was mulling this all over as he inspected the house one more time. He went everywhere Sofia had been. He found nothing. He put the wash in the dryer then collapsed on the bare mattress pad of his bed – his and Sally's bed that was overflowing with delicious memories of Sofia.

He called Sally and was semi-relieved when she did not answer. He left a message that the conversion had gone well and that he would call again when he woke up. When he disconnected, he wondered how he had sounded, and whether she would suspect anything was amiss.

The windows were still open and, even with the ceiling fan on, it was hot. It felt good. Maybe he could sweat Sofia out of his system. He shut his eyes and tried to go to sleep, but he could not shut his mind off. He tried counting backwards from one hundred, but by ninety he was remembering Sofia's warm soft lips. He tried a technique he had learned years ago, where he concentrated on his breathing and nothing else. Each time a thought came in his mind, it was of Sofia and he tried to push it away.

Breathe in, breathe out.

He remembered how his body had responded when he found her at his door, and just how obvious it must had been to her in those old shorts.

Breathe in.

He longed to feel her desire again.

Breathe out.

Breathe in.

Breathe out.

14   - 3:06 p.m.

Mars was out cold until the middle of the afternoon. When he awoke he realized that he was still thinking about Sofia. He reprimanded himself for being such a jerk as he made his way to the kitchen. Unable to even focus on what he wanted to eat, he grazed, then went for a long swim, showered, and remade the bed with the fresh sheets.

By then he was worn out again. He set the alarm for six and lay back down. The sheets smelled like lavender dryer sheets. There was no hint of Sofia's scent, but memories of her spiciness occupied his mind as he drifted back to dreamland.

The alarm woke him from a deep sleep. He shaved, dressed, and called Sally again. This time he got her. She was happy to hear that the project had gone well and reported that they were enjoying the last of their days there. The kids had gone with a group to rent Jet Skis so he didn't get to speak to either of them.

"I'll be glad to get home," Sally said. "This vacation stuff is exhausting."

Mars laughed then whined, "I wouldn't know."

"Oh please, you probably love bach'ing it."

"It's okay," he tried to tease before blurting out, "I miss you." He meant it. His wife had been gone less than a week and he had royally screwed things up.

"I miss you too," she replied. "We'll be home sometime tomorrow afternoon."

"I'm glad," he said worrying again if he had missed any evidence of his crimes.

The guilt was eating at his gut.

Nonetheless, after hanging up he took one last look at the cad in the mirror then left to pick up Sofia. In route, he promised himself that he would just collect on the bet - have a couple of drinks, then have that serious talk they needed to have.

Then he would come home, alone.

When he rang the doorbell of her condo he heard the door slide open on deck above him. He looked up. Sofia's wet head and her robe-clad upper-body appeared over the railing.

"Sorry, Mars, I overslept. Go ahead in. There's beer in the refrigerator. I'll be down in a few minutes."

Or I could come up, Mars thought as he made his way to the beer. She had bought a six-pack of the Dogfish Head IPA that they had with lunch. He used the bottle opener on the counter to pop the top off the ice-cold brew.

As he took his first swig, he could hear her blow dryer. He was torn. He wanted to run up the stairs, but he knew he should not.

His better judgment won out; he walked out onto the beach side patio, and sat. It was protected on both sides by a six-foot fence, but it was open to the bay. He watched as a ferry made its way into port from Cape May, New Jersey.

With visions of Sofia in that skimpy robe filling him, Mars worked hard at convincing himself that once would have to be enough with her. As desire drummed, it was a tough sell. He was on the verge of caving in when Sofia joined him on the patio.

Mars had been wondering if the fact that she was not ready was just a ploy to get him back in bed. Apparently that was not the case. Sofia was fully dressed in yet another flattering outfit and had a drink in her hand.

"Can I get you another beer? I'm buying," she teased.

"Not quite yet," Mars replied trying not to be disappointed that she had not waited for him to come up. "I'm still working on this one."

She settled into the chair next to him. They sat silently watching a ferry as it passed the breakwater then she turned to look at him. He was noticing her sad eyes as she said, "I was thinking that, under the circumstances, you might not be entirely comfortable being seen out and about with me in your home town."

She had a point.

She continued. "So, I picked up some stuff for dinner. I thought we would just hang out here. I hope that's okay."

Mars was grateful; he knew she was right. He should not be seen in town alone with Sofia, not after what they had done. However, under the circumstances he wasn't sure that he wanted to risk being alone with her either. Did he have the fortitude to stay out of her bed?

He was fighting twinges of excitement at the prospects. "Hanging out here sounds great, but..." he stopped short of saying what was on his mind. He wasn't sure what he wanted.

"What Mars?" Sofia asked with concern.

"It's just..." He looked at her. "Sofia, I know I didn't act like it last night, but I'm happily married. We can't -"

She looked sad, but she agreed. "Mars, I know. I'm so sorry. I never should have come back to your house. I'm hoping we can forget this ever happened, that we can go on with our lives as if we were never any more than business associates."

Mars felt the tension go out of his shoulders. He was so thankful that she wasn't expecting anything more that he overcompensated; he leaned over and kissed her on the lips. She kissed him back. He pulled away - slowly.

"It was certainly a pleasure doing business with you, but..." He stood up. "I think I better go get another beer."

When he returned, they sat and chatted on a variety of other topics. Mars could not help but notice how in tune they were. The sex had been one thing, but there was something deeper with Sofia. They thought alike. It was as wonderful as it was disconcerting. It occurred to him how unfair it was for him to find her now.

All night, Sofia seemed to be on the verge of telling him something important, but instead they talked about their families and their common interests. They had a leisurely dinner. She had gone back to Striper Bites and picked up his favorite entree that he had told her about at lunch - Blackened Tuna over Penne Pasta with a tomato and fennel cream sauce along with their Caesar Salad. She had him uncork a nice chilled bottle of Pinot Grigio. Everything about the evening was scrumptious except one thing. He had no business being there.

After dinner, the couple of beers and the wine had him thinking that making love with her one more time would be okay. Well, not okay exactly, but he was thinking that - from his wife's point of view - twice wouldn't be much worse than once.

With a burst of lucidity, he knew that he was about to dig himself in deeper. "How about a walk?" he asked, already standing.

She agreed and they set out on the beach along the Delaware Bay. They didn't stop until they reached the point in Cape Henlopen State Park. As they stood and watched the sun set over Lewes beach, they gave in to the chemistry that they both felt. One long passionate kiss led to a second before Mars pulled back.

He put his arms around her, and held her close. "Sofia, I better go home before..."

"Yeah," she agreed breaking free. "I don't want you to be double sorry."

She started back the way they had come. Mars fell in beside her. He didn't say it, but he was already double sorry. He was sorry for what he had done, and he was sorry that it could only be once.

15 – Sunday

Mars spent some time Sunday morning inspecting the house yet again for any trace of his activities with Sofia. He found nothing. Unable to relax in the house, he went out and attacked the garage. By noon the difference was tremendous. In four short hours he got done what Sally had been dinging him to do since spring.

Satisfied with his work there, and knowing that Sally would be tired when she got home, he went to Lloyd's supermarket and got two pounds of hamburger, some buns, a bag of mixed salad greens, and Freeman's corn on the cob. He stopped at King's and got some homemade banana ice cream - Sally's favorite - and some chocolate.

At home he made the burger patties.

Satisfied that he had done all he could do, he retired to his bed with a beer, a sandwich and a big bag of chips. He found the golf tournament then lounged, snacking and watching Tiger and Phil duel it out again - a first since Tiger's rebirth. It would have been compelling, but he was thinking of Sofia, and of Sally, and of the mess that he had made of their lives.

It was depressing knowing that he had put his marriage and his life with his family in jeopardy. At the same time, it was exciting remembering how he had done it. He could not keep his mind off of Sofia or their magical moments together.

He was just finishing a second beer and thinking what a moron he was when he heard Sally and the kids roll in about three-thirty. Butterflies attacked his stomach as he went to greet them.

Beck was racing towards him when he opened the door. "Daddy," she exclaimed as she flew into his arms. "You missed it, Dad. We had the best waves, and oh, oh, Dad you should have seen me on the Jet Ski. Can we buy one Dad, can we? Mom said may-"

"Hello, Miss Rebecca. I missed you," he said, laughing as he gave her a big bear hug.

"Hey, Dad," Peter mumbled as he tried to slide by them.

"Hey, stop and give your dad a hug. I missed you too, Peter." His son obliged and rolled his eyes as he resumed the task of lugging some bags into the house.

Mars went out to the car where he embraced his wife and gave her a kiss. "Welcome home, babe."

"Thanks, honey."

"How was traffic?" Mars asked knowing that the North Carolina beach roads were not adequate to handle the mass exodus of all the rental units each weekend.

"It was awful until we got to the dual below Norfolk." She looked up at him. "How are you? You look tired."

Again Mars wondered if there were a "Cheater" sign aglow on his forehead. "I am, but I'm fine. The project went great." Mars worried that she could see right through him. "Go on in, the kids and I can unpack."

"Thanks," she said as she walked in with an armload.

Beck came back out with Peter and sort of helped as she attempted to convey a week's activities in the first few minutes. She was still going strong when they all collapsed on the porch.

Peter even had a few stories.

As Mars listened, a brief wave of nausea rumbled through him, knowing he had put all of this at risk. He snapped back into the moment and asked about the cousins, the rental house, the waves, and everything else he could think of.

He wanted to hear it all.

That evening, Mars grilled the corn and the burgers. He had Beck and Peter do the rest of the set-up and the clean-up while Sally rested in the hammock. Mars was thankful that none of them seemed to notice that their whole world had just been rocked off its axis.

It was nice having them home. He just hoped the tranquility lasted.

When he and Sally went to bed, Mars had a few moments of angst. He was worried that she would see something that he had missed – maybe he had a scratch on his back. God, he had never checked. Or maybe, in spite of his efforts, she would smell Sofia's perfume, or notice that he had uncharacteristically laundered the sheets. Or worse yet, maybe she would just intuitively sense that something was wrong.

She didn't.

They both read for a half hour or so then Sally turned off her light and rolled over. Mars was thinking that everything was going to be okay when suddenly she rolled back towards him saying, "Mars... what the heck?"

His heart stopped as he bravely looked up from his book. He chuckled when he saw her holding up a *Dorito*. "Oops," he said as he inhaled it from her fingers, not caring that he had already brushed his teeth.

"I can't leave you alone for a minute," she mumbled poking him in the thigh before she settled back onto her side.

"Uh-huh," he agreed hoping that she would never know how right she was.

He felt tormented; it was Sunday, and if not for Sofia he would have issued an SOS call to his wife. But tonight he was thinking about Sofia. It wouldn't be right to have their Sunday-Only-Sex this week. Would it?

SOS? Sofia or Sally?

He needed to get over that wild night, get back on the horse, so to speak, but it was too soon. It didn't seem right.

Luckily, he didn't have to suffer with his indecision long. Sally was fast asleep.

Next week, he promised himself.

He gave up on reading, and turned out the light. In the dark it was easy to persuade himself that he was back in position. His reunion with his wife had passed without incident. He began to relax.

As soon as he did, wonderfully warm memories rushed in. As he lay cheek to cheek with his wife he knew how inappropriate his thoughts were. He tried his breath-in-breath-out mantra to clear his mind, but he couldn't shake the vision of Sofia straddling him, her breasts moving in the soft blue light above him.

He knew he was screwed.

Part 3 – Dog Days of August

continued

16 - Tuesday 7:36 a.m.

After his impulsive night with Sofia, Mars had known his personal life was in jeopardy, but he had no inkling that his professional life and even his freedom were also at risk – until now. Now it was clear, Sofia had used him. She didn't want or need his body it was just a way to make him her patsy.

She had come to his house not once, but twice, and he had played right into her hands – literally. He reflected on how soft and skilled they were, and her lips...

He pulled into the rest stop in Smyrna, not noticing the beds of beautiful flowers that lined both sides of the entrance; he was too busy beating himself up for being such an idiot. Even knowing that she had used him, he couldn't block out those fantastic memories or the feelings that went along with them. It occurred to him that his grandfather would turn in his grave if he knew what he had done.

The parking lot was empty except for two cars. Mars parked facing the brick building and shut the engine off. He banged his head lightly against the steering wheel as if he could knock some sense into himself. He had – oh so willingly - become the victim of what may well turn out to be a perfect crime.

There was no doubt in his mind that Sofia had gotten on his laptop while he was sleeping. She wore him out then sent the e-mail requesting the override to the conversion job. He had been home alone and had not thought twice about leaving his logon activated. Now he would be assumed guilty and any attempts to prove that she had sent the mail could ruin his marriage and the rest of his life.

Looking back, he knew that the offending override was also the one that had been referred to when George Mumford had stopped him in the Command Center on the night of the conversion. He just assumed that Liz had requested the override. He had meant to ask her about it, but somehow - after Sofia arrived - he had neglected to follow up on it. If he hadn't let her presence in the conference room distract him and had looked into the reason for the override, he would have discovered the access to the file she had manipulated.

He cursed himself for being such an idiot. She had played him for a fool, seducing him not once, but twice. She had exhausted him, stole the money, then woke him up like he had never been awoken before – or since, at least in reality. She must have had that planned too, knowing that it would drive him out of his mind. He had been oblivious to his computer. *Was it on when she left that night?* He had no clue.

It was hard to wrap his mind around the fact that the memories - that he had relived hundreds of times over the last month - were not what they had seemed to be at all. She had made love with him and had framed him for embezzlement. They seemed like incongruous acts; as he thought about it, he realized that they were.

The reality sucked the wind right out of his soul. No matter what he had been thinking over the past month, the cosmos had not brought them together. She had only seduced him so that she could embezzle a half million dollars. The only love involved had been some figment of his overactive imagination - again - just like with the girl that got away.

What a dumb schmuck.

One reason that he had been led so easily astray was because Sofia had reminded him of her. Not looks-wise so much - although they were both Italian with olive skin and fantastic lips - it had been how Sofia had made him feel that had made his heart do a flip. She had been the first woman in thirty years for whom he had felt such an immediate and intense physical attraction. And it had seemed like more, like they were kindred spirits.

Yeah right, Mars, what an idiot!

Mars had always considered himself to be a good judge of character, and it shook him to the core to know how significantly he had misjudged Sofia. Granted, he only knew her for two days, but he had felt so connected to her. Now he knew that she had manipulated him as easily as she had the bank's file.

He wondered how she had selected him. How had she known that he would be such as easy target?

Mars remembered that she had seemed worried or upset that weekend. Now he assumed that it had been because she had known what she was going to do, and by the second night what she had done. Still, he wondered if it was more than that, if she had some problem that had caused her to take such extreme measures.

He was stunned to realize that he could not sustain any ill will - he *still* felt connected to her. He imagined her lying in her bed now, silently apologizing to him. Part of him believed that she must have been desperate.

He knew that he had been her puppet, and she had pulled his strings masterfully. Yet he could not help but feel that she had not been driven by greed – there had to be another reason. But no matter what her reason was for stealing the money, Mars could not figure out why she had involved him. He mulled over some possibilities, but nothing made sense.

He realized that he would never solve the riddle. He didn't even know her. He had risked his life, and his family's life for lust, pure unadulterated lust. He had let his entire family down, and was glad his grandfather was not here to witness his failure.

He sat in his car, trying to see a way out of this jam, trying to see how he could do what his grandfather had always taught him to do - get back in position. It seemed hopeless. He knew that it would be his word against hers. His logon had been used. He would be held accountable.

He remembered the employment contracts that he had signed. Leaving your computer unattended while logged on to the bank's network was a breach of security and was subject to termination. Mars, like many other employees, didn't always follow that rule. It was too damn inconvenient to log off every single time you stepped away from your desk. Especially when working at home.

He needed to find a way to clear himself, to expose Sofia without exposing his betrayal to Sally, without ruining his entire life.

The only way that he could see to do that was to get Sofia to confess. He did not want to call her, to give her a chance to run. He needed to confront her face to face.

But first he needed to pee.

17 - 7:42 a.m.

After a quick trip into the restroom, Mars felt much better. Not only was his bladder relieved, but he felt refreshed – sort of. He had splashed water on his face and brushed his teeth which made a world of difference. He was ready to face the new day, to try to get back in position, but he could not help thinking how very unlikely it seemed.

He was anxious to confront Sofia.

But he needed to call the Secret Service Agent in charge of the investigation at the bank and let him know that he would not be able to make the nine o'clock meeting they had scheduled. He wanted to make that call ASAP so that he could - hopefully - avoid actually having to talk to Agent Williams.

He was going to have to lie to a federal agent.

His heart was pounding. He rooted around in his backpack. He found the pills way at the bottom. He took the BP one and his sinus medicine. The sweet smell of the flowers had him stuffed up.

He retrieved the DAS Reactivated Dormant Accounts

Report from his briefcase and quickly found what he was looking for. In the report for Tuesday July 12, a dormant account with a balance of almost a half million dollars had been reactivated. Mars compared the balance of that account to its balance a month earlier on June's report. He confirmed that the balance had grown by exactly $492,374. It was the same amount that was missing from Kathryn Jacobson's account.

Again Mars wondered why Sofia needed almost a half million dollars. He also realized that it was just bad luck that her plan had not worked. If Ms. Jacobson had stayed missing, if she had been dead like many of the other owners of abandoned accounts, then she would have been home free.

Unfortunately, this dormant account owner was alive and well, but fortunately for Sofia she had a back-up plan. Mars was her Plan B.

He was not going down quietly.

He reviewed his notes from his last meeting with Lance and saw that he had another deliverable for this morning. He was supposed to create a list of ex-employees for the agent – and flag anyone he thought could possibly be involved. Mars had already concluded that the one person who had left his team lately was not a likely candidate. Nonetheless, he would give Lance his name.

The misdirection might buy him some time. The man had been smart enough, but Mars was sure it was not in his nature to steal. Then he thought of how badly he had misjudged Sofia. He decided that it would be on the up-and-up to flag his ex-employee who was capable of the crime.

As Mars made the call he wondered if Lance would hear the lie in Mar's voice. He was a trained agent. He lucked out. Lance was not in the office yet. Mars left him a message with all the information. He thought he heard his voice crack when he said his aunt had died, but he managed to keep going.

He hung up and immediately began second guessing lying to an agent. Maybe he should have let Liz tell his lie. Well, one of his lies.

She was his next call. He took a breather. He listened to his heart thump in his ears for half a minute or so before dialing. She wasn't in yet. His voice did not crack as he told the story a second time.

Poor Aunt Jane, prematurely dead, he thought. He asked Liz to communicate the information via e-mail to the rest of the team and to send a second e-mail to the investigation team. Her third task was to print the July 12 DAS report, highlight the reactivated account, and give it to Lance. Finally, he instructed her to send him an e-mail each evening before she left with an update. She could call anytime if there was anything she needed his input on.

Mars's growling stomach told him that in spite of everything, he was hungry. He knew that the perfect remedy was just down the road - Helen's Sausage House.

Minutes later he had a brown bag in his car. He sat in front of Helen's tiny white building, surrounded by a half-dozen trucks, and practically inhaled a sausage sandwich laden with hot sauce. It went down great. So did the second one.

With his belly as full as his mind, Mars got back on Route 1 north. He contemplated his next move. He had Sofia's address on Broom Street in Wilmington. His GPS would find her house, but then what? What if her husband was home? He decided he needed to take it one step at a time.

By eight-fifteen he had found Sofia's house right in the heart of Little Italy. As he rode by, he looked in the driveway on the left side of her property and saw her white Nissan Sentra along with a dark sedan. He hoped that seeing two cars there meant that she might still be in town, not down in the islands. He continued around the block and parked four houses from hers. He could see her front door.

He wanted to look Sofia in the eye when he confronted her, but he did not want to involve the husband, at least not yet. Given that he had just screwed – and had been screwed by – the man's wife, he would like to avoid him. It was complicated enough already.

He decided to call her first. If she was alone he would go confront her. If she ran he would follow.

He dialed her number. It rang three times. She picked up.

"Good morning, Banksall, Sofia Pitasi speaking."

"Sofia, it's Mars, where are you?" he croaked sounding like a teenage boy entering puberty rather than a man - a man resolved not to let her get away with victimizing him, and his family.

"Hey, good morning, Mars, I'm home. Why, what's up?" She sounded surprisingly normal, making Mars wonder if he had misjudged her. In seconds, certainty settled in bringing with it anger. His words stuck in his throat. He wondered again what drove her to it. Why him?

"Mars... are you there?" she asked still sounding too casual, like maybe they had been interrupted by a lost cell signal. She should sound guilty; she had lured him into having sex with him, had stolen the money, and had framed him.

"Sofia, I *know*," he said as emphatically as he could. To him he still sounded weak; no, wounded.

Sofia sighed heavily, but she didn't say a word.

"Why, Sofia? Why did you do this to me?"

Still she said nothing.

He studied her house. It was on the small side, but looked to be in good repair. Her Nissan was just a year or two old, and the sedan appeared to be a late model Lexus. It sure didn't look like they were hurting for money. "Why did you do it?"

"Mars, I... I..." she stammered.

"Please tell me," he interrupted, "my life is on the line here."

"I'm sorry, Mars. God knows I am." She sounded sincere. He tried not to believe her. "You need to talk to your father."

Her words hit him like a hard slap on the face; they made his head spin. "My father?" What the hell does my father have to do with this?" he barked towards her front door.

"You need to talk to your father. Then we'll talk."

Mars was speechless.

"Trust me," she said just before the click.

She had hung up on him.

What the hell is going on?

18 - 8:35 a.m.

Mars had thought that the situation could not get more bizarre; he had been wrong. Why the hell did he need to talk to his father about Sofia's embezzling money and framing him? His instincts told him to get out of his car and go bang on Sofia's freshly painted white door until she answered, but he still did not know if her husband was home.

He sat there watching as two kids rode up the quiet tree-lined street on their bikes with no hands on the handle bars. An old man came out of the house across Broom Street in his bathrobe and slippers and retrieved the newspaper. Mars watched the mundane morning activities as he tried to fathom how his father could possibly shed any light on what she had done.

Maybe Sofia had hired his father as her attorney. *Wouldn't that just be grand?* It was the only plausible explanation he could come up with.

He really did not want to abandon his sentry point. Knowing he was on to her, she might be ready to make a run for the islands. If she got away he wouldn't have a prayer of convincing anyone that he was innocent. Actually, he knew he was far from innocent, but he was not guilty of the embezzlement.

He needed her.

The morning air was just starting to heat up, but Mars was in a full sweat. He shut his window, started the car, and directed the air conditioning vent onto his face. It was all brain numbing. He knew he wasn't thinking clearly, but down deep Mars did trust her – almost. But even if he didn't, the bottom line was that she was holding all the cards. She was calling the shots. Mars had little choice but to do as she said.

He called his parents' house.

"Hello," his mother answered, sounding rushed.

"Hi, Mom." He tried to sound nonchalant. To his ear, he didn't quite pull it off, but his mother did not notice.

"Mars, what a pleasant surprise. How are you? Is everything all right?" It was obvious that she was not used to impromptu calls from her son any more than he was used to them from her or his father.

"I'm fine Mom. How are you?" he answered knowing that anything other than the rote response would waste precious time.

"I'm wonderful, Mars, but I'm just getting ready to run to the club for bridge."

There's always a 'but', Mars thought as he answered, "That's okay, I won't keep you."

Mars could picture his mother in some stylish outfit, her makeup perfectly applied. She probably had one jeweled earring in her hand, "Is Dad there?"

"No dear, he's not. He's already at the club. He teed off early. I don't expect him home until afternoon. Should I leave him a message to call you?"

"Actually, I'm in Wilmington. I'll run by the club, and

try to catch him there."

"That sounds great. I know he would love to see you."
Mars doubted that. She continued, "I've got to run, dear."

"Okay, bye Mom."

"Bye, bye."

Mars could not help but notice that there had been
no suggestion that he come and find her while he was at
the club. As usual, he did not fit into her schedule.

Mars tried his Dad's cell number. His voicemail
kicked in immediately, and realizing that his phone was
off, Mars hung up. He called the pro shop and found out
that his father had teed off at 7:58 on the North Course
with Gerald Ketchum, and Sid Coleman.

The attendant confirmed that no cell phone usage
was allowed on the course, but Mars could join them
when he arrived. For once in his life, Mars had no
interest in golf, but it seemed it was the only way he was
going to be able to talk with his father.

19 - 9:02 a.m.

The tree-lined entrance road to Wilmington Country Club screamed of money – some old and lots of new. Winterthur's steeplechase course - part of the thousand acre museum and country estate of the late Henry Francis du Pont - bordered the driveway on Mars's left. The fifth hole of the North Course was on his right.

Even in his state of confusion, Mars appreciated the beautiful setting. It was a social class removed from The Rookery and was steeped in golf history. The club had hosted U.S. Amateur tournaments as far back as 1913. Their undulating fairways, greens and sand traps all looked perfectly manicured thanks to a Spanish-speaking work force that was combing through the rough.

Mars spotted his mother's black and white "74" tag on a new white Mercedes E-Class wagon as he drove past the stately brick clubhouse. She was parked in one of the spaces reserved for their over-seventy members. He continued into the parking lot and did not see his father's car before he found a space.

Maybe he got a new one too.

Mars had left home in old wrinkled khaki shorts, a tee shirt, and flip flops. He got out of his car, and felt the humid air engulf him as he rummaged in his backpack. He extracted the rolled-up polo shirt, pulled off his acrid tee-shirt and replaced it with the fresh one that was not too wrinkled considering that he had packed it in such a rush.

He opened the rear hatch of his Edge, changed into his golf shoes, grabbed a cap, and tucked in his shirt. Unfortunately, he had forgotten a belt. His attire fell short of the "clean and tailored" criteria in the club's dress code, but it would have to do.

Mars walked through the breezeway. When he checked in at the pro shop he saw a good looking blue and yellow Polo striped ribbon belt. When he purchased it, the kid on the register said his father's group should finish the ninth hole around ten.

After a stop in the men's locker room, Mars busied himself on the putting green for fifteen minutes. Wilmington kept its greens at well over ten on the Stimpmeter. He tried to focus on speed - they were lightening fast - while he debated with himself on how to broach the subject with his father.

The two of them had always had a strained relationship. It was cordial enough, but they were not close. It really had little to do with Mars. It was more a byproduct of the lack of love between his parents. They had gotten pregnant in college, and had married after both sets of their parents convinced them that it was the right thing to do. When their passion died out, they had little left except their vows and their son. They had stayed together, probably thinking they were doing what was best for Mars. Mostly they had gone their separate ways, leaving him to get his emotional support from his grandparents.

So Mars wasn't interested in confiding in his father unless he had to. He decided he would probably need to retain him as his counsel before he could tell him about the night of the embezzlement - if he told him at all, and if he had not already been retained by Sofia. His thoughts were interrupted when the kid pulled up with a cart.

He offered to run him over to the snack bar between the ninth and tenth holes. Mars was weary so he took him up on it. He was hoping to get his answers quickly then walk back in from the twelfth hole. He got an ice water while he waited.

Sid Coleman saw him first. "Marshall, is that you?"

"Yes, sir." Mars walked over and greeted him. "Good to see you again, Mr. Coleman."

Mars's father and Gerald Ketchum pulled up in their cart. "Mars, what a surprise," the elder Stewart said, offering up his standard handshake - no hug.

"Dad, good to see you," Mars replied returning the familiar firm grip. "I was hoping that I could join you guys for the back nine." He hadn't meant to say that, but he wasn't ready to broach the subject in front of the other men.

"Great," Sid chimed in, grabbing Mars's bag and fastening it on his cart. "We'll take on the old guys."

Realizing that they would not be riding together, Mars quietly told his father, "I've got something that I need to discuss with you. Can we talk?"

"Sure, son," his father replied looking understandably perplexed. It was the first time that either one of them could remember that Mars had shown up unannounced, let alone with a pressing issue to discuss. "We'll talk over lunch," he said over his shoulder as he headed into the men's room. Mars did not want to waste two hours on the golf course, but he was too tired and confused to press the issue.

By the time his father returned, the two older men had made bets on a better-ball match. Sid had initiated it – he and Mars would give Gerald and Mars's father three strokes. The bet was five dollars a man. With the exception of Mars they were all very wealthy, but they played like the small wager was the world to them. The tenth hole was a dog-leg right par five with a huge elevated green. Sid was delighted when Mars cleared the bunkers and got on the green in regulation. His joy was short-lived. Unable to focus, Mars overshot his first putt up the hill then proceeded to miss the short downhill slider.

As they walked off the green Gerald guffawed and loudly commented, "When I was in the army, I saw penises longer than that putt."

And so it went for nine holes. It was the most fun that Mars had ever witnessed his father having – especially when Mars went in the water on his approach to eighteen, and Sid missed a short putt to lose the match.

"Sorry about your luck, son," his dad chided as he and Mr. Ketchum sped over the bridge. The three of them were still chuckling, as they paid off the bets.

Mars, knowing just how bad his luck really was, did not join in.

20 - 12:07 p.m.

Mars hated to ruin the moment, but he knew he had to get some answers. Gerald and Sid were in lock-step with them as they left the parking lot. Mars was afraid they were about to share a table for lunch which would be their normal routine.

"Dad, I hate to break this up, but I really do need to talk," Mars said in a hushed voice.

His father eyed him. "No problem, but let's order first; I'm starved," he said as the foursome headed for the clubhouse.

"We need to speak *privately*," Mars insisted.

That raised his father's eyebrows. Seeing that his son was serious, he made apologies to their playing partners and started towards the grille. "Oops, there's your Mother, we better go say hello."

Mars followed his father's gaze to the terrace and dutifully followed his dad over to a table of four perfectly coiffed women. His mother looked remarkably cool and fresh - totally oblivious to the mid-day summer heat. Her hair was almost pure silver; it shimmered in the light, competing with her jewelry.

As they approached, she did not get up, but joyfully accepted her son's peck on the cheek as she introduced him to the other ladies.

"We're taking a little break from our bridge game, the cards were atrocious," she announced sipping on a glass of white wine. She slid her chair back slightly and gave them the once over. "What are my favorite men up to?"

Mars felt her critical eye, and realized that she was silently - but firmly - admonishing him for being rumpled. He was, no doubt, embarrassing her in front of her upper-crust friends.

"Mars has some business to discuss with me," his father explained as he too planted a requisite peck on his wife's cheek. "We better go."

"Can you join us for dinner, darling?" she asked.

Mars had the distinct feeling that his mother was making the invitation more because she thought that her bridge partners might think less of her if she didn't invite him than because she felt any real desire to spend time with her son.

Some things never change.

"No thanks, Mom, another time," he answered pleasantly, giving her a second peck before he and his father excused themselves.

They found a quiet table in the air-conditioning. Mars had not realized how hot he was and now his overheated damp skin was suddenly covered in goose bumps. They ordered drinks and lunch: a bourbon and a burger for his father, and an iced tea with a BLT for Mars.

While they waited for the food, Mars got down to business. "Dad, does the name Sofia Pitasi mean anything to you?"

The color drained from his father's flushed face as he nearly choked on his first sip of bourbon. "Why do you ask?"

"I can't tell you... yet." Mars looked his father in the eye and continued, "Dad, this is important. You need to tell me how you know her."

His father took a healthy swig of his drink. It apparently gave him the courage he needed. As soon as the glass was back on the table, he gave Mars the shock of his life. "She is Sofia Angela Ignazio."

Mars could scarcely breathe or hear anything other than the ringing in his ears. His father continued "... the oldest daughter of Carmen Ignazio. Do you remember her from the deli when you were a teenager?"

Oh my God. Sofia is Angela? Angela Ignazio had been the girl of his dreams, the one that got away. *Angela framed me? No way!*

Mars found his voice. "That's impossible. She wouldn't, she would have told me if she... I would have recognized -", but as he said it Mars remembered her eyes. Sofia had Angela's eyes – those dark brown sad eyes that probed his soul and drew him in.

"Trust me, son. Sofia Pitasi is Angela."

Mars was starting to believe him, but it didn't make sense that his father would know anything about her. "How do you know?" He studied his father's face. "*Why* do you know?"

"Mars, I really prefer to have this conversation elsewhere." He drained the bourbon. "Why don't we go home? We can talk there."

"I don't have time for that. Tell me." Mars said banging his fist on the table unintentionally rattling the silverware. "Tell me now," he hoarsely whispered.

His father glanced around the room. Sid and Gerald were engrossed in CNBC's stock report. A few other members were having business lunches on the other side. No one seemed to be noticing the scene being played out at their table.

His father continued in low sure voice. "Think back to the mid-seventies. Do you remember sleeping with Angela?"

Mars could not fathom how his father knew. What the hell was going on?

"I remember," he said as calmly as he could while thinking, *I could never forget that night.*

"Carmen Ignazio came to my office in late August that year with the news that Angela was pregnant with your child."

The news pinned Mars against his chair. His head flailed as if he had just been overpowered by G-forces on a wild amusement park ride. *Oh my God, Angela had my child.* They had only had one night together; one magical unforgettable night. *Pregnant the first time? No way.*

His father continued, "She was nineteen and engaged to Vincent Pitasi, who was already running Ignazio's deli on North Union. Carmen was counting on him to be his son-in-law, to help run the family business. He did not want those plans ruined just because you and his daughter were irresponsible."

His father paused long enough to lift his empty glass, signaling the waitress for another. The sandwiches were delivered and ignored. The smell of fresh-grilled bacon did not even penetrate Mars's senses. He was speechless as he tried to focus on the reason he was here - Sofia had framed him - but his past and his present were colliding in ways he had never dreamed possible. He felt like he was mired in a nightmarish Stephen King plot, or maybe a bizarre Dean Koontz one.

This is crazy.

His father's voice filled the void of rational thoughts. He sounded more sincere, more personal, than usual. "I did not want you to suffer my fate; a shotgun wedding followed by a difficult marriage. I wanted more for you son. I wanted you to finish college." He reached out towards, but did not touch, Mars's hand. His eyes were downcast, but he raised them to meet his son's glaring gaze. "I wanted you to fall in love, to have a life-long wonderfully fulfilling marriage like my parents had – not what I have with your mother."

Mars remembered his grandfather warning him about being responsible, about not getting a girl pregnant. He had used Mars's father as an example of how his life could turn on a dime - for better or for worse. His grandfather had admitted that Mars's parents had married because they were pregnant with their only child. It had been the responsible thing to do, but his grandfather had concluded that they did not love each other enough to make the family work, at least not well

Mars knew that he had loved Angela enough. He would have gladly married her.

"What did you do?" Mars asked suspiciously.

"Carmen wanted monetary compensation to make your problem go away - to free you from your obligation," he said simply, as if there were anything simple about it.

Mars was incredulous. "You paid for an abortion?" He could not believe it; they had killed his first child, and they had kept him from the one woman he had truly loved - Sofia Angela.

Until I fell in love with Sally, of course, he told himself.

"No Mars, abortions were illegal then." He sounded like that had been unfortunate. As an afterthought he added, "Carmen was a good Catholic, he would never have allowed that anyway."

Mars tried in vain to coax bourbon from his father's empty glass. He needed to numb his mind as he waited to hear about his child, his oldest son. Or did he have another daughter?

"I paid Carmen one hundred thousand dollars – which incidentally was a lot of money back then."

"Who cares about your damn money? I loved her," Mars hissed.

His father ignored his son's anger and his declaration of love. He continued matter-of-factly. "In return, he agreed that you could live the rest of your life unencumbered by that kid."

"That *kid*? My God, Dad, that kid is my child and your grandchild."

"You sired a son, but he is not yours."

A son. I have another son, Mars thought only vaguely aware that his father was still talking.

"I made sure that he would never be your responsibility. He is Vincent's – Vincent and Angela's. Not yours." His father said this with an assurance that Mars could tell that he was no longer wholly convinced of.

Mars did not know the man across the table. He had never known him. He never would. He hadn't known Angela either; he had just known how he felt about her. He wondered aloud, "Why didn't Angela tell me?"

The air conditioner shut off. The room was suddenly quiet except for some news about more Apple stock gains on the television to which all other eyes were glued.

It had been a rhetorical question, but his father answered. "Her father signed a contract guaranteeing his family's silence."

Mars looked at the stranger across from him. "What is this, some long lost episode of the *Godfather*? What, did you threaten her life if she told me?"

"Of course not, Mars," his father barked. Realizing that heads had turned at his outburst, he added in a quieter but firm tone, "I am not some kind of monster." His father straightened in his chair, assumed the self-confident position of the attorney he was, "It was a simple legal contract. If any member of the Ignazio family ever spoke of it, if you ever found out from anyone other than me, her father would have had to repay the hundred grand, plus a rather sizable penalty."

His son eyed him, shaking his head in disbelief.

"Son, I wasn't just going to hand that kind of money over without a guarantee that you would be spared."

Spared? Mars thought as he stared blankly at the bottom of the bourbon glass; *spared from a life with Angela.* That was all he dreamed of back then. His father and hers had cheated him of that life, his destiny.

No wonder he had been so taken with Sofia. *My God, it all makes sense.* The attraction that had always been there with Angela was still there, even when he had not known that Sofia was Angela, three decades later, he still felt the same way.

He heard the refill of bourbon arrive. His father pushed it across the table. Mars blindly grabbed the ice-cold glass, and took a pull. He felt its heat mingle with his anger, with the smoldering desire for Angela. He had to go to her.

He stood.

His father grabbed his arm as he left the table. "What's going on, Mars? Why are you asking about her now, after all these years?"

Mars shook loose of his father's clutch. He did not have the energy or the inclination to explain. He had to get away from his father. He had to get back to Angela. He had to see her, to talk to her, to know why she had framed him. Nothing made sense.

He muttered, "I have to go," as he fled.

21 - 12:43 p.m.

Mars left his father alone with his unfinished lunch and with the unanswered question of why he was asking about Angela. As far as he was concerned, his father did not deserve to know; Lord only knew what he would do if he found out that Angela had framed him. He would probably have her incarcerated by the end of the day, and he would - once again - ruin his son's life... if it was not already in ruins.

Mars couldn't focus on the embezzlement. He was dumbstruck by the fact that Sofia and Angela were one and the same. Sofia was the woman that Angela, the girl of his dreams, had grown up to be. She was the mother of his eldest child, a son twice as old as Peter.

And she is the woman that framed me.

As Mars drove out the club's long drive, he did not notice the beautiful grounds. He turned left onto Kennett Pike with thoughts swirling through his mind like debris caught in a tornado. He had been betrayed by his father who had sold his child, and by Angela's father who had bought him. Together they had robbed him of the life with Angela that he had so desperately wanted.

He knew that he should also feel betrayed by her, but he could not help but feel that she too had been victimized. He would have made her happy, kept her safe and secure. She wouldn't have needed to steal the money.

His cell phone vibrated in its holster. He expected it to be his father, but it was Sally. He could not talk to her. Not now. He declined the call.

Sally. Poor Sally. He loved her, but he never would have married her if the fathers had not manipulated things. He would have married Angela in a heartbeat. But he had not been given a chance.

Had Angela not wanted him to know? The fact that she hadn't contacted him when she found out that she was carrying his child must mean that she had not cared for him anywhere near as much as he had cared for her. If she had loved him then no contract, no amount of money, would have stopped her from telling Mars.

Instead she had gone ahead with her plans to marry Vinny.

Maybe she hated Mars for what his father had done. Maybe that's why she sought him out and framed him. It was her revenge. *Damn him.*

Mars wondered if his first son knew his father was not Vinny. Mars did the math and realized that their son was almost thirty, surely by now they would have told him.

He wondered what he looked like. Is he tall like me? Is he dark like his mother? Does he have her hair and her soulful eyes? Is he a jock? *My God, he's probably married ... with children. My grandchildren! Oh my God, I may be a grandfather.*

As if on auto-pilot, his car threaded its way through the traffic, past the pricey shops of Greenville with preppy-clad windows, past the car dealers on Pennsylvania Avenue, back into the quiet streets of Little Italy.

As he approached Angela's house he saw that her Nissan was gone. Only the Lexus sedan remained. *Damn.* He pulled over to the curb in front of the house next door, no longer caring if Vinny - the man who had raised his son - was home.

He went to the door and rang the bell. No answer. He banged. Nothing.

He turned his phone back on, ignored the 2 Missed Calls and dialed Sofia's number. No answer. *Oh my God, she ran!* He dialed her cell and was transferred to her voicemail after the first ring. "Sofia, um," he stammered, "call me on my cell. We have to talk. Please, Angela," he begged.

As he leaned against his car thinking about Sofia and Angela, he felt a connection again. *Angela please, call me... now!* He stood with the sun beating down on him staring at his phone, willing it to ring.

It did not.

He could not sort out his emotions. He should hate her, but did he still love her? One thing was clear - he had to find her immediately.

A plump woman peered out from behind the lace curtains of the small brick house next door. Mars watched her watch him as he dialed Sofia's office number in Philadelphia. He glanced across the street and saw that the man that had been out getting his paper in the morning was now watering his roses. They must have a Neighborhood Watch program; he was watching Mars too.

There was no answer on her office number. He pressed zero and got Sofia's secretary.

"Ange – Sofia Pitasi, please."

"One moment… I'm sorry. May I ask who is calling?"

Mars hesitated for a few seconds debating if he should lie then decided there was no point. "This is Marshall Stewart from Lightship Bank and Trust."

"I'm sorry, Mr. Stewart, but Sofia is not in the office."

"Is she working from home today?" he asked knowing full well that she was not.

"No, she's on an emergency family leave. We're not sure when she will be able to return. She will be picking up her messages. Would you like to leave a voicemail?"

Yeah right, emergency family leave, he thought. "No thanks, I left a message on her cell, so I'm sure I'll hear from her soon. Thanks for your help."

They hung up. He wasn't sure. Now what?

Mars glanced at the neighbor's house and saw that the woman was still at the window studying him. He pushed himself away from the car. The man across the street turned his back suddenly and resumed watering his plants. Seconds later the neighbor woman's door opened and she stepped onto the porch with her hands on her abundant hips. Smells of garlic and tomato sauce wafted over her small heat-distressed lawn.

Mars did not want to startle her. He approached her house slowly.

"Can I help you?" she asked eyeing him as if he might be the incarnation of Jack the Ripper.

"I hope so," he said trying to sound casual. "I'm looking for Sofia Pitasi. I work with her."

"Sofia," she said with a humph. "She'll always be Angela to me," she said confirming in one breath what his father had just revealed to him; Sofia Pitasi is Angela Ignazio.

"You look like a nice man," she said pensively, then immediately followed it with, "but so did Scott Peterson." She eyed him some more without offering any information about Sofia.

Mars did his best to look trustworthy in his sweaty golf clothes. "I'm supposed to drop off some papers that she needs, and unfortunately it looks like I missed her." Then he remembered what her secretary had said. "Sofia is taking an emergency family leave, but she asked me to bring her some files."

He saw the woman let her guard down. "I guess I watch too much TV," she said. A crooked smile formed on her chubby wrinkle-lined face. Then she was serious again. "I heard that her son is being operated on today so I expect she's on her way to Baltimore."

Mars took a guess. "To Hopkins?"

"That's right," she said as she nodded towards the rose man, "I heard her tell my brother this morning. She left a couple of hours ago with a suitcase. So I doubt she'll be back for a few days."

Damn, I guess she really does have a family emergency. Then it hit him. Sofia – Angela – told him over lunch that she only has one son. *Oh my God, my son is sick.*

Mars had a million questions, but he needed to get on the road. He returned to his car, opened his door and said, "I'm sorry I missed her. Thanks for your help."

She waved him off as if it were nothing, and retreated into her house where she watched again through her lace curtains.

Once he was out of view, he accelerated towards Interstate 95 South, to Baltimore, to Angela and his sick son.

22 - 1:14 p.m.

About a half a mile before the Delaware Avenue ramp onto I95 South, Mars encountered stopped traffic. He had lost track of the time and glanced at his watch. It was too early for rush hour. He heard sirens approaching.

Sitting there looking at the heat rising off the pavement, Mars cranked up the air conditioning and caught a whiff of just how grungy he was. He examined his tousled hair and unshaven face in the mirror, and realizing that he may well meet his son today, he made a split-second decision to go to his parents' house and get cleaned up. He jerked the car out of the unmoving queue and into an apartment complex. He circled the parking lot and headed back north to Greenville.

Ten minutes later Mars rushed up the ivy-bordered, oak-shaded slate walkway to the back door of the fieldstone house where he had grown up. He peered in the garage windows and saw that both of his parents' cars were gone – they were still at the club. A spare key to the back door was in its usual place, hidden under a rock in the corner of the garden that bordered the manicured lawn.

He proceeded across the terra cotta tile floor, noting that the kitchen had been recently remodeled with stainless steel appliances. He continued down the hallway with its wide-planked cherry flooring. He paused in the foyer in front of his mother's most prized possession, an Andrew Wyeth oil painting which hung over an antique table where a day's mail sat.

He hollered "Hello" a few times.

No answer.

Thank God, he thought, *I can get out of here before they get home.*

He made a beeline for his old room which was still decorated in Tower Hill High School jock motif. His walls were Hiller green on the bottom and white above the chair rail. Sports memorabilia still lined the walls: varsity letters in football, baseball and basketball, assorted trophies and team pictures. He wondered where his oldest son had gone to high school; his bet was Salesianum, an all-boys Catholic school. Maybe if he and Angela had married, his son could have been a Hiller like him, but Sallies had a great sports program too.

Mars looked at the picture of his parents and him at his high school graduation. It pissed him to know that he had not been a part of his oldest son's life. Another man had stood in his place when his son graduated. It should have been him. He had missed so much.

Mars peeled off his sweaty clothes and practically ran through the shower chasing a thousand loony thoughts about the son he did not know, about Angela, and about the fathers that had betrayed them.

Even in his state of confusion, he felt a hundred percent better when he toweled off. He grabbed a razor and got rid of his day old beard, brushed his teeth, put on a fresh polo shirt and shorts then quickly packed up and headed back downstairs. As he passed his father's den door he stopped. He needed to call Sally back. He glanced at his watch. Rush hour would be starting soon. He wanted to get on the road.

He took back roads to Newark. Once he got on I95 and the traffic thinned, he called Sally.

"Hello?" she said expectantly.

"Hey, babe, it's me." He felt refreshed, but even to him his voice sounded tired.

"My God, Mars. I've been so worried. Honey what's happening? Framed? Are you all right?" She sounded as frantic as Sally ever had.

"I'm fine," he lied.

"Where *are* you?"

"I hate to be secretive," he said as he considered his answer. He wasn't prepared to tell her about Angela, at least not yet. "Sally, I don't want you to have to lie if the Secret Service contacts you, so I don't think you should know where I am, but-" he tried to sound upbeat, "I'm okay. Try not to worry."

"Mars don't be ridiculous, of course I'm worried. I'm worried sick. You said someone framed you for the embezzlement. Who? How?"

Mars measured his response. Unfortunately, he hadn't thought the call through. He should have planned what he would and what he wouldn't tell her.

"That's what I'm trying to figure out, babe. I'm sorry... I can't talk long; I just wanted to let you know I'm okay. And I wanted to see how you are, and the kids."

"The kids are fine," she said, this time sounding more melancholy than manic. "I told them that your aunt died. They were sad for you, but neither of them even remembers meeting her." She paused. "So *they* are fine."

Implied in her answer was that she was not.

"What about you, Sally, are you okay?"

The dam holding back her emotions broke. "No, Mars, I am definitely not okay. I lied to my children today, my husband has been framed for a felony and is on the run, and he won't even tell me where he is... So *no*, Mars, I'm not having a great day."

Mars was hoping for more sympathy, but he couldn't blame her, it was overwhelming - and what she knew was only the tip of the iceberg. "Okay, Sal, here's the Reader's Digest condensed version," he said as calmly as he could. "Someone embezzled the money under my logon." He, of course, left out the fact that the incident had occurred in their master bedroom with another woman with whom he had just had the most amazing sex of his life with a woman he feared he had been in love with for thirty years.

"Oh my God." Sally was computer savvy enough to realize that Mars would be held accountable for anything done on his logon. "How will you figure out who did it?"

I already know he thought as he said, "I have my suspicions."

"Can you prove it?"

"There's no way for me to prove it... I need to convince them to confess." He was careful not to let on that a woman had framed him.

There was silence as they both pondered the seriousness of the situation. Mars knew he couldn't prove anything; he couldn't even tell the truth without destroying his family. It frightened him to think how his life had turned on a dime, just as his grandfather had warned him it could. But he also remembered his advice. He needed to get back in position.

"Sally, I've got to go. I know it's scary. It scares the shit out of me too, but I've got to make the most of this time I have before the Secret Service, or someone else at the bank, finds the mail and figures out that the crime was committed on my logon."

There was another long pause. He thought he heard a sniffle. He didn't have time to acknowledge it. "I'll call back later tonight."

"Okay, I love you, Marshall Hamilton Stewart the third."

"I love you too," Mars answered. A tear rolled down his cheek. He had never meant those words more, but he knew that their life, and love, would never be simple again.

23   - 3:29 p.m.

As Mars started the hour long drive to Baltimore, he barely thought about the fact that Sofia had framed him. Instead he remembered his Angela. Each summer, on his lunch breaks from his lifeguard job at Cape Henlopen State Park, he had gone to Ignazio's. Without fail, seeing her made his face flush, and his groin stir. It was clearly not just a reaction to the aromas - the yeasty smell of fresh-baked breads, mixed with the steamy vapors of grilled onions and steak, mingled with the mouth watering bouquet of freshly sliced salami, prosciutto, and provolone were all enticing. But his had been an involuntary, sometimes unwelcome and painful, reaction to the girl he desperately wanted.

He never saw her in winters - even though they both lived in Wilmington, their paths did not cross - but he dreamed of her year round. The visions borne on cold starry nights were more hopeful, less tortured, than his summer dreams. In those dreary months, he allowed himself to hope that she had broken up with her boyfriend to be with him, that they would marry, and live happily ever after.

At the beginning of each summer, Mars would anxiously await their first encounter. He would catch her eye and ask, "Still?"

Each year, her brown eyes appeared a shade darker as she replied, "Still." Year after year, the impact of her rejecting him was always the same - he felt wounded and empty for days - but then eventually he would get on with his summer.

He was a lifeguard surrounded by gorgeous, scantily clothed, shapely young women many of whom thought that the guards were a hot commodity. Mars rarely got turned down when he asked someone out, but that was relatively rare. Mostly he hung out with the guys and observed their antics.

During those summers, they met plenty of young women in the bars too, especially at the Bottle and Cork in Dewey where a fellow guard, turned doorman at night, never carded them. Mars had been pretty conservative with his partying and with the ladies, at least compared to his animal-house friends. Some of his buddies were the stereotypical insensitive jocks out to put as many notches in their belts as possible, but it all just seemed so superficial to Mars.

He had a few short romances, but he never met a girl that captured his heart like Angela.

Mars ate an Italian sub with peppers at Ignazio's practically every day every summer for five summers. He watched as Angela grew from a long-legged cute girl to a tall, lean and beautiful young eighteen-year-old. Her eyes - that never failed to lock on his - were so deep that he got lost in them more than once while he waited for his order to be filled.

She would quietly but firmly pull him back to reality. "Mars! Here's your hot Italian," she would say with a twinkle in her eyes, knowing that she was the hot Italian he really wanted.

Mars had to settle for the sandwich which he frequently ate outside. Whenever she got close enough that they could talk, her father would suddenly appear. He always seemed to be lurking nearby, guarding his daughter.

Sitting in the lifeguard stand, Mars would pass the time daydreaming of Angela: Angela in a bikini like the hundreds in view; Angela swimming with him like that teenage couple out by the raft; Angela lying next to him like the two under the yellow umbrella. He obsessed about Angela all day and dreamed of her most nights.

In some ways it was torturous, but he couldn't seem to stop himself. Besides she was such a pleasant diversion. He enjoyed thinking about her, wondering what her story was, even though his longings were sometimes painful.

For years she had given him a consistent answer, and any rational person would have given up. But her eyes always gave him hope. Her one word answer to whether she still had a boyfriend was punctuated with a sadness that permeated him. He felt that she wanted to go out with him, and he never understood why she didn't break up with her boyfriend if he didn't make her happy.

He spent hours on his lifeguard stand thinking of ways that he would make her happy, fantasizing about dates that they could go on: a drive down to Ocean City to eat at Phillips followed by some rides at Jolly Rogers, or to the Bottle and Cork to sit on the patio listening to the local bands, then maybe walking, and - in his best dreams - going skinny-dipping on a moonlit night. He had a ton of great-date ideas, and he rarely wasted them on anyone else.

Then one day in July, of his junior year of college,

when she took his order she barely made eye contact. It was so unusual that it instantly made Mars's stomach do a flip. Something was wrong. When she handed him his sandwich, her eyes were averted and she turned away quickly.

Confused and concerned, Mars went back out to his Jeep. He was parked in the shade of the building. He planned to eat there as he often did – hoping to catch another glimpse of Angela before returning to work. As Mars pulled the sub from the brown bag a note fell on his lap. It read, "Mars, please meet me on top of Timmy's Tower at 8:00 tonight. It's important. Angela."

24 - 4:10 p.m.

The Susquehanna River and Havre de Grace slipped by his windows unnoticed as Mars remembered their night on Timmy's Tower.

It was one of the many World War II observation towers located in Cape Henlopen State Park. They had been constructed and used to successfully spot German submarines in the surrounding ocean and bay waters. The cement structures had long since been abandoned except by young locals who found them to be a great place to hang out. They were an attractive nuisance; they were not safe yet they provided panoramic views of Lewes beach and the Delaware Bay. You could see south to Rehoboth and the Henlopen Hotel, and out over the ocean Cape May was visible on clear days.

Mars had witnessed many sunsets and beautiful night skies, and even a sunrise or two from the towers. They varied in height from forty to seventy-five feet, and were about sixteen feet in diameter. They had rows of gun-slit windowless openings that provided observation points from each level.

The ladders and stairs inside were in various states of disrepair making the climb risky, but the view was worth it. Mars only knew of one guy that had been hurt; a few years earlier Timmy Sweeny had been climbing down one of them in the dark. When a rusty rung gave way, he fell to the cement floor some two flights below. Luckily for him sand had drifted in over the years and had created a relatively soft landing. Someone had drawn "Timmy's Tower" on his arm cast, and the name had stuck.

What might transpire that night was on his mind all day. He wondered what it was all about. He fantasized about what he wanted, and about what he wanted her to want. He had imagined how the evening might unfold. Fantasies occupied his mind and teased his body, distracting him from his guard duties. Fortunately, the waves had been calm, and swarms of red jellyfish had kept the crowds out of the ocean making his job easier that endless day.

Anxious, Mars arrived at the tower twenty minutes early. It was a clear evening, and the heat was dissipating. The park was quiet with late beach-goers making their way home and only a few bicyclers out and about.

Seagulls flew overhead.

Over the years, one of the slits at the ground level of the tower had been chipped away to create an opening just wide enough for Mars to squeeze through. Once inside he started the climb with a backpack full of necessities; a flashlight, a beach towel, and four cold beers.

When he reached the top he saw Angela was already there, sitting on a blanket with her back to the ladder, her arms and chin were resting on the lowest railing. Her legs were dangling over the side. Her long brown hair, which had always been pulled back in the deli, hung loose and was blowing towards him in a breeze off the ocean.

Mars sat next to her, his backpack on his lap. He was feeling awkward about the feelings that she aroused in him. Embarrassed, it took him a few seconds to realize that she was crying. It was not the greeting that he had imagined.

"Angela, what is it?" he stammered. "What's the matter?"

She looked up at him with tears streaming down her cheeks and more spilling out of her beautiful, miserable brown eyes. Without saying a word, she held up her left hand displaying a small diamond ring.

Mars's heart sunk as he hugged his knees to his chest. "You're getting married?" he croaked, his fantasies instantly deflated.

She nodded, looked out to the bay, and resumed her silent sobbing. Instinctively, Mars put his arm tentatively around her shoulders and tried to comfort her, wondering - given her news - why in the world she had asked him to meet her.

After several minutes, the sobs slowed to the point where she managed to say, "My father forbids me to date you – to date any Protestant."

What she said confirmed what Mars had always thought - she had wanted to go out with him all along. She looked up at him with her inconsolable eyes then stared back out to the horizon. "I've known Vinny my entire life. We've dated since I was a freshman. He's my best friend. He's good to me ... and to my parents."

She let her head fall onto his shoulder. He could smell her fruity shampoo and could feel her tears dampen his shirt. "Do you love him, Angela?" he had asked bravely. "You shouldn't marry him... I mean... if you don't love him."

She exhaled heavily then sucked in fresh sea air. Her answer came out on an exasperated sigh. "I do. I'm sure I do... but I dream of you, Mars. I have for years."

Those were words that he had always wanted to hear from her, but now that he knew that she was marrying Vinny they cut like razor blades stinging his soul. He wanted to tell her that he dreamed of her too, but he didn't; he didn't want to make this any harder for her.

He didn't know what to do or say. He didn't understand why he was there. He just held her while she quietly sobbed.

They sat there like that - his arm around her, her head on his shoulder, his head resting lightly on hers - as darkness fell over the ocean. He could have stayed like that forever. After a while Angela stopped crying, and he could feel a slight chill where his wet shirt was catching the evening breeze.

The coolness was soon replaced by a heat that built up between them. Mars was trying to ignore it, thinking that it was just him. Then Angela put her hand on his chest and pushed him firmly back on her blanket. The last thing Mars remembered clearly was her cool hand sliding up under his shirt, across his chest, and then back down his torso moving torturously slow as it made its way under the waistband of his shorts.

When she grasped him in her hot hand, she defiantly whispered in his ear, "I'm going to marry Vinny, but tonight I want to be with you, Mars."

It never occurred to Mars to object. Even as it was happening, he knew that once with Angela would be infinitely better than never.

He had been more experienced, but Angela had apparently given it much thought. She was the aggressor: undressing him, toying with him for what seemed like hours before she stopped to perform a tantalizing striptease.

The sun had just set, and its warm light was igniting the low clouds in hot shades of red just as she removed her bra revealing her small firm breasts. He reached for them in near darkness, and as his fingers found her hard brown nipples her hands found him again.

Angela was in charge that night. She teased him until he was practically delirious. He remembered, in his fog, hearing her wince when she took him inside. The pain did not deter her; she was a woman on a mission, and he was her eager accomplice.

By the time she was still, it was dark and when Mars was able to focus his eyes he saw that it was a mostly clear starry night. He felt as if he and Angela, high on their perch, were two more stars forming yet another constellation, one that should grace the universe forever.

Not wanting to break the magical spell, Mars did not speak of what could not be. Instead he pulled the beach towel out of his pack and covered them both, sealing in their heat.

By the light of the rising moon, his lips found her eyes then traced her cheekbones and her nose before they locked onto her soft full lips again. He pushed the towel aside and kissed his way down her long salty body, all the way to her perfect toes. On the return trip he lingered breathing in her musky scent which mingled with the salty ocean breeze until she tugged lightly on his hair pulling him back up to her hungry lips.

Mars had wanted that night to change everything, but it did not. Some days he even imagined that it had all been a wild and fabulous fantasy. But his abraded back and knees - from the cement decking of the tower - and her knowing smile each day at the deli assured him that the images seared in his mind were indeed memories.

He was thrilled each day when he saw her, and

depressed each night as he longed for more. Then one day he saw tears welling in her eyes, and they formed in his too. He knew that she would soon be gone. And she was. Before the summer was even over, she disappeared from his life. A month later he overheard Carmen Ignazio talking about his daughter's wedding.

Mars was devastated then and even more now, knowing she had married Vinny carrying his child.

25 – 4:50 p.m.

As Mars exited I-895S, he surmised that when Angela had cried those heart-wrenching August tears three decades earlier, she had probably already known that she was - that they were - pregnant. He should have had protection. The only other times he had had sex before Angela, he had initiated it, and he had been prepared. He had taken his grandfather's warnings very seriously.

He and Angela had never even been out on a date, so he hadn't dreamed – well, he had dreamed of it often – but he had not imagined that it would be a reality that night. Even after Timmy's Tower, it never occurred to him that she could have gotten pregnant. A far as he was concerned, that was just something health teachers said to scare you.

But it had happened.

Angela had their son with Vinny. The two of them had raised his son. His son was being operated on at Hopkins. He sped up as he approached Baltimore. He tried to convince himself that he needed to focus on the embezzlement, on getting Sofia to clear him, on saving his marriage and his family, but his thoughts kept drifting back to Angela and to the child they had created, and the feelings he still felt.

After circling the hospital, in what was a poor neighborhood of Baltimore, Mars turned into the Broadway parking garage. He had no idea where Angela would be, so he followed the signs to the main entrance.

The elderly woman at the Patient Information desk wore a tag indicating that she was a volunteer named Kitty. He held his breath as he gave her the patient's name -"Pitasi." As he said it, he realized that he did not know his son's first name.

Kitty hen-pecked on the keyboard then pressed Enter, while peering at the monitor. Her chin was raised so she could see through her reading glasses that rested near the end of her nose.

A green screen flashed up, Mars tried to read it as she looked over her glasses at him. "Anthony or Christine?"

"Anthony." He was grateful his offspring was not named after Angela's husband Vinny.

"He's in O-482B. Are you family?" she asked turning away from the screen.

"Yes." Mars replied, wondering if he went by Tony. Tony Danza's image from the days of *Taxi* flashed through his mind. *No, too Italian,* he thought. Her son was half-WASP.

Kitty handed him a guest pass. "This must be displayed at all times." She pointed him to the elevators and instructed him on how to navigate to the Osler Building.

Mars took a detour into the cafeteria planning to just get a cup of coffee, but as the aromas of the food hit him he realized that he was starved. He had not touched his lunch at the club. He selected a personal pizza -

usually harmless - and a bottle of water then settled into a table.

As Mars wolfed down the first slice, he considered the possibility that Angela would not be the only visitor; her husband Vinny might also be there, or maybe - God forbid - her father Carmine Ignazio, a man that had never liked Mars.

How would he explain his presence?

If she was just Sofia, the woman that framed him, maybe he would just burst into the room and confront her. But she was also Angela, the mother of his child, the girl he thought he had loved thirty years ago.

Sofia Angela Ignazio Pitasi held the key to his past and his future. He decided to call her cell phone. No answer. Maybe she had heeded the no-cell-phone warning. He hoped she was there and he hadn't made the trip for nothing.

Mars was about to find out. He inhaled the last slice of his pizza then made his way to the elevators where he crammed into a full car, trying not to touch anyone or anything; germs were everywhere.

He walked past the visitors' lounge on Tony's floor and glanced in, figuring if any other family was there they would probably not recognize him. No Angela. He proceeded down the hall past 476, 478 and 480. The door to 482 was open. Mars passed by slowly and noticed it had two beds. The one by the door was empty. There was a young man in the one by the window, but he was on his side facing away from the door. Mars could not get a good look him.

Shit, which one is B? He had not asked and Kitty hadn't volunteered that information. He approached the nurse's station. A nurse in lavender scrubs looked up from a mountain of paperwork, "May I help you?"

"Yes, I'm looking for Anthony Pitasi."

"They just took him down to surgery." She offered without looking up. She grabbed his file, opened it and added, "Operating Room Three. There's a map just outside the double doors." She glanced up to make sure that he was satisfied before continuing to shuffle through her papers.

Mars had many more questions, but he left anyway. He still had no idea what Anthony's problem was, or if Angela was in the building. He had no choice but to go try to find her.

He found the Cardiac Surgery Waiting Room. Again he made a slow pass by the door noting the foul smells of human waste mixing with bleach and antiseptics. His stomach churned. The waiting room was a busy place where at least a dozen people were sitting. A large group was huddled around an elderly woman, consoling her. No one looked familiar there. A couple was watching MSNBC.

Then he saw her sitting alone flipping through a magazine.

26 – 5:12 p.m.

Mars watched her for a few minutes. Now that he knew who she really was, he could see Angela in Sofia. He had noticed her bottomless brown eyes before, but now he saw that there was something familiar about the way she held her head.

He walked across the waiting room. She was looking at a *People* magazine, just glancing at the pictures, not reading. She looked tired.

"Angela." His voice was soft, purposely non-confrontational. Still, it startled her.

"Oh my God, Mars." She put the magazine down. "You came."

Mars felt anger rising as he remembered that she had sent him to see his father then had run off. "Lucky for me your neighbor knew where you were or-"

She cut him off. "Didn't you get my message?"

"What-?" Mars started then remembered he had missed a couple of calls. He had not checked his voicemails.

"Right after you left to see your father I got the call

saying that Tony was having his surgery. I had to leave, but I called from the road."

Mars realized that he had misjudged her - again. He sank into the chair across from her.

"Mars, I know we need to talk, but I can't," she said sounding exhausted, but she was firm. "Not now, Mars."

"I know it's not a good time, but I deserve some answers." Mars looked around, "Are you alone?"

"Yes," she said softly looking down at the magazine in her lap before making eye contact again. "So your father told you?"

"He did. I know about... about the pregnancy."

"So all these years, you really didn't know? Your father had never told you?" She asked suspiciously. Her eyes moved to the television. They were welling up.

"No," Mars said, wanting her to look him in the eye again. When she finally did, he added, "Angela I swear, I never knew. It never occurred to me ... You were getting married. You told me not to contact you again. I tried once, but... I had no idea. "

A family came into the room, and plopped down in a group of chairs behind Angela. The man had blood on his shirt. The kids were crying.

"Angela, why didn't you tell me?" he asked, feeling betrayed.

"I can't do this here, Mars," she said, the pain painting her words with a sadness that seemed to have accumulated for thirty years. There was an edge of desperation that was fresh and alive.

"Angela, at least tell me how my son is."

A look of surprise came over her face. She studied his face then stood and walked quickly out into the hallway and onto a full elevator that was going down. Mars blocked the doors from closing and crammed in too.

They didn't speak. He stood next to her looking down

at her strained face and realized that he was feeling sorry for her. He reminded himself that his life was on the line. She owed him some answers.

When they exited in the lobby, she proceeded out the front doors. Mars wondered where she was going. Was she going to run again? She stopped next to the first unoccupied bench. She turned slowly to face him.

"You don't know about our son?"

Tears flowed down her cheeks instantly disarming Mars. He was confused. "I do. My father told me today. What's wrong with him?" He wondered if he could donate blood, or maybe he needed a kidney or something.

She sat. "Oh my God, Mars, I -" Tears ran down her face. She seemed incapable of finishing her thought.

"Did you steal the money for our son?"

She stared at him through big tears. Lines formed on her brow. "Mars, he's not yours." She dropped her head into her hands. "Oh God, what a mess."

He couldn't understand why she was denying Anthony was his. "We'll figure it out." He couldn't see her face. He lowered his and tried to soothe her. "I'll try to help you, Angela - and him - but you've got to help me too. The Secret Service is going to find that e-mail you sent, and then they are going to come for me. You have to tell me what's going on."

"I was hoping the owner-"

"Ms. Jacobson," he interrupted.

"Yes, Ms. Kathryn Jacobson. I know her name Mars. I didn't mean to hurt her... or you. It's just - all that money was lying there dormant. I was hoping she would never surface, that her money would never be missed."

She sat back up. Her shoulders slumped. She looked at her watch. "It's a long story. I have to get back to Tony. I need to be there when he comes out of surgery."

Mars didn't want to wait a minute longer, but he

would. He stood and pulled her up by her out-stretched hand. "I'll come with you; we'll wait together."

She pulled her hand free and looked him directly in the eyes. "No, Mars. He is *not* your son. I need to go back in there. Alone."

Still eye to eye, not understanding, he asked, "Angela, do you have *two* sons?"

"No," Angela sighed heavily, "I don't, I -" Again, she stopped mid-sentence and sighed heavily. She looked utterly distressed.

"Look I know that my father-" he hesitated wanting to say 'sold my son', but he feared he would upset her further. "My father gave up my rights, but that boy is my flesh and blood and if he needs me -"

"Mars, Anthony is *not* your son. Please," she pleaded. She hit her forehead lightly against his chest. He drew her closer. "Please. I'll tell you everything, just not now. I need to go back in."

She seemed to summon her strength. Her shoulders straightened and she raised her head. She was ready to go, but she could see that Mars was unconvinced. "Mars, the story has waited three decades ... Please just let it be for a few more hours."

He tried to read her; tried to see a lie in her face. He didn't. He saw young Angela, older now, but she was in there. He should have recognized her, if not by her looks then by how she made him feel. "Okay, Angela. Go. But then we have to talk. Tonight."

She wasted no time moving away from him.

Immediately, he second guessed himself. "Am I a fool to trust you, Angela?" he called after her.

She turned, but continued backing towards the hospital. Mars matched her pace, keeping a constant distance between them. "No, Mars. I *need* you too. I know this is hard for you to understand, it's hard for *me* to understand. I needed your help."

"Lord knows I need you," Mars blurted back.

"I'm staying at the Inner Harbor Marriot," she said.

"What about Vinny?"

She stopped, and turned back to him. "He's not coming. He has to stay home; the deli is open nine to nine. Mars, I've got to go."

She disappeared through the door.

Mars started to panic. He knew what would happen if she did not clear him, but he couldn't cover all the doors. He had no choice but to go wait for her.

I am a fool.

27 – 5:26 p.m.

Mars watched Angela go back into the hospital. He returned to the bench and sat. He couldn't figure out why she wouldn't admit that Anthony was his son. He didn't get it. Maybe her father had lied to his father to get the money. Maybe she was never pregnant with his child.

The sun was beating down on him. No wonder no one else was sitting outside; they had all taken refuge in the air conditioning of the building. Mars did not like cities. All the paved surfaces bugged him. He needed beach and bodies of water. He thought of that ad that used to run on television – the old American Indian weeping over what we have done to our earth. Cities with their traffic and noise always made him feel off-kilter. The extreme heat was not helping.

He knew that he must be crazy to let Angela out of his sight again. He had no more information than when he arrived. She could be exiting the other side of the building with her bags packed full of bikinis and sunscreen.

A vision of him with her on a beach popped into his

mind. He was applying the sunscreen to her warm tan skin. Caribbean blue waves lapped at the powder-white sand beach.

A man in scrubs whizzed by on a bike, waking him from his alluring fantasy. Maybe they could take the money and run off to the islands together. Mars stood and tried to shake off the thought. He could not run off with her, but he realized somewhere deep inside, he felt that he could trust her not to run from him.

He stood and walked back to the parking garage convinced that she would call him. She would do what she said. He would find out what was wrong with their son, and if it was in fact the boy's health that drove her to embezzle the money.

By the time he pushed the card-key into the lock of his hotel room, Mars was very hopeful that she would take responsibility for what she had done. He was supposed to be on a non-smoking floor, but it was obvious that someone had recently had a cigarette there, and whatever spray they had used to camouflage it had not done the job.

He opened the window and let the hot humid air fill the room. The city smells were a slight improvement. He was disappointed that the hotel was not adjacent to the Inner Harbor, but it was adequate.

The bed had snow white linens; an array of pillows that beckoned to him rested against the walnut headboard. A maroon reading chair with an ottoman was in one corner; a desk with an Ethernet connection was in another. Even the carpet – a maroon and beige leaf pattern – looked fresh. They must have remodeled recently. Too bad it stunk.

Mars put his bags on the luggage rack, lounged on the bed and checked his voicemail. There was nothing interesting. He called Liz at the bank to see what was going on there, but she had apparently gone home for the day. He knew that she would have sent him an update, so he set up his laptop and connected to the internet using his Secure-Away fob. Once on the bank's system he checked his work e-mails.

There were several pertaining to the embezzlement investigation, but they were all fairly benign. Liz had sent a progress report on his other projects as well as on the fraud research. So far – thankfully – their efforts had not yielded any clues. He hoped the other recipients had deleted their copy of the mail.

It occurred to him that even when someone found it, the override request may seem innocuous. But Liz was on the ball. She would question it. He hoped that she would not be the one to uncover it.

Mars reread his copy. Sofia had overridden the conversion process to take her test file as input instead of the production file. He copied the filename out of the override and searched for it. No surprise, it had been deleted. Even without seeing it, he was confident that she had moved funds from Jacobson's dormant account to the dormant one that she reactivated a week later.

He also knew that she must have withdrawn the money. He toggled to the Deposit Account System online transaction history screen. Mars reviewed the history for July twelfth, the day of the account reactivation that he had found that morning. *Bingo.* A wire-transfer had moved almost all of the money to an account in another bank. She left ten cents.

By now that money is offshore. Hopefully, she is not on her way to join it.

Mars made notes in his planner then sent a brief e-mail to Liz thanking her for the update. He asked some questions about what the Secret Service agents were up to, and reiterated that he planned to return to work on

Monday. He would try to get up with her during business hours tomorrow.

Mars was about to sign off when he decided to Google Tony Pitasi. No hits. He tried Anthony Pitasi. Nothing. Not even Facebook. Disappointed, Mars logged off and stretched out on the bed. He could not relax. Fears about his future and his son Tony's health swirled through him. He decided to go for a run - maybe down to the harbor - in hopes of clearing his head.

The summer daytime heat was giving way to more pleasant evening temperature, but it was still humid. He was dripping when he ran past the aquarium, but kept up a good pace for fifteen more minutes then turned back. He stopped in the hotel gym, used some of the free weights then took a shower.

Feeling saner, he called home.

Peter answered. "Oh hey, Dad." He was obviously unconcerned; and after a brief conversation that felt a little like pulling teeth, Mars found out that Sally and Beck were at some kind of function at Beck's field hockey camp. They would be back in another hour or so. Peter promised to leave his mom a message that Mars had called and that he would try back later. Mars did not want to call her cell and get her all stirred up in public.

He tuned in to the CNBC station. The market was down again. He watched for Apple on the ticker tape. He kicked himself again for not buying it earlier in the year. He could be rich - like Angela, but legally.

The ringing phone jarred him out of a deep sleep. He glanced at his watch – eight-forty-seven. He had been comatose for well over an hour.

"Mars? It's Angela." She sounded pooped.

He sat up. A slight smile of relief formed. She called. He had known she would. "Hey, are you at the hotel?"

"Yeah, I just got in. Have you eaten?"

"No. Would you like to go out?" He was trying to remember what restaurants he had seen when out running. There was always Phillips Crab House. It was not as good as the original in Ocean City, but it would do.

"Not really... I was planning on ordering room service. Do you want to go grab something for yourself, or do you want me to order for you too?"

"I'll do room service with you. Hang on." Mars got up and found the menu. He felt the now familiar twinge in his shorts at the thought of being alone in a motel room with her. He was an idiot. "Order me a plain personal pizza, a side salad, and a Diet Coke."

"Okay, I'll call. Then I need to jump in the shower. Why don't you wait a half hour then come to my room - two-fourteen.

"Okay, see you then."

Mars stared blankly at the television not even noticing as Apple's price rolled by, up another forty cents.

28 - 9:22 p.m.

When Angela answered the door she was fresh out of the shower. She was one clean woman – at least in that way. Mars had an almost uncontrollable urge to wrap his arms around her. She was dressed in gray Capri sweat pants with a pink strip down the outside of each leg. A matching top was unzipped to the point of distraction. Her hair was towel-dried and combed back off her forehead. Her face was make-up free, her cheeks flushed from the heat of the shower.

She smelled like spring.

"Come on in," she said, her fatigue obvious as she walked back into the bathroom. "Make yourself at home," she said before turning on the hair dryer.

Her room was the mirror image of his. He opened the armoire exposing the television. With the remote in hand he was tempted to sprawl out on the still-perfectly-made bed. Instead, he settled into the reading chair. He found the weather channel. He didn't really care about the weather; he just wanted to be doing something, or – more accurately – he wanted to appear to be doing something while he focused on tamping down the too-warm feelings that he was having for Angela.

Not again, you idiot.

He knew that it was utterly ridiculous - reckless his grandfather would say - to want her under these circumstances. *You're happily married.* Then there was the fact that she had framed him. He knew it should matter. It did not. The physical attraction that he had always felt for her was, in spite of everything, still there, and he was pretty certain that she felt the same way.

That night could not have been an act, could it?

Flashes of Elaine on Seinfeld demonstrating how she faked orgasms morphed into thoughts of Angela thirty years ago, and of Sofia a month ago. It was a compelling montage that threatened to drown out all rational thoughts. The voice that told him that he could not go there again, that he had already made that mistake – twice - was barely a whisper. The first time she had gotten pregnant and left. The second time she framed him and left.

The trend was obvious. A sane man would not tempt fate. He was feeling anything but sane. He resolved to keep his distance.

He tried to think about Sally, Peter and Beck, but found himself thinking about Tony. What was he going to do about him? And Angela, as the mother of his first child was - in a bizarre twist of fate - family too. He could not see how to fit all of the pieces into the puzzle that was his life.

He knew that, after his own childhood experiences, he could never leave his kids. And he would not leave his wife. But now that he knew about Tony, he could not abandon him either.

And deep in his soul, he knew he could not abandon Angela, certainly not right now. She said she needed his help, and he certainly needed hers.

"Sorry, Mars." Her voice jolted him back to the moment as she came into the room.

She was ravishing. He tried to focus on something else. "How's Tony?"

"He's resting well, thanks." She sat on the bed and nestled into the pillows against the headboard, facing him.

"What surgery did he have?" Mars asked, feeling like he had a right to know long before now.

"He needed a heart valve replacement. He's doing well though. Says he hasn't felt this good in years. It's a miracle." She closed her eyes, let her head fall back.

He wanted to be next to Angela to comfort her. Instead, he leaned back in the chair resting one ankle on the other knee and waited for her to continue; to tell him more about his son. Her eyes stayed closed. "Dinner should be here any minute; I haven't had anything since breakfast." She sighed, as if she was about to drift off to sleep. "I promise I'll tell you everything, just give me... a few... more... minutes."

Mars did not press her. He let her rest as he wondered if he had passed some congenital heart defect to his son. His father and grandfather both had heart disease.

Angela's head listed to one side.

Mars realized that she had been through a lot, but he resented the delay. She had framed him. She owed him an explanation for that and about his son. He tried to be firm with his self-talk, but it was no use. Truth be known, he was content just being in the same room with her.

29   - 9:31 p.m.

Mars sat in the chair watching Angela resting on the bed. He considered his predicament until the room service guy knocked. Mars signed and brought the tray to the table next to him.

He considered letting Angela sleep, but he had waited long enough. Besides, she had heard the door. She rolled her face into the pillow, and moaned a quiet protest before sitting up on the side of the bed.

Mars brought the desk chair over to the table and sat in it, leaving the upholstered one for her. She folded herself into it and immediately uncovered the food. He saw that she had ordered the same thing: pizza and a salad. They both dug in. In the background, the weather channel was giving an update on Tropical Storm Hallie. They made some small talk about the busy hurricane season, coastal erosion, and the pros and cons of beach replenishment as they ate.

It was crazy, but Mars was patient. It was easy to be patient. Spending time with her was enough... well, almost enough.

After consuming half of her pizza, Angela abruptly started telling the story that he had been waiting to hear. "I missed my period that August, and I knew. I had been nauseated for weeks. I just felt... *different.* It took me another couple of weeks to tell my Mom. I was afraid to tell my father. Mom told him... It was as awful as I thought it would be. Pop was furious."

Mars believed it. The guy had never liked him.

Angela pushed her food aside. "You need to understand that my dad had two daughters. No sons. I don't know about the rest of them, but Italian men want sons. Oh sure, daughters are blessings too, but sons carry on their proud names. They grow up to run their businesses.

"My husband Vinny lived just up the street. His father was one of my father's best friends. He died when Vinny was only twelve."

It was a sad story and Mars could see where it was headed. Vinny couldn't carry on the family name, but he could marry a daughter and run the Ignazio delicatessens.

"That first year after his dad's death, Vinny helped around our house doing yard work and other chores. My sister and I were delighted not to have to do boys' work anymore. When he was thirteen Pop hired him to work at our deli."

Bingo, Mars thought.

"He was two years older than me, but he was always so nice. By the time I was a teenager, I had a huge crush on him. He flirted with me for years. I was crazy about him."

"I can relate," Mars said.

Angela smiled knowingly at him, but continued the story. "When he was fifteen, he asked me to his

Homecoming Dance, and Pop let me go.... I felt so special; Vinny Pitasi the soon-to-be-varsity-star quarterback for Salesianum was taking *me* to the dance." She seemed to drift back to that time, smiling faintly. "I never dated anyone else."

"I can relate to that too," Mars said with a dramatic wince. It had been painful year after year to find out she was "still" dating someone else. Then that night on the tower she had told him the real reason, her father wanted her to date a Catholic boy. Now he knew, not just any Catholic boy; her father had the one all picked out.

"Mars, you know I wanted to date you. I was torn, but I couldn't."

Mars had believed her now just as he had that night thirty years ago. The hours on Timmy's Tower had been like magic to him. He had been under her spell for a decade after. It crossed his mind that he had been set up both times. Maybe, if Tony was not his child, maybe she used him back then to extort money. His mind was like warm tapioca. He had no idea what to believe.

He looked up.

She had been watching him as he mulled it over. She could see his confusion. "I defied my father by being with you. Suffice it to say, when I announced that I was pregnant with your child, all hell broke loose."

Her eyes welled up just thinking about it. She looked tired again. "Pop said there was no way that his daughter was going to get an abortion, and no way on God's earth she was marrying a Protestant."

Mars felt his fury for the man in his cheeks and ears. "There was no way you weren't marrying Vinny. That's what it was all about. It was a freaking arranged marriage, Angela. You might as well have been in some third-world country."

"I know it seems like that, but it all went back to him

not having a son and Vinny not having a Dad. And there was the fact that I thought I loved Vinny until -"

Mars felt his chest swell. "You shouldn't have gone along with it." She frowned hard, left the table, and plopped back down on the bed where she sat leaning against the headboard again. Her arms hugged her knees to her chest. She looked like a frightened teenager. Mars felt bad.

She recounted her ordeal. "Pop told me that I would break Vinny's heart if I told him what we'd done. I thought he was probably right." She paused.

Mars could understand that feeling. He knew he would break Sally's heart if he left their marriage, or if she ever found out what he had done with Sofia / Angela in their bed.

His wife was in love with him. He loved her too. He had betrayed her, but he never meant to and he was not going to abandon her, no matter how much he wanted to be with Angela.

She was continuing. "He even thought it would be better for everyone if I slept with Vinny then told him that I was pregnant with..."

"That's asinine, not to mentions wholly un-Catholic."

"I agree." She studied his face, "I knew that I could not start our marriage with a gigantic lie." Then in measured tones, going slow to make sure he got it, she added. "I told Vinny the truth."

"And he still married you?" Mars was amazed. As much as he loved Sally – and Angela – he wasn't sure he could have married either one of them if they were pregnant with another man's child.

"Guess Vinny must not be all bad," he offered with a wry smile. Angela looked up in time to catch it.

"He came around, but he didn't speak to me for weeks. I used to think that those were the worst weeks of my life." She laughed a laugh that said she knew just how wrong she had been.

Mars understood that her worst days were in the process of being redefined – so were his. It was easy to see how horrible that ordeal must have been for her. And, he realized, this must be too. She had to have been desperate to commit a felony.

"My parents even found a *convent* where I could go and have the baby."

"God, they still have those?" Mars asked unable to visualize her in a habit. *What a waste that would have been.*

"But Vinny came back." She smiled sadly. "He still loved me. He looked horrible. He hadn't slept in days. He decided. He didn't want to live without me. All I had to do was promise to be faithful and he said he would forgive me."

"Did he?"

"He tried. Maybe he did, but he never really trusted me again."

It occurred to Mars that Vinny might be more insightful than his name conjured up. Mars caught her eye again. She must have read his mind. "I've kept my promise until you – again. You are my weakness. Imagine me giving myself to you when I didn't know anything more about you than you liked hot Italians."

"Just one hot Italian. And I don't have to imagine, Angela, I remember very well." He was smiling a true smile. Those were some of the most blissful hours of his life.

"The only other thing I knew about you was that you were a lifeguard – you were so cute in those blue trunks with your sun-bleached hair."

He blushed.

"Not to mention persistent."

Flattered, he laughed, but Angela was already continuing her sad tale. "The fact that he was willing to marry me, and raise someone else's child, made me certain that I loved him – or that I should. He married me that September."

Mars had finished his pizza. He had totally lost interest in his salad. He didn't know what to say, but Dr. Phil's line - *How's that working for you?* - ricocheted around in his mind as he fought against the bitterness. She had feelings for him. She should have stood up to her father.

He wished now that he had gone after her. Maybe if he had shown up in those two weeks before Vinny came back he would have had a chance. Maybe if he had promised to convert to Catholicism.

"Well, I guess that was better than a convent," Mars offered.

"Yeah, but I was consumed with guilt. I worried endlessly that Vinny would never totally forgive me, that he wouldn't be able to love the baby, and worse that maybe I didn't love him enough to be there." Her eyes found Mars's as she bit lightly on her lip. "I never felt the attraction to him that I felt for you. From the first time you asked me out, I dreamed of you, Mars. But I figured it was just a case of the forbidden fruit, of wanting what I couldn't have."

"But you could have had me Angela," Mars said. "If you had come to me we could have made it work even without our fathers' blessings."

She looked up at Mars, with those deep brown eyes, "It was complicated Mars. I knew that I had strong feelings for you, and believe me I thought about going to you, but I barely knew you – I barely know you now. Plus, Pop told me about the deal that he made with your father. He had accepted money in exchange for a promise. I could never tell you. It was a done deal. That's why I made you go to him this morning. Your father had to tell you; I still couldn't go back on my father's word, Pop would've turned over in his grave, and your father would have made me pay the money back with the interest penalty."

"Someone should have told me-"

"I know, Mars. But I was so young. I was scared." She continued, determined to get the story out. "My father used the hush money to buy us a house, and he gave it to us as a wedding present so Vinny would never know about the payoff."

"So you did lie. You let your father look like a big man," Mars said.

"Perhaps," she agreed not wanting to argue. She went on. "I was torn about you Mars, but I felt lucky to still have Vinny." She looked perplexed as she remembered. "I didn't know how to feel about the house, it seemed dirty, like some kind of a bribe. I was excited to have a baby on the way, but at times I felt trapped."

"You *were* trapped in the marriage your father arranged."

"Some days – and nights – it felt like that, because part of me was always thinking about you - my memories of our night were so vivid." She looked slightly embarrassed.

"Now there are two nights to remember," Mars added smiling lustfully before stopping himself. They both let their minds drift back to those precious hours.

"We're good together," Mars noted.

Angela smiled a silent agreement. "I loved Vinny enough to make it work for him and the baby. I figured that I would be happy eventually."

"Were you?"

"I never had a chance. At eight months I lost the

baby." Her voice trailed off. Mars could hardly hear her. "He stopped moving and I knew." He saw a tear roll down her cheek. "Our baby died inside of me."

"Oh my God." The news hit him like a brick in the solar plexus.

30 - 10:13 p.m.

Mars closed his eyes and shook his head as if he could shake the truth away. Tony was not his son. He tried to sort through his feelings of loss and relief. When he looked up again, Angela was crying alone on the bed.

He crossed the room in two long strides and sat beside her. He took her in his arms and kissed her hair as the full impact of her nightmare struck him.

"It was awful, Mars. I only saw him for a few seconds then they took him away... forever. He was so perfect, except..."

Perfect except he was dead, Mars thought. How horrible. He hugged her tighter, letting the news sink in. His son had died. Tony really was not his son. He is Vinny's son. "Angela, I'm so sorry."

"I just knew that it was my fault. I had been consumed with guilt and worried sick through my whole pregnancy."

He gently pushed her back, held her firmly by the shoulders, and waited for the eye contact. "It wasn't your fault, Angela." He didn't say it, but he was thinking that it was their fathers' fault. It was not hers.

He pulled her close again, his heart wrenching knowing that she *still* felt guilty. Her head was resting on his shoulder, her breath was warm on his neck, and her tears soaked his shirt again as he kneaded her back and kissed her hair. Finally her breathing returned to normal.

She sat up. "Everyone told me, *It's God's way*, or y*ou're young, don't worry, you'll have another...* as if my little boy could be replaced."

She seemed to reflect on that for a while. Mars's head was spinning. He couldn't think straight. He felt inadequate, he wanted to comfort her, but he didn't know how.

She continued, "Tony is my second child. He was born a year later... There was never any time to grieve for my dead boy. No one wanted to hear about him, let alone talk about him. They told me not to dwell on the past. Maybe it would have been different if Vinny had been the biological father, but I sensed that my whole family was relieved. I know that sounds cold, and they would never admit it, but deep down, I know that they felt it was a blessing in disguise. In some ways maybe I did too, and realizing that made it worse."

Mars stroked her hair and her shoulder.

"Vinny married me knowing it was your child. He was good to me, but he couldn't feel what I felt for my unborn child - what you would have felt." She snuggled a little closer, and Mars felt bad that he didn't feel more grief. He was relieved. He hadn't shirked his responsibilities after all.

"Vinny wanted to forget the past, and I couldn't blame him. After a few months no one spoke of my dead baby any more, but I could not stop thinking about him."

She looked up, "I was obsessed with *my* loss, and

even more with my baby's loss: he never got to breathe his first breath, never cut his first tooth, or walked a single step... I felt that I had robbed him of his life."

"It wasn't your fault, Angela," Mars said again as he brushed some stray hairs out of her tear-soaked eyes. "I'm so sorry I wasn't there for you," he held her tighter. Angela had no way to know just how true that was, how he had longed for her for all those years. She would never know how he had looked for a woman that he felt the same way about.

He wondered if their child would have lived had they been allowed to marry. *A moot point,* he thought, but still he wondered...

31 -10:42 p.m.

Mars held Angela in his arms as he thought about the trauma of her losing their baby. When Sally had been pregnant with Peter, by eight months they were carrying on conversations with her belly, singing to it. They had painted the nursery a safe yellow, and had stocked up on all of the other necessities for when the baby first came home: formula, powders, lotions, and diapers - lots of diapers.

He knew how bonded they must have already been - Angela for sure, and hopefully Vinny. He could not imagine the loss she had felt or her sense of isolation when her family had not shared her grief. It was unfathomable.

He agonized, wishing that he had been there with her sharing in their loss. He knew that the sorrow he felt now was less for the baby than for Angela. Their fathers had played God with his and Angela's lives, and consequently their child had been still-born, like their love. It may have been perfectly formed, but it had not been given a chance at life.

His heart broke for them, then and now. Then they may have been able to make it work. Now there was no chance for them. He had a family, and so did she. Mars realized that there was no way to win.

He kissed the top of her head, and mournfully whispered, "Our fathers should have let us work it out."

Her smooth hand covered his. They were wrapped around her belly. Her thumb mindlessly stroked his fingers, as if they were guitar strings and she was playing a sad ballad. "I blamed them too, Mars, but not as much as I blamed myself; I shouldn't have met you on the tower that night. I knew what we were going to do. I wasn't on the pill. And I blamed myself for not telling you." She paused as if she wasn't sure she should continue. "I worried that things wouldn't work out with Vinny, that - that maybe I loved you."

"I *knew* I loved you," he said softly. He closed his eyes and the whole world disappeared; he floated with Angela on a cloud that was the life they should have had.

The dream was short-lived.

"When our baby died I was sure that I killed him. Some days, I figured God had punished me for my sin." Mars pulled her closer. "Other days, I knew that there was no God."

She was crying again. Mars kissed her cheek. "Geez ... I can't even get a grip now," she laughed. "You can only imagine what a basket case I was then." Then she was serious again "When I got pregnant just months later - my hormones only made it all worse. I was afraid that I might lose my second child too."

"Wasn't there anyone that you could talk to?"

"No. My family had moved on. They expected me to too."

How cold, Mars thought. "What about your sister, or your priest, or a nun?"

"I did talk to our priest. He assured me that it was not my fault, that I should accept that it was *God's will;* that I was blessed to be pregnant again so soon... I never told him that Vinny wasn't our baby's father. Pop forbade me to tell anyone."

"Even your priest?" Mars tried to keep the incrimination out of his voice.

"He was so ashamed of me. His daughter's sin was not to be discussed."

Mars lay there blaming her father, and his own. He wanted to blame Vinny too, but he couldn't. Vinny must have loved her very much. "Had you picked a name?" Mars asked.

"His headstone just says Baby Pitasi, but if it was a boy, he was going to be Carmen Louis Pitasi after my father and Vinny's."

As if it mattered at this point, it bothered Mars that his son would have been named after Carmen Ignazio - one of the two men that had pushed Mars out of Angela's life. It didn't seem right, and he found himself visualizing his son, if he had lived, with his WASP-ish features and that strong Italian name. The whole thing was stupid.

Angela brought him back to her reality. "I had no outlet for my feelings until I started writing poetry," she laughed a sad laugh, "bad poetry at that. My poems were dark and depressing - all about my dead baby - but it was therapeutic, and over time, I started to feel better.

It took years, but I finally wrote a poem that captured how I wanted to feel about our child," Angela tilted her head up to look at Mar, "and about you. It became my mantra. At night, or whenever I feel blue, I still mentally recite it until the emptiness goes away."

"Can I hear it?"

She turned to face him, her deep eyes probing his. "Do you remember the sky that night?"

"I remember the stars and then the moon rising right over the tower."

She continued, "From then on, I could not look at the moon without thinking of you. Later, it was comforting to envision our son in heaven, somewhere up in the sky, with that moon... and with a father that loved him."

Mars smiled. He liked knowing that she had never gotten over him either. He could feel her relax into him as she recited her poem:

Two Ladders

Two ladders to the moon, my son
We climb them in my mind

And there I hold you close and warm
'Til moonlight turns to dawn

And through each day I dream of you
And miss you while we're gone

Two ladders to the moon, my son
We'll go there for all time

"That's beautiful, Angela," Mars said pulling her closer. Thoughts of their fathers and of the embezzlement were a galaxy away.

32 - Wednesday 6:18 a.m.

Mars felt the first light of morning on his eyelids even before he opened them. Through the gap in the half-open curtains, he saw that the sun was rising over Baltimore's skyline. It cast a wedge of orange on the white comforter and on Angela's shoulder. It warmed the side of his face.

He was waking up *with Angela*. It was a dream come true, albeit thirty years too late. He pulled her fragrance deep into his lungs.

He was on his left side under the blankets, spooned against Angela. Her butt was nestled against him. The backs of her thighs rested lightly on the front of his. He could feel her heartbeat under his hand, and he knew from the rhythm of her breathing that she was still fast asleep.

She had been exhausted, and - as if on cue - had dozed off just after reciting her poem. Mars had not been able to bring himself to wake her to talk about the embezzlement. He had meant to go back to his own room, but obviously he had drifted off to la la land too. It had been a long day for both of them.

Even though they were both still fully clothed, every breath she took stirred him. But his mind and body were not in sync; unwelcome thoughts streamed into his head trying to drown his pleasurable feelings. He knew that he had no business being here with Angela, but in his heart he felt it was where he belonged.

Past tense he noted. She had been right for him, but she wasn't anymore. He needed to focus on the present and the future which, with all of its risk and all of its rewards, loomed in front of him. It was not staring him in the face, but was pressed against his crotch. With each long exhale, Mars grew more certain that Angela had been his destiny. He had known it then, and he knew it now.

This is lunacy, he thought as his eyes shot open again. *What would Gramps do?*

He knew he needed to get back in position, but he had less of a clue how to do that now then he had a day ago. His grandfather had not advised him on what to do if you were married to one person, and found you were in love with someone else too. And his mentor certainly had not addressed what to do if that other someone was a felon - a felon that he could never get enough of.

Anxiety trickled down from his brain and crawled into his limbs. It filled them with a restless, antsy feeling. He broke into a sweat. He knew he had to get away. He needed to think. He had to figure out what to do before he dug himself in any deeper... even though deeper was exactly where he wanted to go.

He eased his hand away from Angela's breasts, inch, by inch, until it was free then waited to see if she would wake. She did not. He rolled clear of her, and eased himself out of her bed. He went to the window. With the sun on his face, he stretched, and tried to slow his breathing, his heartbeat, and his mind.

He tried to remember her mantra. *Two ladders to the moon, my love...*

He could just barely see the mast of a tall ship flying the Maryland state flag as it slid out of the Inner Harbor. Baltimore was waking up. Cars, and an occasional pedestrian, were already moving on the streets below.

Miraculously, the world was still turning.

Mars began to see and feel the possibilities of the new day. He was a problem solver by trade and by nature. He would solve this one - somehow.

He went to the desk, and wrote a note. He was going for another run. He asked Angela to call him when she got up. They still needed to talk. He still had no clue why she had framed him. It would be one thing if he was Tony's father - maybe she would have felt that he owed it to his son - but he wasn't.

He left the folded hotel stationery leaning against the bedside clock then stood for a moment watching her. She was smiling faintly, and he wondered if she was dreaming about him. She looked peaceful and content - maybe on her poetic moon.

It took all of Mars's resolve not to crawl back under the comforter.

As the door clicked shut behind him, he instantly regretted his decision, but he knew that his fate had been sealed thirty years ago. Their fathers had locked him out of Angela's life. He needed to deal with it.

33 - 6:38 a.m.

Mars jogged east on Pratt Street along the harbor trying to figure out a plan for his life. When that failed he focused on a plan for the day.

He needed to call Sally. He was sick about what he was doing to her. He had never meant for this to happen. Looking backwards would not accomplish anything. He needed to go forward, but did not know how the hell to get out of the mess he was in.

He tried again to imagine what advice his grandfather would give him, but all he could think of was that he never should have let himself get in this position in the first place. It still seemed impossible. How could it be that hc, Marshall Hamilton Stewart III, had messed up this badly? He was such a conservative guy, totally committed to his wife and his family. He had been content with his life; yet in one moment of weakness everything had all changed.

But has it? He dodged a group of people getting off a bus thinking that the jury was still out on the embezzlement, and on a personal level the only thing that had actually changed so far was his feelings. In his heart and soul he knew he was in love with Angela. But he also knew that in the grand scheme of things it was a moot point – at least to everyone else.

So if that was all that ever changed, things could still work out. No one would ever need to know how he felt. He just needed to protect his family. He needed Angela to admit to stealing the money.

His feet made familiar contact with the pavement. His life was hanging by a thread, but so far it was intact. He was determined to do everything in his power to keep it that way. Mars passed the aquarium, with its glass atrium shimmering in the morning light.

The whole relationship with Angela aside, his big problem was that he could be arrested any day now. Surely the Secret Service with all of its resources had found, or would soon find, the e-mail that Angela had written. When they did, they would discover that his aunt had not died. They would devote resources to finding him.

Mars remembered the first time he saw Special Agent Lance Williams. He had been the only one in a business suit at that emergency Sunday meeting. Mars glanced at a few of the guys in suits that he passed. He guessed he was safe unless one of them started jogging after him. But they could be contacting Sally any moment.

He started his mental To Do list again. First call Sally. Then check in with Liz at the bank to see what was up with the investigation. He kind of doubted that the agents would tell her about the e-mail if they had found it, but she might know something.

Third on the list was his father. As much as he hated to draw him any further into this, he figured that his dad owed it to him, and to Angela, to help get them out of this mess that he and her father created thirty years ago.

Mars intended to collect on the debt.

Then there was Angela. It made him ill to think of her going to jail, but if it came down to him or her, it had to be her. No doubt, he had screwed up morally, but she had committed a crime, not him. He needed to hear her say that she would not let him take the rap for her. They had not gotten around to discussing that yet, but he was pretty confident that she had too much integrity not to come forward. He had to know that for sure before he went home. It was, after all, what he had come here for.

Mars turned and started sprinting back to the hotel, back towards Angela, trying to focus on his plan, trying to ignore his heavy heart. He wanted to make sure that he and Angela had plenty of time to talk before she had to leave for the hospital. As he retraced his steps his mind wandered to the bigger problem.

He wasn't exactly sure what it meant to be *in love* with someone versus simply loving them, but he was confident that the term applied to his feelings for Angela. It had not been a simple crush or a phase he was going through. It had been the real thing, and it had endured the decades. It was just as compelling now as it had been then. There was no denying that it was more intense than the love he felt for Sally. He had absolutely no idea how in the hell he was going to live his life knowing that.

As he ran, he imagined how wonderful it would be to share his life with Angela, to wake up with her every day as he had today - and be able to make love with her in the morning light - to spend his days with her, and to share her bed each night.

For a moment it seemed like nirvana, but that was quickly replaced with an overwhelming sadness, a sense of grief as he acknowledged - again - that it could not be.

34 - 7:25 a.m.

As soon as he got back to the room from his run, Mars called home. Sally answered on the first ring. She was relieved to hear from him again, but he could tell that she was still upset that he wouldn't say where he was.

"The good news is that I'm pretty confident that I won't be arrested," he said wanting to make her feel better. Angela had not yet said that she would confess, but he believed that she would.

"That's great news, Mars," she said instantly sounding better. "I knew you would figure it out. Who did it?"

He sat in the chair eying his still perfectly made bed feeling guilty. She had so much faith in him; he was undeserving. "Sally, I can't tell you yet; again, I don't want you to have to lie to the Secret Service."

"Okay," she said, reluctantly agreeing to his logic.

"You know that you are incapable of lying to a federal agent."

"I guess you're right.... but you think he'll confess?"

"I do." Mars winced as his choice of words reminded him of his broken vows. Again, he did not correct her assumption that he had been framed by a man. He stood and paced as he changed the subject. "Have you seen any strange cars around, anyone watching the house or anything?"

"No," she said thoughtfully then added, "I'm not sure that I would notice with all the tourists around."

She was right; it would be hard to spot the feds, but still he felt reassured. "How are the kids?"

"They're enjoying the end of their summers and looking forward to you getting home from your *aunt's funeral.*"

"I hate lying to them."

"Well, that works out well, Mars. *You* didn't have to lie to them. *I did.*"

Mars instinctively lashed back, "If you think they should hear the truth, Sally, just put them on the phone. I'll tell them that I've been framed for a felony, and that life as they know it may be over. Is that what you want?"

As soon as he said it, he realized how unfair he was being. He was tired. He had barely been gone from home twenty-four hours yet it seemed like a week. So much had happened, but he knew that was no excuse. In fact, it was all the more reason not to rock the boat.

He took a deep breath. "I'm sorry, Sal," he ran his hand though his hair still damp with sweat. "I'm sorry that you had to lie.... I'm sorry any of this happened." He flopped on the bed, and looked heavenward. He focused on the pimpled white plastered ceiling. "I'm trying to fix it; I'm doing the best-"

She saved him. "I'm sorry too, honey. I don't mean to make matters worse, Mars. It's just that," she spoke in a hushed tone, "I'm scared."

Mars could hear her take a couple of deep ragged

breaths. He knew that she was fighting to keep her composure. He could almost see her chin quivering. He felt like such a louse for bringing this on his family.

"Sally, you know I wish I could be there with you... but I have no choice. I have to be here." He paused, thinking about the double meaning. He had to be here in order to get Angela to agree to clear him, *and* he *needed* to be here with Angela, just a little bit longer, for selfish reasons.

"I need to go to work on Monday or they'll get suspicious, if they aren't already. So I'll be home Sunday at the latest."

"Not until Sunday? That's four more days."

"Sally, please, I said *at the latest.*"

Angela had said that Tony might be released by Friday. Once she left, there would certainly be no reason for him to stay in Baltimore, but he knew he might need to go back to Wilmington to consult with his father. Even then he should be able to get home by the weekend, but he didn't want to get Sally's hopes up.

"I'll be home as soon as I can, Sally," he added softly. "I have to run. I'll call you later. Try not to worry. And call me if anything strange happens. I love you, Sally Morgan Stewart." That was the way they said it when they wanted to add an exclamation point, and Mars definitely wanted to today. No matter what happened from here on out, he needed her to know how very much he loved her.

"I love you too, Marshall Hamilton Stewart the third."

He hoped that she always would.

35 – 8:05a.m.

When Mars hung up from Sally, he had a voice message. It was from Angela. She had ordered room service breakfast and wanted him to come down when he got back from his run. She said that she would be ready to talk about *it*.

Mars was nervous. He was finally going to hear what drove her to embezzling the money, and why in the hell she had framed him. When they talked the night before, she did not seem to blame him, or even his father - so why had she framed him?

His shower and his call to Liz would have to wait. He did pause long enough to pull off his sweaty tee-shirt, dry his pits with it, and put on a clean one – one that just happened to match his blue eyes.

When Angela let Mars into her room, he gave her a kiss as if he had been coming home to her for decades. She was fresh out of the shower yet again. Mars had a strong urge to take her in his arms; he wanted to do all the things he had been considering doing just before he had extricated himself from her bed earlier that morning.

But he knew that they needed to talk.

Apparently Angela was on the same wavelength; she moved away after the single kiss as if she knew - as he did - that some separation was needed if they were going to finally have this conversation.

"There's a bagel and some other stuff on the tray. Help yourself." She settled into the upholstered chair, and sipped her coffee.

Mars fixed a plate. He was trying to muster up the anger that he knew he should feel, but he found himself thinking how odd it was that his lips always found hers so easily. There was no awkward jockeying for position with their noses, no too-wet-near-misses; their lips met perfectly. It seemed like more evidence that they belonged together.

As soon as he sat, she began. "Tony lost his job when his bank was acquired two years ago. Once his severance period was over, he had to shop for his own health insurance – he's too old to be on our policy. Unfortunately, he had a history of heart problems, and he had to take a policy that excluded cardiac coverage related to his pre-existing conditions." She let out a big sigh, "To make a very long story short, he ended up needing a new valve. For some reason, it was considered elective surgery. The only way the hospital would do it was if he could pay out of pocket. The timing was awful. Vinny had just mortgaged everything that we have to open a second deli. The banks wouldn't lend us any more. We were tapped out."

"I figured it had to do with Tony's illness... but Jesus, Angela, embezzlement? Didn't you have some more conventional options?"

She drained her coffee cup, pulled her legs up under her, and continued. "We couldn't come up with the money. I couldn't risk losing him."

Mars could see how afraid she had been of another son dying. No parent should go through that once, let alone twice.

"For years, I had seen ways that someone could embezzle money in our conversion processing. I had even joked about it with a few of my co-workers, confident that *I* would never do such a thing." Looking at him, she asked, "Did you ever think about it, Mars?"

"Yeah, I did too. I even told the agent in charge of the investigation that I had thought about it. It was one of their questions they asked us all when they first interviewed us."

"Oh geez," she said realizing how it would look for him if they found the e-mail.

"Yeah, I'm a dumb-ass – a real choirboy my boss says - I told them the truth - that I wouldn't ever do it, but that I had seen ways it could be done. I hope those words don't come back to haunt me."

"Yeah, well, I'm dumber; I actually did it." She looked as if she could hardly believe it herself. He was thinking she wasn't all that dumb, she had framed him. "I was hoping that the dormant account owner would be deceased, that no one would ever realize that the money was gone." She set her empty cup down. "So much for that theory."

Mars knew that if Ms. Jacobson had been dead everything would have worked out.

Angela sighed heavily and recalled, "Tony kept getting worse. The timing of your bank's conversion was perfect, too perfect. I convinced myself it was a godsend. I decided to do it." She sat back lost in thought again.

"I can almost understand that - who knows maybe I would do it too - but why in the hell did you pin it on me?" Nothing she had said yet gave him a clue. "What did I do to deserve this?"

"Nothing, Mars. You didn't deserve it. I didn't plan it this way. I knew that you were on LB&T's conversion team, so I knew we would have contact. I was hoping you wouldn't recognize the older grayer me." She tried unsuccessfully to smile. "Careful what you ask for."

He could see that she had been hurt that he hadn't known it was her. His eyebrows shot up. "Is *that* why you framed me, because I didn't recognize you?"

"No," she answered unpersuasively. "But I was more pissed than I expected." She looked him in the eye, "*I* would have recognized *you* anywhere – but especially in bed."

She had a point there. He hadn't had a lot of partners, but she – as young Angela and again as a more mature Sofia – took love-making to a new level. It was passion perfectly channeled; it was sport; it was exhilarating in a way that he had not experienced with anyone else. "I looked for you in every Italian woman I saw, but in my mind you were frozen in time, Angela; you were eighteen with long dark hair, with smaller boobs and -"

"Pre-pregnancy boobs," she interjected with a thin smile.

He laughed then got serious again. "It might have helped if you didn't have an entirely different name. Why in the world would I have thought that some woman named Sofia was," he stammered, "was you, Angela?" He looked at her as if his gaze could measure truth. "Seems pretty coincidental, not to mentions clandestine, that you changed your name."

"I didn't," she fired back before gathering herself. "Really. I know it looks bad." She sighed heavily, as if she were almost too spent to explain. "Angela is my middle name, but that's what Pop always called me - he always said I was his Angel. Obviously he was wrong, but that's what I went by until I started working. Then it was just easier not to correct everyone when they used my first name."

Her eyebrows pinched together, her brow furrowed, she sighed with exasperation. "I know it may seem like a set-up, but I never intended to frame you Mars."

She had such believable eyes. "Then *why did you,* Angela? Why did you come back to my house? "

"When I first saw you in the conference room, I felt that same old connection. I never understood it, and feeling it again, I don't know," she bit her lip as she pondered. "It caught me off guard. It confused and unnerved me. I started second guessing my plan." She studied him.

He didn't want her to see that he felt the bond too, that he felt that somehow he could trust her, when he knew damned well he shouldn't.

She went on. "I know it's nuts. We don't even know each other - maybe I was grasping at straws - but I started thinking that you might help me. I knew that your dad was a lawyer, and that your family had some money, and you have a million dollar beachfront property."

"That my grandparents left to me."

"I know it was nuts, but I started thinking that maybe you would lend us the money."

"Maybe I would have. Why didn't you ask me, Angela? That would have been a whole lot simpler."

"I was going to. That first day that I walked the beach to your house, I was going to ask you for a loan - just until we could sell one of the delis. Then I saw pictures of your wife and your kids. And over lunch, I could tell what a great life you had. I knew that asking for a loan would make no sense at all, especially if I didn't tell you about our baby. I had promised Pop I never would."

"So committing a felony is better than breaking a twisted promise to your dead father?"

"I was ready to risk him turning in his grave, but I was afraid that if I told you, if I dragged up our past, that I would just mess your life up too." She leaned her head back against the chair. "I know it sounds ridiculous-"

"It is ridiculous. How could dredging up our past be as bad as this?" His arms became the beam of an unbalanced bar as he weighed out the choices. "Break a promise to Pop," he said curtly, as he shifted to the weighty Option B. "Or break a federal law and frame an innocent man."

Even as he said it, he tried to imagine how he would have explained the loan to Sally. Maybe he could have gotten his father to help her.

"In hindsight, I agree, but I never consciously made *that* choice. Her hands weighed out the options from her perspective, "Let Tony die." She shifted her left hand down and her right one up. "Or save him."

"Okay, I get the save Tony part – well almost – but somewhere along the line you decided to frame me."

"Please, hear me out." Her eyes plead her case.

They won.

"I was going to ask to borrow money at lunch, but I chickened out there, and again on the golf course. Then later that night, when I only had a couple of hours before the conversion, I went to your house again. I had already decided not to ask you for a loan, to request the override myself so I don't know why I went. Maybe so you could talk me out of it."

They both remembered the torrid scene that had followed. There had been very little conversation. Mars's heat changed from anger he could not sustain to desire he could not suppress. He was as crazy as she was.

"I remember thinking – afterwards, when you were

talking to your family, and I was out on your deck – that time had run out. I wouldn't be able to substitute the file I had altered. I was sort of relieved, but when you fell asleep I saw you hadn't shut your computer off. You were still logged on to the bank's network. I thought about Tony." She listed these things as if describing all of the conditions leading up to a personal perfect storm.

Her sad brown eyes bore into his. "I'm so sorry, Mars, but I saw my opportunity, and I took it. I made a split-second decision, and it saved my son. God help me, but I can't regret it. I prayed that the account owner would never come forward, that this would never come back on you." She sat up straighter. "I do not regret it, but *I will* own up to the consequences."

Her eyes stayed focused on his. He felt a weight lift off him, off his family, but he knew this was not over for either of them. She could go to prison. He could still lose his job for leaving his bank logon accessible. And if they weren't careful they would both lose their families.

The whole truth could never come out.

Before he even thought about what he was doing, he had closed the gap between them. She took his hand. He pulled her up out of the chair, into his arms. "I want to help you get through this, Angela," he whispered into her hair.

She leaned into him; her head was on his chest. "I shouldn't have dragged you into it."

They stood there quietly. His hands were rubbing her back unconsciously, while his mind tried to focus on a small kernel of a scheme. "I have a couple of ideas."

She pushed back so she could see his face. Her eyes brightened with anticipation. "What do you mean, Mars? They already know the money was stolen, and they are bound to find-"

Mars cut her off. "I shouldn't have said anything." He

didn't want to raise her hopes, or his own. "I need to think about it more, but *maybe* I can help."

She bear hugged him so hard that he stumbled backwards onto the bed. She landed on top of him squirming with excitement. "Oh God, do you think – Oh Mars, I hope-" She stopped short. She felt the effect that she had on him. Her lips found the hollow of his neck then moved up to his ear. "I knew you would come *up* with something," she teased.

"I definitely did," he growled softly into her ear as he rolled her over.

She half laughed and half sighed as she slid her hands down his back, under his shorts, and onto his bare butt.

36   - 8:31 a.m.

Mars was trying to convince himself that Angela's just-scheduled appointment with Tony's surgeon had been fortuitous, that it had saved them from being reckless yet again. When the alarm on her phone had gone off, she had left his arms and the room abruptly.

He was still in a fog.

Intellectually, he knew that he should be thankful, but he was not. He wanted her so much that he could scarcely concentrate on anything else. He felt like he was just going through the motions as he returned to his room, set up his laptop, and got logged onto the bank's system. He had quite a few e-mails, but he went directly to the one from Liz.

****

SUBJECT: Team Update
TO: MStewart@LBnTrust.com
FROM: EMaloney@LBnTrust.com

Mars,
Sorry to hear about your aunt. I hope that you and your family are doing okay.

You are not missing too much here although it is rather exciting. The Secret Service has Jason and me providing printouts showing every line of code that we changed in the month before the embezzlement. Agent Williams is directing the show. Jason and I are working with the other two agents: Jose and Amanda. So far, we haven't found anything weird, but we are only through about a third of the analysis. They are very detail oriented, not taking our word for anything, so it is a slow go.

Our MVP is hovering around, being his usual charming self. I can't wait for your return so that you can run interference. Are you still planning on Monday? No rush, we're fine. Family is more important.

In the meantime, let me know if you need more information. I'll leave you an update each day before I go home.

Liz
****

Mars thought about her news. Since they were only a third of the way through, he was hopeful that it would take them the rest of the week to complete their analysis. That would work to his benefit since he did not want them to start looking elsewhere - especially at e-mails - for an answer.

He started mulling over his plan. The more he thought about it, the more sure he was that it could work if he could get back in the office and implement it before they found Angela's e-mail.

He fired off a quick response to Liz.

****
SUBJECT: Team Update
TO: EMaloney@LBnTrust.com
FROM: MStewart@LBnTrust.com

Liz,
Thanks for the update. Sounds like you are making
slow progress. What's next after reviewing the
software changes? Do you have any other ideas?

After the memorial service, I won't have much to do
here, so if I can get an earlier flight, I may return to
work on Friday. If not, I'll see you Monday for sure.
Thanks for your help,
Mars
****

He hated lying to her, but Liz was the least of his concerns at the moment.

Knowing that Angela was going to confess just made him desire her all the more. She was a good person who had used bad judgment. He tried to stay focused on the big picture. Family is most important.

He needed to go face his father in Wilmington. He was still pissed at him, but he needed his legal advice. He had no idea what his work schedule was these days since he was semi-retired, so he decided to give him a call.

"Stewart Law Firm, how may I help you?"

"Hello, Barbara, it's Mars."

"Mars, it's so good to hear your voice again." She was a sweet lady; she'd been his dad's secretary forever.

"Thanks. Hey, is Dad free for lunch tomorrow?"

"Let me see." Mars could hear her keystrokes; they must have automated the old man's calendar. "It looks like he is. Can you hold for a minute while I check with him?"

"Sure." While on hold, Mars was serenaded by Enrique performing "Hero." He started thinking that maybe he could be Angela's savior after all.

Barbara interrupted his thoughts. "Mars?"

"Yes."

"Your father said that will be fine. He'll be available for lunch at one o'clock, and he'll be free the rest of the afternoon."

"Great, Barbara, I'll see you tomorrow. Thanks."

"You're welcome dear. See you then."

Mars hung up. It was set. He would need to leave Baltimore by 11:30. He would meet with his father and be home with Sally by dinner time. He called his wife to let her know. She didn't answer their land line or her cell. He left a message and was immediately contemplating the fact that he had just one more night to be with Angela.

One night, he thought hearing the Etta James tune with that name playing in his head. In his mind, she belted out the blues; his soul joined in. A smile formed as an idea for a compromise came to him. He would live the rest of his life without Angela, but first they would have one night to make a lifetime of memories.

Mars and Angela were seated at a quiet table in a little alcove of one of Tio Pepe's dining rooms. The red candles on the white tablecloths added to the romantic feeling. He remembered when he and his grandfather had discovered this famous Baltimore eatery. They had stumbled upon it shortly after the restaurant opened in the early seventies. It became their favorite spot when they were in town for an Orioles' game.

Wrought iron sconces lit the whitewashed walls and made Angela's face glow as they enjoyed the Sangria. Mars had forgotten that they required men to wear jackets. He was now clad in a tan blazer that the restaurant kept on hand. It had tacky gold buttons and was ill-fitting. He felt conspicuous.

"So how was Tony today?" he asked, tugging the sleeves down.

"His doctor says that he is progressing on schedule. He's up walking, so that's good... but to me he looks twenty years older."

"His body's been through a trauma. He'll recover. Is

he on track to be released by Friday?"

"I think so, but he won't be able to go home. I Googled information on rehab centers in Wilmington." Her cheeks were wine-flushed; she looked beautiful, but tired. All that sitting around the hospital would make anyone weary, and Angela had a lot of other stuff going on.

"I'm sure there are some good ones around Christiana Hospital."

"There are. We'll pick one tomorrow." She took another sip. "How about you, how was your day?" She picked a cherry out of the glass and ate it seductively. A smile formed on her wonderful lips. "Did anything new... come up?"

"Not since this morning," Mars replied with a sheepish grin, feeling a primal urge even as he answered. "I got an update from Liz. The Secret Service has them plowing through all of the changes that we installed, looking at every detail. So far they haven't focused on the e-mails, so they haven't found it."

"Do you think that they will?" she asked being serious again.

Mars refilled their glasses from the colorful pottery pitcher. "I do, but maybe not until they finish looking at the more obvious stuff. We should have a few more days."

"But you think they will eventually find it." This time it was not a question. "I was hoping that they wouldn't." She sounded dejected.

"I guess there's always a chance they won't, but we shouldn't have false hope. Even if the Secret Service doesn't find it, my team will." It had taken him less than two days to find it himself. He knew Liz would eventually do a keyword search on their e-mails, just as he had.

"You haven't changed your mind, have you?"

"No. I'll confess... if I need to. But this morning, you

said that you might have a plan. I was just hoping ..."

Her voice trailed off.

"Angela, I have an idea; it's not a plan yet. I need to ask-" Mars fell silent as the waiter brought the garlic shrimp appetizers. It smelled wonderful. He was glad they had both ordered one.

He leaned towards her. "Where's the money now?"

"I wired it all to an off-shore account. Then last week I wired enough back to Tony's account to pay for the surgery."

"So how much is left?"

"More than half, but the bills are going to keep coming – who knows how much rehab will be, and the prescriptions, and I need a lawyer..." Mars could tell she could keep adding to the list when she looked up and asked, "Why, what do you have in mind?"

"I need to consult with my father. And we need to get you an attorney first. But I'm thinking we need to come forward before they find the e-mail."

Angela sat back seeming to shrink before him. "So your plan involves me turning myself in. I thought this morning that..." She stopped herself, and with renewed courage added, "Okay, tell me more. Why did you ask about the money?"

"I'm thinking that if you turn the rest of it over to the authorities, it should help your - our - causes. The bank could cut its losses."

Angela thought about it. "The surgery is done, and that was the most important thing.... I can wire it back, if you think it'll help."

Mars reached across the table and took her hand in his. He looked her in the eye. "Let's wait, and see how things pan out. Maybe we can use it as a bargaining chip." He squeezed her hands and caught her gaze.

He looked deep into what he hoped really was her

soul. "Angela, we have to agree to try to keep the fact that the embezzlement happened in my bedroom - in *Sally's* and my bedroom - off the record."

"I know. The last thing I want to do is wreck your life, Mars. You want me to tell the truth - just not the whole truth." She let go of his hands. "That'll work for you but-"

He eyed her, tried to read her thoughts. Was she still playing him? "Angela, even then I could lose my job." He folded his arms across his chest. This was not going the way he wanted the discussion or the evening to go.

"Why? If I confess, why would they fire you?"

He noticed that she hadn't said *when I confess*, but decided he was reading too much into semantics. "I left my computer signed on. It's against bank policy and is grounds for termination. For obvious reasons."

"But Mars, everyone does that at one time or another."

"I know, but they will be looking for a LB&T employee to offer up as a scapegoat to the media. I'm not going down without a fight." His mind started wandering down that tangent... He reined his thoughts in. He didn't want this one night to be this full of tension.

"Angela, let's just forget all about the bank for the rest of tonight." He held out his hand to her. "Okay?"

She hesitated than laid her warm soft hand on his. He folded his fingers through hers. "Easier said than done, Mars. I've made such a mess of things."

She was right on both counts, but by the time they finished their meal - they shared his filet mignon and her paella then filled the remaining nooks and crannies with a pine nut cake roll - thoughts of the stolen money were far away.

Thoughts of the life they could have had together filled the space.

As they sipped on the house coffee, he wanted to float

away in her deep brown eyes. "Angela, you know how I feel about you, don't you?" She didn't answer, but he could tell from her half-smile that she did. "You know that I wish things had happened differently, but...I'm married. I love Sally. I love my kids. I love my life."

"I know you do, Mars. And I love Vinny and Tony."

Relieved that they seemed to be on the same wavelength, Mars continued, "I have to leave tomorrow. I have to go home." Her eyes saddened, but her jaw set determinedly as he added, "I want us to make the most of tonight Angela." He squeezed her hand then let go. He raised his coffee cup signaling a pending toast.

Angela raised hers and clinked it against Mars's as he toasted, "To tonight, our night. May it be... enough."

"To tonight," she echoed.

38 - 9:35 p.m.

After dinner Mars and Angela strolled hand in hand on the brick sidewalks along Pratt Street in Baltimore's Inner Harbor. Mars knew it was a bit careless, but the odds of running into anyone either of them knew were slim.

It was their night; they took chances. It crossed Mars's mind that his grandfather would call their behavior this night reckless for sure, but being with Angela with the cool night air blowing off the water was heady stuff.

"There's our moon, Mars." He looked up and saw it full and bright, reflecting off the Glass Pavilion of the National Aquarium.

They were lost in a long deep kiss when a teenage kid in baggy-low-slung jeans yelled, "Get a room!" as he click-clacked by on his long skateboard.

Mars laughed as he nuzzled Angela's flushed neck and whispered, "He's got a point; let's get out of here."

The three blocks to the hotel seemed to take forever, and the elevator ride was endless. Angela had his belt unbuckled before the door to her room clicked shut under their weight. He unbuttoned her blouse, but not fast enough; she helped.

Discarded clothes dropped to the floor.

Mars pulled her to him. He gasped as he felt her soft skin hot against him. Again, Etta's song "One Night" played in his head. Angela was his dream come true. They were meant for each other. Deep in his soul he needed this one night.

The lyrics rolled through his mind, while he guided Angela onto the bed. As she pulled him down to her, the blues rushed through him knowing that they should have had a lifetime together.

They made love slowly this time. Hands and mouths explored and teased, bringing each other to the brink, and then backing off, over and over, until they could not stop.

Afterwards, Mars lay on his back feeling more content than he had in years. Angela's head rested lightly on his shoulder; her leg was sprawled across his fatigued groin. As she played with the hairs on his chest, he floated beneath her.

"I wish we could stay like this forever," Angela said softly.

"Me too," Mars agreed as he kissed her hair. The smell of them co-mingled on the strands was intoxicating. His eyelids fluttered shut.

He barely heard Angela as she asked, "What time do you have to leave in the morning?" Her breath was warm on his chest.

"Late. Maybe eleven-thirty," he answered wondering where he would find the strength to leave her bed.

Her hand moved down, over his belly. "Maybe we should try once more."

Mars groaned, unable to even think about it. "You are

insatiable; *that* must be why I love you so. But you're dreaming if you think-"

"*Do you* love me Mars?" Angela interrupted. She had pushed herself up onto her elbow, and her eyes found his even in the darkened room.

He did a crunch, kissed her square on the mouth then collapsed back on the pillow. "I do, Angela, I always have. I spent the decade after you left trying to convince myself that I didn't, but I feel something for you that I have never felt for anyone else."

"Not anyone?" she asked softly as her hand moved back up his body. Her finger traced his nose then found his lips.

He kissed her fingertip. "No one. I definitely love Sally, but my feelings for her evolved over several years... What I feel for you is," he struggled to find the right word. "Innate." He nibbled on her finger.

"You make me hungry," he laughed, as he rolled her onto her back. He pinned her hands over her head then kissed her eyes, her nose, and her lips. He lingered on each breast then released her hands as he ran his tongue down past her navel, stopping just long enough to declare, "I love you too much, and I hate that I will never get enough of you."

Later, there were no words, no more talk of love, no questions about the past, nor was there any discussion about the future that they both understood that they could not have.

39 - Thursday 6:55 a.m.

Mars woke in virtually the same position as the previous morning. The back of Angela's body was spooned against the front of him, but unlike the day before, there was nothing between them. They were skin to glorious skin.

She was so wonderfully warm and musky. She smelled of them. It dawned on him that it was a scent that he would never wake up to again. That reality made his gut lurch even as she stirred him.

Yesterday he had left her bed, but this time - this one and only one morning - Mars did not even consider pulling away. Instead he moved even closer until he was firmly pressed against her. Her breathing had not changed. She was still fast asleep.

Mars inched his hand deliberately down over her right hip. He waited motionless for a long moment until he was sure that she was still slumbering. By the time she awoke they were both more than ready.

Minutes later they were snoozing again.

The alarm woke them at eight o'clock. They had set it

so they could savor the few hours that they had remaining together. They were back in the spoon position when Angela lifted his hand and kissed it. She whispered, "I'm going to miss you *so much.*"

"Ditto," he sighed, knowing what a gaping hole he would feel when he went on with his life. Was he supposed to pretend Angela did not exist?

Unwelcome frustration, then anger, crept in as he thought again about how their fathers had betrayed them. "We should have had a life together," Mars said obviously feeling self pity.

Angela pushed him until he rolled onto his back. She laid her head on its now familiar place on his shoulder. She sounded artificially cheerful as she said, "Yeah, but look on the bright side, Mars. If we had been together for the last thirty years, I doubt we would still feel like this."

Mars rolled his head enough to kiss her nose. "That may be true, Angela," he smiled half-heartedly, not ready to play, "but somehow I doubt it. Maybe it wouldn't be this intense, but -" His voice drifted off.

She tugged not so gently on a chest hair as she interrupted him. "Who knows, we're probably not even compatible," she said lightly.

He frowned. He was not in agreement.

She pulled another hair harder this time, "Well except for the yummy stuff."

"Speaking of yummy," he countered, "I know you like food, which I also happen to like. And we are both addicted to golf... What else is there? I say we are completely compatible," he joked back, but still half-heartedly.

He could see her struggling to come up with an example. "You would probably hate my cooking."

"I love Italian food," he countered. He pushed her hair away, kissed her ear, and whispered, "Almost as much as

I love Italian women."

"Wo*man*," she corrected. Then she laughed her infectious laugh. For a few seconds she sounded like a child being tickled. "Then maybe I would hate how you squeeze the toothpaste, or -"

"I squeeze perfectly." He said tweaking her nipple.

"Well then, it would drive me crazy that you leave the toilet seat up-"

"No way," Mars said with conviction, "I am well trained."

"Oh yeah," she said turning her head and biting his earlobe, "then how come when I got up last night, I dropped onto ice-cold porcelain?"

"Okay, you caught me," Mars said surrendering the point just before he kissed her with a passion that he wished he could follow-up on, but he was exhausted.

He pushed away, and looked into her brown eyes then softly, but vehemently said, "You will never convince me that we wouldn't have had a great life together."

Angela's eyes glistened. "Now I know we would have Mars, but I didn't know it then. It's not just our fathers' fault. You should blame me. I should have fought for what I felt, but I figured it was just my imagination. How could I love someone I didn't even know? I *knew* Vinny. And I knew he loved me - enough to marry me even though it wasn't his baby." She clinched her eyes shut.

Mars kissed the salty tears that pressed out of them. "It's wasn't your fault, Angela, it was our fathers'. They're the ones that manipulated us. They should have let us figure it out for ourselves. They didn't give us a chance."

"Yeah, but Mars, we had already screwed up - I was pregnant." She opened her wet eyes and found his. "I believe they thought they were doing it for our own good. They were trying to save us from a bigger mistake."

"Well they blew it, Angela. We were meant to be

together. And now... now it's too late. We can't have each other without ruining everything else."

"I know, Mars," she sighed as she turned away from him, onto her side. "You're going home to your family, and I am going home to mine."

Mars snuggled against her back. "I know *what* we have to do; I just don't know *how* I am going to do it." He blinked back his own tears. "How do we just go back to our lives knowing that we are missing *this*?"

He rubbed his nose along her spine.

"We'll find a way. We have to." She pulled his arm around her. "Remember our toast. We had our one night. And this... It has to be enough." She didn't sound too positive," especially when she added, "And -" Her voice trailed off sadly. She didn't finish her thought.

"And what?"

"And... at least you'll have your life; I'll probably be in jail."

Mars felt like such a heel; he hadn't even been thinking about that. Part of him wanted to tell her not to confess, that he would go to jail if it came to that. He wanted to be her hero, but he knew he couldn't be Sally's slayer.

He held Angela tightly knowing that he could not shelter her; he had to save his family.

40   - 9:33 a.m.

Mars went back to his room to pack, while Angela showered. He had turned his cell phone off before dinner and was just now turning it on. He had three messages.

The first one was from Sally just after eight p.m., returning his call. She tried again at eleven sounding a little worried, but saying that she was going to bed, and that she would talk to him in the morning. The third was from his father an hour ago, saying that he would meet Mars at the club instead of the office.

Mars dialed home and got Sally on the first ring.

"Mars, thank God. I was worried."

"Sorry, Sally, but I got in late, and I went for a run first thing this morning." *More lies* he thought. "Is everything okay there? How are the kids?"

"Everything's fine here, considering..." She apparently decided to change course. "We miss you."

"I miss all of you too," Mars said truthfully. Part of him longed for the calm settled life that used to be his. The rest of him ached knowing he had only minutes left with Angela.

"Good news, I'll be home tonight," he said hoping to sound cheerful. *It is good,* he told himself, trying to focus on the positive.

"Really?" she sounded surprised, and excited.

"I'm *almost* positive," Mars said hating to commit. "If anything changes I'll give you a call."

"So it's going well, Mars? Everything is going to be okay?" she pumped.

"I think so. I'll explain when I see you," he said wondering how much he would tell her.

"Okay Mars, I'll let you go. See you tonight. I love you." Her voice was strong again and filled with a happiness Mars knew was all too tenuous.

"Love you too babe," he replied.

He had been sitting on the edge of the bed, and as soon as he hung up he fell back hard, and studied the ceiling. *What a mess.*

He glanced at his watch. Angela would be out of the shower. He wanted to spend as much time with her as he could before she left for the hospital. He could figure out how he was going to explain this all to Sally later.

Just as he was about to go to her room there was a knock on his door. He found Angela standing there without her bags.

No, not yet, he thought as he let her in. He wondered what had changed. Before the door closed behind him, Angela said, "I've got to go. The nurse called. Tony hasn't been doing well this morning. I need to go see what's going on."

They kissed. Their mutual hunger was tempered by the circumstances.

"Okay." Mars said not relinquishing his hold on her. He pulled her tight and swayed back and forth. Their sadness was palpable.

He took a deep breath. "I hope he's okay. Can you let

me know?"

"That's what I wanted to ask. How should I contact you?"

"I guess the best thing would be to call my cell. If I can't talk, I won't answer. Leave a message. Can I call you back on your cell?"

Angela thought then answered, "Yeah, I'll do the same thing. If I can't talk to you, I won't pick up. Leave a message. I'll be here until at least sometime tomorrow, so I'll be able to talk. But once I get home... You can call, though; you're a legitimate business associate."

Suddenly she looked overwhelmed. "Mars, if I need to turn myself in I will. Just let me get Tony home first. Please."

He squeezed her unable to make that promise, especially if there were complications with her son's surgery. He could be in the hospital a lot longer. Time was a factor working against them. He didn't want to give the investigative team time to find the mail, to arrest him. He wanted to execute his plan.

"Please," she pleaded again.

Mars placed a finger on her wonderful lips, "Shhhh... Angela, don't worry about it now. You take care of Tony. Let me see what I can figure out."

As he had seen her do before, she summoned her strength. "Well no matter what happens, Mars, I'll always appreciate you trying to help me. After what I did, I don't deserve it. "

He couldn't help but think about the parallels with what Vinny had done - he married her after she betrayed him. He must really love her too. Mars knew that should make him feel better, but in ways he did not want to admit even to himself, it made matters worse.

She stood on her tip toes, and pulled his face down to hers. "No matter what," she slipped into a bad Bogart impression, "we'll always have Baltimore."

She laughed until he kissed her one last time. Then she was gone again.

41 - 12:02 p.m.

Unable to bear the loneliness, Mars left the hotel shortly after Angela. He arrived at Wilmington Country Club an hour early, went to the pro shop, got a bucket of balls then took a cart out to the driving range. He hit them all without thinking once about his swing.

All he could think of was Angela. He replayed much of their night together as shot after shot went long and straight. He remembered how they had moved so fluidly together – like a pair of dolphins swimming effortlessly in sync.

"Marshall."

His father had arrived. They exchanged their customary handshake before his Dad suggested that they eat before playing. They settled at a table on the terrace. Mars suspected his father was afraid of another scene in the grille. He had to know that Mars was still seething over the thirty-year-old misdeed.

As soon as they had ordered, Mars got out his wallet, extracted a dollar bill, and offered it to his father.

"Paying up already, son?" his Dad chuckled, inferring

that Mars would lose their golf match.

"No," Mars said not joining in with the uncharacteristic attempt at banter. "Actually Dad, this is payment for your professional services. Much as I hate to, I nccd to retain you as my lawyer."

His father snatched the bill out of the breeze, tucked it in his trousers and leaned back in his chair. He studied his son. "What's going on Mars? You were so vague the other day."

Mars dropped his guard; his anger spilled out. "You ruined my life. Is that clear enough, *Dad.*" He practically spat the last word.

His father looked around. No one had noticed. "Why is the Ignazio girl coming up now?" his father probed quietly, not arguing Mars's point.

Mars sat there still not sure he wanted to confide in his father, but he knew it was his best option. Like it or not, he needed his father's help. Reluctantly, he began, "Did you happen to read in the paper recently about money that was embezzled from LB&T?"

The elder Stewart's eyes got larger and his slightly wild eyebrows pinched together forming a uni-brow. "I did, but what does that have to do with you?" He leaned forward. Suspicion tainted his voice as he asked, "Why do you need a lawyer?"

The fact that his father thought that he might have committed the crime added more fuel to Mars's smoldering anger. "What? You think I stole the money?"

His father softened his tone. "No son. I don't think that you did, but you aren't answering my question, *why* do you need a lawyer?"

"For one thing, I need to make sure that everything that I tell you is protected under attorney-client privilege."

"Okay," his father patted the dollar in his pocket.

"Tell me."

"I've been framed," Mars said bluntly.

"For the embezzlement?" his lawyer asked with fatherly shock.

Mars nodded.

"What evidence is there against you?"

"An e-mail was sent from my address requesting the changes that caused the embezzlement. It was sent from my computer, under my logon."

The elder Stewart was not very computer literate, but he understood the implications immediately. He knew that Mars would be held responsible, and it would be a case of guilty until proven innocent. He leaned back, and contemplated the situation. His eyes squinted. "What's Ignazio's daughter got to do with this?"

Mars leaned back, crossed his arms over his chest. His voice was full of sarcasm when he replied, "Well *Dad*, that's where this gets really interesting. Do you believe in karma?"

The color drained from his father's face, "What did *she* do now?"

"Don't you -" Mars was interrupted in his defense of Angela by the waitress delivering their lunch. His father seemed to be on some new health binge. He had ordered a salad and no booze.

As soon as the waitress was out of ear shot, his father leaned forward, and jeered, "I always knew that girl was trouble."

"Well for your information, *that girl,* the one I thought I loved when I was a kid, is a woman now. A beautiful, intelligent, kind and wonderful woman, and guess what?"

The rhetorical question was not answered. His father grabbed his water glass, and took a big gulp.

His son went on, "I *still* love her."

The senior Stewart scanned the terrace for the

waitress, apparently wishing he had ordered his usual bourbon. He had turned an unhealthy shade of gray, except for his nose and his ears, which now had a purplish hue. "You do *not* love that woman. You are confusing love and lust *again.*"

"How could you possibly know that?" Mars demanded. With hushed vengeance he added, "Just because you had to marry Mom, and it didn't work, it does not mean that we would have suffered the same fate."

He remembered his grandfather recounting how both sets of parents had pushed his parents to do "the right thing." He could almost see how his father would not want to push him to the same fate.

Mars continued this time with a touch of empathy, "You wish it were true. If it were, then the deal that you made with Angela's father would have been a good one. But I love her, and she loves me. You *robbed* us of our life together."

The shot hit its mark. Wounded, his Dad sat back. He mopped his napkin across the sweat beading up on his forehead, all the while studying his son.

"My God, Mars, you're serious, aren't you?"

42   - 1:31 p.m.

His father looked so devastated that Mars actually started feeling sorry for him. He remembered what Angela had said - that their fathers had meant well. He hadn't believed it when she had said it, but now he could see that she was probably right.

"You may have thought you were helping me, but you were wrong. We should have been together all of these years."

His father was still having trouble comprehending the situation. "Mars, you hardly knew her. You were dating Sally. As I understood it, you never even dated Angela," his voice trailed off as if he were no longer sure of anything.

"I didn't know her, but I loved her. I know it's hard to believe, even for me. I spent years convincing myself that it wasn't true, but trust me it is." He said the next words like an alcoholic admitting his addiction. "I am in love with Sofia Angela Ignazio, and she is in love with me."

"It's Ignazio Pitasi, and, Marshall, you are not in love with that woman," his father exclaimed, while meeting his son's gaze. Mars did not back down. "What about Sally, and Peter and Rebecca?"

"I have no intention of leaving them," Mars replied dismally. It was impossible to ignore how powerful his feelings were for Angela. It was going to be excruciating to leave her behind, but he loved his wife and children tremendously too.

"Well that's good... I guess." His father ate a few bites of his salad as he pondered the situation. "Let's go back to the embezzlement. I hate to assume anything, so tell me just what the connection between Angela and the embezzlement is."

Mars knew that the information that he was about to give his father was not going to present Angela in a favorable way, but there was no avoiding it. "She framed me," he said candidly.

His father put his fork down, and with all of the composure he could muster said, "So I'm to believe that she's in love with you, and yet, she framed you." He looked up at his son again, his disdain for Angela apparent even before he spoke. "Doesn't that seem a bit far fetched, son? Isn't it just possible that she is using you again?"

Mars felt his blood boil, but at the same time he knew the situation was unfathomable. "I know it looks bad, but she did what she had to do to save her son."

Sounding a smidgen sympathetic, but still very skeptical his father asked, "Her son from you is sick?"

"Well... actually, no." Mars hesitated knowing that this next bit of information was going to shock his father. "Our son was stillborn."

Unable to control himself his father blurted out, "So what the hell did they do with the hundred grand that I paid them for that child's support?"

This time it was Mars that glanced around the terrace

to see if any heads were turning their way. Only one woman seemed to be tuned in. He didn't know her. Through clenched teeth he whispered, "Dad, that money is irrelevant now."

His father's eyebrows shot up as if to say *maybe to you.*

Mars continued. "Angela's father bought them a house in Little Italy while she was pregnant. He had no way to know that she would lose the baby." Then feeling like he was being too generous with both fathers, he snapped. "What the hell difference does it make anyway? You and Mr. Ignazio made a deal. It was hush money as much as anything else."

Glaring at the man across the table from him, a man that he had never really known, he continued, "Angela said that you implied that you would ruin her family if they ever breathed a word about me being the father of her child. They kept their promise. They earned your payoff."

Silently acknowledging the truth of that statement, his father moved on. "Okay, so the baby died and she framed you to save another one of her children – do I have that right?"

Mars elected to ignore the sarcasm; it was almost justifiable. "That's right, except her son, Tony, is an adult now, an uninsured one at that."

Mars ate some of his BLT while he thought about how to explain it. As he mulled it over he realized that there was no way that his father was going to get it, so he might as well just give him the facts. He recounted the story, bedroom scene and all.

To his credit, his father listened intently, raising his eyebrows and smirking a couple of times, but he did not interrupt. Even when Mars was done, his father took his time. He finished his salad, and weighed his words before speaking.

"Well, Mars, I am not convinced that she loves you, but I do concede that you must love her." His tone implied that his son was being a fool, that he was blinded by irrational feelings.

"So what now? Surely you aren't planning on being noble. You can't take the rap for her."

"No I can't," Mars replied wishing he could.

"Is she willing to turn herself in?"

"She is, but you have to help her." His look dared his father to refuse.

43 - 2:34 p.m.

Marshall Junior was leery about his son's plan, and was quick to offer his professional opinion. First, Mars should get Angela to turn herself in immediately - while she seemed willing to do so. He knew that if she changed her mind it would be his son's word against Angela's. He pushed Mars to instruct Angela to contact the Secret Service as soon as she could - as if Mars was in a position to tell her to do anything.

On a personal level his father was sympathetic and obviously felt some guilt. Although he still didn't buy that the two were really in love, he no longer seemed to totally dismiss the possibility. At a minimum, he apparently understood that no one wants someone that they love - or think they love - to go to jail – guilty or not.

They decided to get a cart and play some golf while they discussed it further. As they waited on the first tee of the South Course Mars's father asked him what he was going to tell his wife.

"Sally knew Angela from the deli, too. She'll remember that I had a gigantic crush on her," Mars said as he tried to work through the problem himself. "I'm thinking that I should go ahead and tell her everything that happened thirty years ago, as well as the legally important points regarding the embezzlement."

His father was skeptical, "So you'll confess that you had sex with Angela that summer. And that you got her pregnant? Weren't you dating Sally then?"

Mars thought about it. "We were dating, but just casually...Sally won't like it, but everyone knew how I felt about Angela. They all kidded me about her. If I tell her what really happened, I think she will understand. She won't like it, but she'll find it perfectly believable that I took advantage of the opportunity."

"So then you plan to tell her about the deal that I made with Ignazio." It annoyed Mars that his father sounded overly concerned about how that might reflect on him.

"I need to," Mars said, "It's one of the most important facts. The first hole was a four-hundred-and-twenty-three-yard par four. Mars's mind was not on golf, but just as on the practice tee, he hit it straight and long. His Dad's shot was also straight, but quite a bit shorter.

Back in the cart, Mars continued, "I have no intention of telling her that I was and still am in love with Angela. So as far as she is concerned your intervention will come across as a good thing. If you hadn't interceded, Sally and I might never have married, and Peter and Beck would not exist."

Although he had meant to be sarcastic, as he was saying it he realized that it was the truth. Sally had been a loving wife and a wonderful mother. "I do love Sally, Dad, and I don't want to risk losing what we have created together. I'm going to have to provide some sort of explanation for why Angela would do this."

"Maybe you shouldn't say who it was that framed

you," his father suggested as he got out of the cart to hit his second shot. It went straight again leaving him a nine iron or a wedge to the green. They rode up to Mar's ball. He had one-eighty remaining. He hit a five-iron thin. It leaked right, and ended up in a green-side bunker.

"I don't know, Dad. If I don't tell her it was Angela, and she finds out later - in the news or in court - I will be totally screwed."

He father considered it some more. "You're probably right. Even if we can make a deal for Angela, she may still be prosecuted. If so, it will be public information, and Sally would find out."

They both mulled that over as they finished the hole with a bogey each. They had to wait again at the next tee for the group in front of them – four older guys. It was going to be a slow nine holes. Mars looked at his watch – two-fifty-two. He wanted to be on the road by four-thirty at the latest. He should be able to make it.

"Maybe you need to present Angela as being a bit more manipulative than you believe her to be. What if the embezzlement was an act of revenge?"

Mars hated the thought of making Angela out to be a villain - his father evidently thought she was - but he conceded that it might be a good way to deflect any suspicions about what was really going on. It was certainly plausible. Actually, it was more believable than the truth.

"But then why would I be trying to help her? It wouldn't make sense."

"Son, I don't think you can tell Sally that you are helping Angela. What possible explanation could you give for helping her after she framed you?"

Mars thought it over as they played the next hole. It was slightly shorter than the last par four. He got on in regulation, missed his birdie putt, and made a tap-in par.

His father got on the green in three, and made another respectable bogey. His game had improved in his semi-retirement.

"I think you may be right, Dad." As he said it, Mars realized that it felt good to work through his problem with his father. They hadn't done much collaborating over the years.

Life sure was full of surprises.

44   - 4:30 p.m.

Mars and his father abandoned their golf match after six holes. It had been excruciatingly slow and they had come up with a plan for what Mars would tell Sally. They had also agreed that his father would contact one of his colleagues who did pro-bono work, and who owed him a favor, to see if he would represent Angela.

Mars got hung up in the traffic just south of Wilmington, near the airport. He lost about fifteen minutes, but he relaxed knowing that he would make it home for dinner as promised. Even as he thought of exactly what he would say to Sally, thoughts of Angela's warm body kept running through his mind.

He decided to give her a quick call since it might be his last opportunity for a while. His heart raced when she answered.

"Hey Angela... it's me."

"I miss you."

"Tell me about it," Mars replied feeling an emptiness that he figured would be with him for a long time; he hoped not forever. "How's Tony?"

"He's doing much better now, thanks. His temperature had spiked to a hundred and three. They think that he has an infection - probably from the catheter - so they gave him mega-doses of antibiotics and he's much better."

"Good," Mars replied feeling selfish as he hoped that meant that Tony would be released on schedule. His hopes were quickly dashed.

"His doctor did say that he may have to stay put for an extra day or so. I'll know more tomorrow, but I think it would be best if he does."

For him, but maybe not for me, Mars thought as she continued, "So how are you? Did you meet with your father?"

"I just left him," Mars replied, but his mind was on having left her too soon now that she was going to be in Baltimore an extra day. "I wish I had stayed one more night, Angela."

"I know. I wish you could have too. But hopefully our memories are enough. So far it's working for me. I for one have been playing scenes over and over in my mind all day." She laughed. "You've turned me in to some kind of pervert."

"Moi?" he exclaimed, using almost all the French he knew, as he laughed, "You're the one. You should see what just the thought of you -"

"I wish..." she interrupted, saving him from his own lewdness. After a short silence, she got serious again. "Did you and your father figure anything out?"

"I think so, but..." he hesitated not wanting to hurt her feelings.

"But what, Mars?" she said apparently fearing the worst. "Let me guess, he wants me to turn myself in immediately?"

"Honestly, he does. And he doesn't understand me

wanting to help you. He finds it incomprehensible that we love each other."

"Well he has a point. It is hard to comprehend. Even to me it seems surreal, so I can certainly understand him having a problem accepting it. Framing you did not help my cause, so don't be too hard on him."

"Yeah, I know," Mars answered still not ready to forgive his father.

"So is that the *but*? He doesn't think I love you?"

"No. He and I were trying to figure out what I can tell Sally. We agreed that there is no way that I can tell her that you framed me *and* that I am helping you." Mars hesitated, "He thinks that I need to paint you out to be revengeful. That I should say that you incriminated me because of some repressed hatred of our family."

Angela was quiet for a bit then generously said, "I think he's right, Mars. Obviously you can't be completely honest with your wife without risking your marriage. So do it. What difference does it make if she thinks the worst of me?"

"I suppose," Mars said, but he still hated the idea. "Anyway, he's going to represent me, and - good news - he's planning on contacting a lawyer friend of his to see if he'll represent you."

She didn't respond.

"If that's okay with you, Angela."

"That would be great, but the only money I have is LB&T's and you want me to give that back, so I don't know how I would pay a high-dollar attorney. Maybe I need a public defender."

"Dad's going to call in a favor, so you'll just have to pay a token fee, if anything."

"Have I told you that I do love you?" she asked softly.

"Hmm, I forget," Mars paused for effect, trying to lighten things up. "I do remember hearing something like that, but I wasn't sure, it was kind of muffled." He smiled broadly at the memory. "I think your thighs were over my ears."

She laughed. He groaned. They were both silent as the memory bound them together again. Neither seemed to have more to say, but they did not want to end the call either.

Finally Angela spoke. "Well, I guess we better go. Are you going to be okay, Mars?"

"Yeah," he said less than convincingly. "How about you?"

"It's weird, but I feel more hopeful than I have for a long while. Thank you for helping me. No matter how it turns out, I'll always be grateful."

Mars wondered if she was thanking him prematurely, but he kept his concerns to himself; he didn't want to burst her bubble, or his own.

Trying to get his head on straight, Mars found the George Strait CD and played "On the Other Hand" over and over as he drove south where his wife was waiting. She definitely would not understand.

He fingered the golden band on his left hand.

45 - 6:00 p.m.

Mars arrived in Lewes just after six o'clock. As he drove over the canal bridge on Savannah Road, he shut off his air and opened all of the windows. Marsh scents and salt air filled his lungs as he caught his first glimpse of the bay.

He was home.

Home was with Sally, Peter and Beck, not Angela. She was a hundred miles away, and that realization hurt, but he knew it was best... under the circumstance.

He took the obligatory drive around the Lewes beach parking lot, and watched as several families enjoyed the still-hot evening with their DQ ice cream cones. He paused in one of the beach-front parking spaces and watched an inning of a multi-generational wiffleball game. They all seemed so happy.

Mars wondered what secrets they were keeping. He doubted that any of theirs were as big as the ones weighing him down.

He was feeling sorry for himself as he pulled in his driveway. Rebecca came running out yelling, "Daddy!"

She was in his arms the minute he got out of the car.

He knew he was a lucky man.

"Hey, Becky Bear," he said grinning as he hugged her back. "I missed you." He had. She was a joyful child. It was contagious.

"I missed you too, Daddy," she said holding his hand as they walked towards the house. "Mom's been sad without you. She said you weren't coming home until Sunday."

Knowing that his daughter had noticed Sally's condition tore at his heartstrings. "I know. I was sad too, that's why I flew home early."

He felt horrible that the lie had come out so easily.

When Sally came out onto the deck, Mars realized that the lying was just beginning. His gut churned as he swallowed that reality.

"Hi, honey," Sally called. She was smiling as if all their problems were over. Had he given her false hope?

"Hey, babe," he said walking to her. He released Beck's hand and gave his wife a big hug as they walked inside. "How are you?"

"Better now that you're back," she replied.

"Me too." He gave her a squeeze. Even with the uncertainties, it felt good to be back in his home, with her, where he had always felt comfortable. "Where's Peter?"

"He's out on his sailboard. He should be in soon. I told him dinner was at six-thirty"

"Yum, what is it that smells so good?" The aromas reminded him of the ones that had wafted from the house next to Angela's in Little Italy. He thought again about her thighs covering his ears and smiled broadly.

"We made spaghetti and garlic bread for you," Rebecca answered, obviously proud of whatever assistance she had provided.

"Double yum, two of my favorites made by my favorite two girls." he said to Beck, winking at Sally who was already back at the stove, stirring a big pot.

"So dinner's in fifteen minutes?" he asked massaging Sally's shoulders as she stirred the sauce.

"Uh huh, why?" She was on to him.

"No big deal, I was just thinking about taking a quick swim and getting a shower. I need to wash the city off of me."

Before Sally could answer, his daughter was rushing out of the room yelling over her shoulder. "Wait for me Dad, I'm coming too."

"Go ahead," Sally said, "this will keep."

"You sure?" he asked.

Sally didn't answer, but she turned the burner off. As soon as their daughter was out of earshot, Sally turned to Mars and asked, "Is everything okay, Mars?"

"I think it will be," he answered trying to look and sound reassuring. "Dad is going to be my lawyer, and we have a plan."

Beck's foot steps were already back at the top of the stairs. As she reached the bottom, with bathing suit in hand, she exclaimed, "Da-ad come on. Get ready."

Mars kissed his wife on her cheek, grabbed his bag, and went to his room to change. Five minutes later he was diving into the bay right behind Beck. As usual, the water felt like ice at first, but by the time he had swum a few strokes it was fine.

Rebecca was a good swimmer and could keep up with him as long as he didn't go full tilt, so he stroked at a leisurely pace.

He thought of Angela as the water caressed his body.

Father and daughter swam parallel to the beach for a quarter of a mile then turned and swam back. When they stopped, Mars said, "Your backstroke looked good, have you been practicing?"

"Yep, "she said proudly as she dove towards him. When she came up she said, "Throw me."

"You're getting too big for this," he said, but he obliged. He did a deep-knee bend holding her feet in his hands then thrust her out of the water and up in the air. She splashed back down, laughing and holding her nose as she went under.

"Again," she demanded still grinning.

"Okay, but just one more, and then you need to go get your shower so you can set the table." He threw her again. When she surfaced she obediently swam to shore then ran across the beach, up to their outside shower.

Mars saw Peter sailing in and he swam out towards him. When they met, Peter dropped the sail and said, "Hey, Dad, welcome home." He actually sounded like he had missed his old man.

"Thanks, Peter. It's good to be back. Mind if I sail for a few minutes?"

"Help yourself," Peter said, removing his life vest then diving towards the beach. He was probably glad not to have to put the Windsurfer away.

Mars sat on the board, while he put the vest on. He stood and pulled the sail slowly up, letting the water drain off as he raised it. As he caught the breeze he found himself thinking again about Angela and the life they could not share.

The sailing soothed his ragged soul. He had a great life. Not perfect, but very close.

46 - 11:05 p.m.

"So, Mars, what's going on? What did you find out?"

He and Sally had just retired to their bedroom. It was their first chance to talk about the embezzlement since he got home.

"You better sit down," Mars said not knowing any way to ease into it. He plopped onto the end of the sofa so that he could face her. She looked scared. So was he. He could feel the tension creeping up his neck and into his temples. He was not looking forward to telling his wife the sanitized, yet still convoluted and unpleasant tale.

"Is it that bad?" Sally asked obviously sensing his tension. "I thought you said it was going to be okay."

"I do think that it will be... at least I don't think I'll be arrested."

"Well that's a good thing isn't it?" Sally asked trying to sound optimistic. She was a trooper. She got down sometimes, but she always rallied back, and whenever she saw that he was having a rough time, she made a special effort to look on the bright side.

"Yeah, that part is good... very good. But I could lose

my job –"

"What for, Mars? You didn't do anything – you were framed."

"I was, but I also broke the bank's security policy, and that's terms for dismissal."

"What policy?" Sally asked with a tone of disbelief; she knew how conservative and rules-oriented her husband was.

"I left my computer on while I was away from my desk," Mars said. It was true, but it was a lie of omission. He couldn't mention that the desk was the one in their master bedroom. It was a huge lie, but the truth would hurt her worse.

He hated himself.

"That's no big deal is it? Doesn't everyone do that?"

"Yeah, they do, but *I'm* the one that got framed. Trust me; my job is definitely on the line. Someone at the bank will have to be held accountable. That someone is me."

It was true no one logged off every time they left their desk, and most of them had disabled the screen locks that were set up to kick in after three minutes. It was a pain to have to keep re-entering your password. Mars normally followed the procedures at work. Unfortunately, at home, he rarely did, especially when home alone monitoring an installation like he was doing that night. He just left it on so he could get his updates quickly.

"So someone got on your computer and stole the money?"

"Yep, they sent an e-mail from me requesting an override to one of the conversion jobs-"

Sally interrupted, "The big project last month while we were in Hatteras?"

"Yeah," Mars was losing his train of thought. A dizzying array of images of Angela moving above him illuminated by the blue light of the monitor flashed through his mind. They were so vivid for a second that he felt as if his wife may have seen them too.

When he refocused Sally looked concerned. Now she understood. They both knew that there were not many other jobs like his in the area. If he lost this one, he might have to do what many other technical people did; he would have to commute to Wilmington, Philadelphia or Baltimore, or worse, he would have to take a consulting job that would involve week-long trips to cities. He dreaded the possibility, but it was the least of his concerns.

"Mars, do you really think they would fire you just for leaving your computer on?"

"No, they would fire me because they'll need a scapegoat. I'm telling you, babe, they always need an employee to blame." He had seen it happen before. He knew that someone would have to be let go, and given the circumstances, he knew that he would be the best candidate. "I may just have to prove that everyone breaks that policy. It may not stop them from firing me, but it'll make it a lot harder for them. I'll call the ACLU if I have to."

Sally gave him a nervous look. "Mars, what are you going to do?"

He raised his eyebrows and gave her a silent you-don't-want-to-know look.

"Mars, please don't make matters any worse." She sat studying her hands on his toes then looked up. "The most important thing is you won't go to jail."

They sat in silence for a minute. Mars wrestled with how to tell her the other news. Before he could get started, she asked the perfect lead in question. "Who did it, Mars? Was it someone on your team? If they fire them, won't that be enough?"

"No, it wasn't an employee. It was one of the

consultants." As he said it, he toyed with stopping right there, not telling her who the consultant was. But he knew that he needed to. His pulse thumped in his ears. It seemed abnormally loud.

He didn't get to mull it over very long - she asked, "Which one?"

He inched bravely ahead. "Do you remember Angela Ignazio from the deli when we were kids?"

Suspicion thinned her lips. Her eyes were reduced to blue slits. "How could I forget Angela? She was the girl that you had that big crush on when I had one on you." She sat straight up pushing his feet off her lap as she eyed him. "Mars, why are you bringing her up now?"

Mars barely had the courage to look at Sally, but he did, to gauge her reaction, as he blurted it out. "She's the one that framed me."

His wife's jaw dropped, her forehead furrowed and he could see the wheels turning. Her squinting eyes did not leave his. "How did *she* have access to your computer?"

"Angela was one of the consultants that Banksall assigned to the conversion process." Mars answered with as much innocence as he could muster.

She spat out, "Angela Ignazio was a consultant working with you while I was out of town, and you didn't bother to mention that to me?"

Hurt and disappointment pooled in her eyes before fire leapt in. Then she was gone off the couch and out the sliding doors not hearing Mars gulping for answers.

Mars sat there knowing that if Sally ever learned the whole truth, if she ever found out that Angela had been here in this very bedroom, *in their bed*, his marriage would be over - no if-and-or-buts.

Just my butt kicked the hell out.

Burdened with that certainty, he pushed himself up on weary legs, and pursued his wife.

She was not on the deck. He walked out over the dunes and saw her standing in the light of the moon.

Two ladders to the moon, my love... and to a freaking nightmare.

He went to his wife and stood beside her. The bay was lapping at their ankles as he put his arm around her shoulders. She shrugged it off.

"Come back inside, Sal," Mars urged.

"I *do not* want to have this conversation where the children might hear us."

"Babe, I didn't know it was Angela."

Sally's "humph" made it crystal clear that she did not believe him.

Mars moved in front of her, held her face lightly in his hands, and tried to make eye contact in the moonlight. "Sally, it's true. She is not the Angela I knew thirty years ago. She is a middle-aged woman named Sofia Pitasi."

"And I'm supposed to believe that you didn't recognize her. *Come on, Mars,* you were crazy about her."

"I had a crush on a teenage girl. Sofia Pitasi is not that girl." Knowing that he had not convinced Sally, he foolishly went on, "I admit, she did remind me of Angela, but lots of women-"

"Oh great," Sally jerked away from him, ducked under his arms and started walking. As soon as he caught up to her she stopped and glared. "That makes me feel much better. *Lots* of women remind you of her. I guess I deluded myself, Mars. I thought you got over her a long time ago."

"I did." It was true. It had taken him a decade, but he got over Angela, or at least he thought he had. He wouldn't have married Sally if he hadn't believed that.

But when he saw Angela again, even not realizing who she was, the attraction was still there - magnetism just like in the movies. It was undeniable. But he had to deny it to his wife.

They had stopped walking. Mars managed to get his arms around her, but she stood there like a statue. "Sally," he pleaded. "You know how I am, I'm terrible with faces."

Her whole body had been different. In hindsight, he knew he should have known it was Angela as soon as he saw those eyes, or certainly when her lips -

"Well *your* name hasn't changed. You are still Marshall Hamilton Stewart the third, right? Come on Mars, even if you didn't recognize her, surely she recognized you." She pushed her husband away.

"Sofia - uh, Angela - knew who I was, but she didn't tell me who she was."

Even in the darkness he could see disbelief still contorting her face. He continued pleading his case. "I didn't know until my father told me."

"Your *father*?" She backed away from him. "What the hell is going on, Mars?"

47   - 11:33 p.m.

As he watched Sally's reaction, Mars second guessed whether he should have told her about Angela. Maybe his father had been right. He should have taken a chance that it would never come out in the news. He should not have told her the truth about who had framed him. But he had told her. And now that he had mentioned his father having a role in the saga, he had to tell her what he had just learned a few days ago about why Angela had disappeared from his life so completely.

"It's a long story, Sally. Let's sit," Mars said as he led her away from the water.

He gently pulled her down on the cool dry sand. She sat across from him, and studied a shell that she played with as he told her the truth about thirty years ago. Mars confessed to being intimate with Angela - once - and that, unbeknownst to him, she had gotten pregnant. He recounted the deal of their dads – a payoff for a promise that Angela's family would never tell Mars. He explained about Vinny, and her losing the baby then finally having a son with her husband Vinny. He told of her fear of losing him too if he could not have the surgery, and how she had decided to embezzle the money to save her only child.

Sally never said a word.

"She said that she had planned to move the money under her own logon, but when she saw an opportunity to frame me, she took advantage of it. To her it felt like a godsend." He tried to make his tone sound as if he really did not believe Angela; he tried to mimic his father's tone. The incomprehensible reality was that he believed Angela.

I'm loony, but I do.

Mars refocused on the moment. He felt unburdened, at least partially, as soon as he had the story out. Everything he had told Sally was true. He had of course omitted the incriminating facts about where she had access to his computer, and about their one fantastic night in Baltimore.

He had told Sally what he could. Now it was up to her.

"Is that it? Is that everything?" she asked as she stood up brushing the sand off her butt.

"Yes," he lied.

Without another word Sally left.

This time Mars did not follow her as she walked away from him down the beach. Instead, he waited for what seemed like hours lying in the sand, observing the absolute order in the night sky. How was it that the galaxies of stars, planets, and moons moved with such predictable precision, and he had trashed his life?

He had no idea what his wife would do next. Had she, with her woman's intuition, seen the truth? Part of him wished that he could tell her the whole story. He wanted to come clean. He doubted that she would tolerate his infidelity, but maybe - to preserve the family for Peter and

Beck - she would. He liked to think he would be able to forgive a one-time act - eventually - but he would never want Sally to stay with him if she were in love with someone else.

In his heart of hearts he knew he was in love with Angela, but he was just as sure that their ship had sailed and had been torpedoed. This was where he belonged.

The only way it could work was if Sally never found out how badly he wished that he and Angela had been able to have a life together. Not that he wished away his wonderful family. He did not. He loved their life, but he was certain – in spite of Angela's half-hearted efforts to convince him otherwise – that they would have been extremely compatible. They would have had a great life, too.

He found himself remembering the last night in Baltimore, and her thigh-muffled declarations. He longed to see her again. He wondered if he ever would. Intellectually, he knew that they should stay away from each other, but the thought of them never being together again filled him with profound sadness.

He heard Sally's footsteps in the sand. She was only ten yards away. He wiped his tears away with the neck of his shirt. Her face was obscured by darkness. He hoped his was too.

When she reached him she kneeled down, and kissed him tenderly on his cheek. He wondered if she noticed the salty residue.

"I'm sorry. I overreacted, Mars. It was all a very long time ago. You lost a child." She sat back on her haunches. "Are you okay?"

Mars was relieved but disoriented by her reaction. It wasn't what he expected at all. Somehow her kindness made it worse.

"I'm okay. It's weird; with everything that's going on, I

really haven't had time to focus on... on the boy." He tried to analyze his feelings about his son's death.

Instead, Mars was thinking how wrong it was that his wife was apologizing to him. How unfair it had been that Angela had to deal with all the pain of their son's death alone. He needed to be thinking about the present, but he was absorbed in the belief that it would have made a gigantic difference to Angela if he could have been there for her then. He loved her so much; he would have done anything to be with her back then.

Sally's words closed the time warp. She sounded concerned, but also skeptical. "What's wrong with her son that she needed money that badly?"

She settled in next to Mars, and he put his arm around her shoulders. She leaned against him and her body molded to his as it had for decades - like two pieces of a puzzle that - amazingly - still fit.

Mars took a deep breath of the damp sea air. He did not deserve this woman's compassion, but he was so very grateful for it.

"He needed heart valve replacement surgery; he had no insurance."

"Couldn't they borrow it?"

"She claims that they are leveraged to the max." Again, he made it sound as if he did not fully believe Angela. That untruth floated like chum on his soul. The lies were coming too easily.

Sally took the bait. "Maybe she hates your family." She sounded thoughtful. A bit too eagerly she added, "Maybe she hates *you*."

"Hate me? Why?" Mars questioned wounded by the very thought of it even as he considered that it would be to his advantage if Sally subscribed to that theory.

"If someone had gotten me pregnant, and his father paid me off... I don't know; maybe I wouldn't believe that he didn't know about the baby. What father wouldn't tell his son - use it as a powerful life lesson?"

"My father."

"Good point," she agreed.

Mars thought of several reasons that he knew the hate-theory wasn't true. No one could make love like that if they hated you. *Could they?*

Sally rubbed his arm and continued, "She doesn't know you like I know you, Marshall Hamilton Stewart the third. I know you would have done the right thing and married her, but how would she know that?"

Angela knew it now. Mars was sure of that - almost. One thing was definite; he was a one-hundred percent jerk for letting his wife try to cheer him up.

"How's he doing?"

The question threw him. *Who? Oh yeah. Tony.*

"Angela said that his surgery was successful; he's doing as well as can be expected."

They sat quietly while Sally processed the information and he worried if he could get back in position after his biggest shank ever. He knew it was iffy unless - no until - he could stop thinking about Angela so damn much.

"So when is she turning herself in?"

"I don't know. Dad is representing me. He'll meet with her lawyer as soon as he can. Hopefully we'll know more in the next couple of days." He did not mention that his father was taking care of getting Angela an attorney.

Sally's tone switched from empathetic to threatening. "She better not renege on confessing."

"The thing is Sally," he paused contemplating the seriousness of what he was saying, "If she decides not to confess, it's my word against hers. It was my logon so-"

"She has to," his normally docile wife said with conviction. She stood and brushed the sand off as if that was to be the final word on the subject. Mars sat, unable to see her facial features. He wondered if her new-found fiery spirit was about to be unleashed on him, but she reached down for his hands and leaned back providing ballast as he stood.

They started back towards the house hand in hand.

"She did say she'll confess, right?" his wife asked, needing to be reassured.

"She said that she would."

48 - Friday 12:37 a.m.

Mars lay on his back in bed next to his wife. He could not sleep. He tried his breathing technique a few times. It did not work. He had feared that Sally would be upset that he had been with Angela thirty years ago, or worse, that somehow she would know that there was more, much more, to the story.

Thankfully, Sally had not sensed the whole truth. The bond that had grown between them over a quarter of a century, the trust - that he no longer deserved - had saved him, at least so far.

Sally was a remarkable woman, and he was more convinced than ever of how much she loved him. He felt undeserving, but he was relieved. He found that he was actually hopeful that things would work out between them.

He tried to stay focused on his wife. It was her butt against his hip, but his thoughts drifted back to Angela. *Two ladders to the moon.* His memories were so intense that he could almost feel her wrapped around him, could almost smell her musky scent. *I go there in my mind.* She aroused feelings in him like no one else ever had.

Mars rolled onto his side. He was butt to butt with Sally as scenes from the past few days and nights replayed over and over. His mind would not let go of Angela. Finally, he decided just to relax into them.

When he awoke Friday morning, his first thought was Angela, and it took a few seconds to get his bearings. He was at home, in his own bed, with his wife. He opened his eyes. Sally was already up. He could smell the coffee brewing, and he heard small waves breaking onto the beach. The windows were open. He breathed the salty mix deep into his lungs.

It was wonderful to be home even though he ached for more of Angela. He rolled out of bed to face his life without her. *One day at a time just like any other addict*, he thought.

As he approached the kitchen, Sally greeted him with a surprisingly cheery, "Good morning." Guilt swept through him as she continued. "I almost woke you since you said you were going to work, but you were sleeping so soundly. What time do you need to get there?" she asked from her stool at the counter.

Mars looked at the clock on the microwave – it was seven-twelve. "No rush, they're not even expecting me until Monday." Plus, his plan could not be executed until the end of the day. "I guess I'd like to get there by nine." He rubbed his eyes as if he could rub away the thoughts that were mired in his morning fog.

"Do you want me to make pancakes and bacon?" She asked, closing the Business section of the News Journal. She tucked it neatly into the folds of the rest of the newspaper.

"No thanks, I've been missing my bagel with peanut butter. But first, I need coffee." He poured a cup then asked, "What's on your agenda today?"

"Not much. Since you're going to work, I think Beck and I will go do some back-to-school shopping at the outlets. I'll stop at the grocery store. Do you want anything special?"

I want Angela, he thought then silently admonished himself. He wanted his old life back, but he sure missed her. "How about some New York strips and a salad? If you shop, I'll grill."

"Deal," she said as he walked over carrying a steaming mug. He kissed her cheek and said, "It's good to be home," as much for his own benefit as hers.

It paid off. She looked happy. God, he hoped that she stayed that way. He knew she wouldn't if she ever found out the whole truth. It felt like an unforgivable lie not to tell her, but he rationalized that it was better for her this way. Betrayal was bad enough. He would not abandon his family, nor would he push her away by revealing the whole sordid truth.

Mars vowed to never see Angela again. Unless, of course, he had to for some reason related to the embezzlement. He started to conjure up reasons why they might have to be reunited.

"Let's go sit on the deck," he suggested, anxious to go admire their bay view or at least pretend to as he struggled to settle back into his reality.

His wife followed him out to yellow Adirondack chairs. They sat with their feet up on the silver-gray cedar benches facing the water.

Mars inhaled deeply. "God, I've missed this. I don't know how people live in cities. The air is nasty. I hated running there. The whole damn place is paved. The earth can't breathe and neither could I."

"We're very lucky." Sally said as she often did, but this morning he could hear some fear creeping in. She turned to face him. "Mars, what did you mean when you said that you would have to show them that everyone breaks that security policy? What are you planning to do?"

Mars glanced at her then gazed back out to the horizon where recreational fishing boats cut through the waves. There was a lone Sunfish out just beyond the sandbar. One of Parson's commercial boats was coming into the inlet.

"It's just an idea," he said not wanting to alarm her. "I'm not positive I'm doing anything. I need to go in, and see what's happening. Apparently they haven't even found the e-mail yet."

"I think we'll know when they find it. They'll assume you did it, and they'll come to arrest you, won't they?" Concern resonated in her voice. "She needs to confess now."

His wife was right, they would come for him. In addition to being arrested LB&T would probably fire him, or at least suspend him, on the spot. He would be guilty until proven innocent. He certainly hoped Angela would be ready to confess Monday. He was pretty sure she would get Tony home over the weekend. Then she would have to meet with her lawyer. He couldn't push her for many reasons, including the fact that she might push back.

While he waited for her to do her thing, he was going to do what he thought he could to try to save his job. He had to do it today, while he still had access to the bank and their computers. He knew he would probably go through with it, but he didn't tell Sally. She had enough to worry about.

He patted her leg. "Don't worry, babe. Everything will work out."

Mars breathed in the fresh air, and tried to enjoy the calm in what he feared was the center of his own personal hurricane. This felt like it could be the calm before the back-side of the storm - like when Isabel blew through in 2003. Many thought they had escaped the storm only to have the backside's tidal surges cause havoc.

He hoped that his home and his family would survive, that he would be the only one blown away by Hurricane Angela.

49 - 9:05 a.m.

Mars felt uneasy as he approached his department. He hadn't talked with Liz or anyone else since Wednesday. He had checked his e-mail before going to bed the previous night and there had been no significant news. His team was still analyzing all of the changes that had been installed in an attempt to find a breach in the software modifications. It was a slow go, line by line.

Liz came bustling into his cubicle just as he flipped open the locks on his briefcase. "Welcome back Mars." She sat in one of his office chairs.

"Thanks, Liz," he replied making brief eye contact, trying to read her face. He turned to power his computer on. She looked normal – excited by the investigation – but otherwise the same. As he scanned her face again he was sure she did not suspect him. He was relieved. "What's going on? Sounds like you and Jason are still wading through the changes."

"We were, but late yesterday I got a voicemail." Mars held his breath. "Lance and Amanda and Jose left last night. Apparently they had to go to some Electronic

Crimes Special Agent training class today. They'll be back here Monday, so we are at your disposal today. Got any ideas?"

"Not really." Mars relaxed as he processed the fact that the Secret Service was not on-site today. "Why don't you reserve a conference room at 9:30? Tell Jason to join us. You guys can bring me up to speed on what's been happening since I left."

"Okay, will do." Liz stood to leave "I'm going for coffee, want some?"

"Yeah, sure," Mars answered pulling his wallet out and handing her two bucks. He didn't bother telling her how he liked his. She already knew.

As soon as Liz left, Mars gave his boss Tim a quick call.

"Hey Mars, where are you?"

"In my office."

"Welcome back."

"Thanks.

"Sorry about your aunt. I wasn't expecting you back til Monday."

"Yeah, I wrapped things up quicker than I thought. I was able to get an earlier flight." Mars had told that lie so many times that it almost seemed like the truth. "I'm getting ready to meet with Liz and Jason so they can bring me up to date."

"Guess they told you the secret agents are taking today off," Tim said poking fun at the situation. "How about lunch? We could run up to the club, maybe play nine."

Tim never ceased to amaze Mars with his lackadaisical attitude. "Lunch would be fine, but no golf for me, I need to catch up on things here." *We do have a fraud investigation underway,* he thought.

"Cool, let's shoot for noon," Tim responded, "I'll drive."

They hung up. Mars needed to check in with his main client - Mary Thompson - to see what her perspective was, but when he checked on the time he decided to wait until he got done with Liz and Jason.

"Here's your coffee, we've got conference room B," Liz said as she popped in and out of his office.

Mars signed on to the e-mail system and scrolled through the conversion project folder until he got to the e-mail that Angela had sent. He reread it then just sat and stared as he thought about why no one had found it yet.

He understood why Tim wouldn't find it; he was totally disorganized. Their CIO wasn't much better than Tim, so his copy could have also been deleted. That left George Mumford. As their Modifications Management representative, he certainly should have filed his copy. One would think that he would have remembered it or stumbled onto it by now.

If nothing else, he would expect the Secret Service would have searched the mail system as he did. *Christ, I even told them that emergency changes got installed with e-mails as the only audit trail.*

It made no sense. He sat there spacing out, thinking that maybe he should leave well enough alone, and just wait to see what happened. Maybe they would never find it. Then again if or when they did he would not get another opportunity to execute his plan. So, if he didn't act now he would risk losing his job.

His watch beeped. It was time for his meeting. He closed his e-mail and started to walk out of his office. As an afterthought, he went back and activated the lock on his computer screen.

Live and learn.

50   - 9:32 a.m.

Jason and Liz were waiting for him in the conference room. There were three cardboard file boxes in the middle of the table along with a few papers stacked neatly in front of the empty chair at the head. His two best team members were seated on either side.

"Looks like you've been busy," Mars commented as he sat.

"Yeah, welcome back to our chaos," Jason said. "Sorry to hear about your aunt."

"Thanks," Mars replied then quickly switched to the topic at hand. "So what's the status of the research? Find anything interesting?" he asked knowing full well they had not, and would not, at least not in the software modifications.

"This is a list of all of the changes our team has made to the DAS system this year." Liz referenced the spreadsheet on the top of his pile. "We've been working through the list of modifications that George provided to the Secret Service. The agents divided it using a very scientific method." She smiled.

Jason grinned as he added the punch line. "I got the even number ones, and Liz got the odds. It's based on a complex algorithm they were taught in the Special Agent Academy. Silly me, I would have thought I would get the odd ones." Jason was no doubt referring to his odd looks. His ever-changing hair was now a bleached blond spiked do. That was calm for him.

"You two seem very amused by this," Mars said smiling with them. He was glad that they had been able to maintain their sense of humor. "What's up, don't you think our nation's best are competent?"

Amanda started to weigh in, "No, they seem-"

Jason cut her off. "They're definitely not Obama's brightest. I get the feeling that the agency is stretched pretty thin since the Columbia scandal. For sure they did not send their top dogs to find this loose change."

Mars contemplated how that bit of good news might benefit him and Angela before snapping back into his managerial role. "Well, compared to Bernie Madoff's eighteen billion dollar Ponzi scheme, and seven-hundred billion dollar TARP bail-outs, this may not qualify as big bucks in their world, but I'm quite certain that LB&T and our customer, Ms. Jacobson, do not consider her missing half-million to be small change."

"True," Jason agreed. "Every couple hundred thousand helps."

"Okay, so you are working through George's list of software changes-"

"Programs, sub-programs, called routines, JCL, and database queries are all included," Jason expounded.

Mars's heart skipped a beat as he scanned it looking for the offending JCL override requested by Angela's e-mail. It was absent. Relief spread through him as he thought, *Modifications Management my ass – George Mumford should be fired!*

The list included check marks indicating what had been reviewed to date. They were about three-quarters of the way through. "You've made good progress. Anything suspicious?" he asked again studying them.

Both Liz and Jason shook their heads soberly. "We've been paying particular attention to the direct file accesses, but there were only a few of those," Liz reported. "They're highlighted in yellow."

Mars glanced at the list, seeing that all of the yellows had been reviewed. He noticed a file access requested by Angela, and knew that it must have been how she had copied the production file to make the test file that she had manipulated. Thankfully, it had a check next to it too.

Under the circumstances, he was not disappointed to learn that his best employees and the Secret Service had not thought it to be suspicious. He realized he wouldn't have thought so either if he didn't already know about the e-mail. As far as they knew, all she had done was create a test file; that was a common occurrence. Reading the test file into a production job was the taboo thing. Without Angela's override request the file access was innocuous.

"Did Lance want you guys to do anything with this today?"

"No, they specifically told us not to while they are not here to look over our shoulder. We are not capable of doing this without them. We must wait until we can explain the reason for each line of code. Then and only then are we allowed to check it off. We are not to be trusted," Jason mocked. Apparently his intelligence had been insulted, but he continued on a lighter note, "We were going to take the day off - maybe go to the beach - until you showed up."

Dutifully, Liz set the record straight. "We were going

to help out on the Student Account Enhancement project. They're behind schedule with the new federal regulatory changes."

That had been the big project on their plate; they had all been working on it before the embezzlement was uncovered. Everyone except Liz and Jason still was, but Mars couldn't get too excited about it. Worst case it would go in a week or two late, and he and his team would miss out on bonus pay. He was much too preoccupied with Angela and the embezzlement to be personally concerned, but he would feel bad if his team missed out on the incentive money after all of their hard work.

Mars leaned back, studied his two prodigies, and asked what he was afraid to ask. "So, do you two have any clue how this was done?"

"I believe that someone manipulated the file directly," Jason said making Mars's stomach gurgle again. "Unfortunately all of SYSOUT from that time period was purged."

Jason was referring to an audit report of sorts that the Operating System spews out each time a job runs on the computer – system output listing all of the input and output files along with other components used in a job. If the SYSOUT still existed it would show that a test file had been read into one of the conversion jobs. Fortunately it had been auto-deleted. The bank had strict criteria for how long it kept all kinds of electronic records. SYSOUT was only kept for one month.

Mars started to think that maybe Angela was right. Maybe no one else would ever figure out what had happened. His optimism was squelched when Liz piped up, "Rumor has it that they have a crew running scans of everyone's hard drives. I heard they copied them all that first weekend before we came into work. Remember, they took all of our laptops for a few hours?"

Mars felt sweat form under his arms and across his torso. He hoped he could execute his plan before they found the incriminating mail and gave him the boot.

51 - 12:25 p.m.

After deciding how Liz and Jason would spend the day, Mars had lunch with his boss. They ate in the cafeteria even though Tim had planned to go to The Rookery North where he had promised they would just hit one bucket. Mars knew that it would have turned into at least nine holes, and he didn't have time to waste.

"Liz and Jason are still busy double-checking all of the modifications we installed over the past two months. They've made great progress. What else are the agents looking at?"

"I really don't know. Feds are leaving me out of the loop which suits me just fine. Not my party, not my problem. I endeavor to keep it that way." Tim was more interested in his burger and fries drenched in malt vinegar. They smelled like the boardwalk - much better than Mars's healthy meal.

Mars tried to read Tim and decided that nothing had changed. The Secret Service was not on to the e-mail yet, or if they were, they hadn't alerted his boss. Unfortunately, he wasn't going to learn anything from

Tim, so he finished his salad and yogurt, and got moving.

On his way back from lunch, Mars paid Mary, the manager of the Deposit Account Systems client area, a visit. He found out that they had been researching the account where Angela had put the stolen money. She had confirmed what Angela had said; the money had been moved out of LB&T via a wire transfer. It was long gone and was untraceable.

Mary's group had rewritten their procedures for dealing with dormant accounts to insure that something like this never happened again. They would begin working the DAS Month-end Dormant Account Detail Reports as well as the daily ones that had been ignored due to man-power issues. To that end, they were approved to hire one more person and interviews were underway.

Angela's own stimulus plan at work.

Mars was glad to see that Mary was in relatively good spirits. He had been worried about her. At the Sunday meeting she had seemed close to tears, blaming herself. Mars knew she was not at fault, but he also knew that her job, like his, was on the line. LB&T was going to have to do something public to regain customer confidence and firing the two managers closest to the crime just might do it.

After leaving Mary, Mars spent the afternoon checking on his team. All the while he was struggling with whether to invoke his plan or not. He wished he could take a chance that they would never find the e-mail, in which case he would never be implicated and neither would Angela.

On the other hand, if he didn't take action today there was a good chance that the Secret Service would find it via their automated searches of his and everyone else's disk drives. He would lose his job.

To make matters worse, he could *not* stay focused. His mind was trying to multi-task, but he was not doing a hell of a good job of it. Thoughts of Angela seemed to run in parallel with all other thoughts. Several times an hour he found himself just daydreaming of her. His imagination was bounded only by the unfathomable; he could not see how he could live the rest of his life with or without her.

Marshall, you better get a fucking grip.

He locked his screen, walked out of his office down the long hallway and out to his car. He decided not to fight it any longer. He called Angela.

"Hello," she answered in a hushed voice obviously knowing who it was.

"Hi Angela," Mars said, his voice full of longing for all he could not have.

"Hey Mars. How are you? Are you at work?"

"I am," he replied. "It's amazing. No one found the e-mail yet."

"Great, maybe-"

He cut her off. "But, as we speak, they're scanning the backups they took of everyone's hard-drives."

"So you'll wait and see?" she asked hopefully.

"I don't think I can afford to. Once they find the override request it'll be too late, I'll be escorted out of the building. I'll lose my job."

"So...what are you going to do?" Angela asked sounding worried.

"I need to make sure that management knows that a lot of employees leave their computers on and unattended."

"Mars, please don't do anything stupid," she pleaded then added, "I won't let you go to jail for what I did. Can't you just wait?"

"I know you won't," he said softly, "but I can't afford

to risk losing my job either." He changed the topic, "How's Tony doing?"

"Good," she answered, but he noticed the lack of enthusiasm. "He'll be released to Brandywine Rehab tomorrow. It's just a few miles from home."

"That's great news," Mars said knowing that should mean that she would be able to meet with the lawyer, but he also knew that once she was home it would be harder for them to stay in touch. "Do me a favor; leave a message on my cell once you get him settled there."

"Okay, I will."

"I miss you, Angela." Mars said realizing what an understatement it was.

"I miss you too, Mars. I could hardly sleep last night. The bed seemed empty without you."

Vinny will keep you company soon, Mars thought, hating the jealousy that welled up in him.

They sat in silence, content for the only connection they could have.

Finally Angela said, "Be careful, Mars."

"I will," he replied, wondering if he was about to make matters worse.

52 - 3:33 p.m.

Mars waited until three-thirty to start scoping out the situation. As was typical on Fridays, almost everyone had left for the weekend, but there were still a dozen or so co-workers around. He walked over to the MVP's office knowing that Nick's secretary usually left early on Fridays. Luckily, today was no exception.

He passed her reception area and poked his head into their CIO's office. His briefcase was still there. He was somewhere in the building, hopefully engrossed in chatting up some young blond female employee. His monitor faced away from the door.

As Mars walked around Nick's desk and the stacks of unfiled papers, his pulse pounded in his ears and temples. His MVP had come through for him; he had left his computer on. His screensaver - one of the unimaginative stock ones - was rotating across the monitor. Mars said a silent prayer of gratitude that even the head of IT had not followed bank's logoff policy.

Mars used his pen to press the ENTER key. Bingo. Nick's desktop flashed onto the monitor. His e-mail session was still open. Adrenaline shot through Mars. He walked back out to the hallway and looked in both directions. No one was in sight. He rushed back into the office, sat at the Chief Information Officer's desk, and quickly typed his message.

****

SUBJECT: Confession
TO: RGregory@LBnTrust.com
FROM: NCollins@LBnTrust.com

I am guilty of a breach in LB&T's security policies. I left my computer on and unattended.

****

Mars broke into a sweat as his cursor lingered over the SEND button. It was now or never. He did it. Then he toggled to the SENT MAIL folder where he deleted the MVP's copy so he would not see it before their CEO, Randal Gregory, received it.

Mars hustled back to his desk and collapsed into his chair. He was concerned about his racing pulse and paused to do some deep breathing. Once he settled down, he continued as planned.

He walked through the department and stopped at each desk checking to see if they had shut down their computers properly. Whenever they had not, he sent the same mail. An hour later over twenty employees had made the same confession including his boss Tim and himself.

Once he was done he quickly packed up his stuff and left the building hoping it would be enough to save his job.

53 - 4:21 p.m.

Knowing that the confessions would be a moot point unless Angela turned herself in, he called her as soon as he was on the road home.

"I did it," he said as the Friday night tourist traffic pushed him down Route 1.

"Okay." She waited. When he did not elaborate she asked, "Are you going to tell me what you did?"

"I got on our MVP's logon and sent an e-mail from him," Mars confided. "I was going to have him confess to the embezzlement, but I was worried that might be a felony in and of itself."

"So what did your message say?"

Mars noted she sounded anxious. "Don't worry; I didn't embezzle any more money."

"Not funny, Mars."

"Sorry. I just said that he breached the bank's security policy by leaving his computer on and unattended."

"Okay... What's the point?"

"I'm just making my case that many employees don't

adhere to that policy and therefore - when you confess - you having access to my computer should not be grounds for my termination. I not only sent it from Nick's computer, I sent it from about twenty others including my own."

Neither spoke while they considered his actions. They both knew he still needed her to confess for them to matter.

"What if they catch you?"

"I don't think that they will. No one saw me."

"Won't they know from the security system that you were in the building?"

"Yeah, they can tell that I was there, but I made sure that there were quite a few others still in the department. They would be hard pressed to pin it on me."

"So what do you think is going to happen?"

"I don't know, but they certainly can't fire us all."

"I see your point, but won't that give them a heads up on how the embezzlement happened?" She sounded worried when she asked, "Or are you planning on telling them what I did?"

"I have to consult my father, and you need to speak with the lawyer he got for you. Did you hear from him yet?"

"I did. We set up a meeting for first thing Monday morning. Thanks."

"Good. Maybe you should get his opinion on whether it would be better for you if we came forward before they find your e-mail. Personally, I think it would be."

"I'm sure you're right *if* we assume that they will find it. But obviously, them not finding it would be my best case scenario, and yours."

"True," Mars said thinking that it was a pipedream. "Well, ask your attorney and let me know. No great rush since I don't think anything will happen here over the weekend. Monday would be good. So everything lined up for Tony to go to rehab tomorrow?"

"Yep, he's doing great. In fact, I'm on my way home. They'll take him in a medical transport in the morning. He wanted to come home, but the doctor says that he needs a week or so of rehab before he releases him. That suits me."

"So you'll be home tonight - with Vinny." He immediately felt foolish; he needed to get his head on straight, but he couldn't help thinking he should be with Angela, not anyone else.

"I will. And you'll be with Sally and your family," she said sadly. "This is harder than I thought it would be, Mars."

"They say absence makes the heart grow fonder." Mars offered the cliché, trying to get them both to look on the bright side.

"If that's true, I'm in big trouble," she replied.

Mars knew that he was already in crisis mode; if he were any fonder of Angela he wasn't sure how he could go on with his old life. It had been a stupid thing to say, and it had not lightened the mood.

"Well then let's hope they're wrong, whoever *they* are," he said, but even as he spoke the words he could feel that they were right. The little time they had had together was never going to be enough.

"Uh huh," she agreed. "Well, I'm almost home so we better go. I'll call you Monday after I meet with my lawyer."

"Okay, Angela. I hope everything goes well with Tony, and all. I'll be thinking about you." As he said it he realized that he was becoming the master of understatements. Words just didn't seem to cover what he felt about Angela.

"I'll be thinking about you too, Mars. Have a nice

weekend."

They hung up leaving Mars feeling empty and alone. It was frightening how attached he had become to her - again - in just a few short days. He knew that they could not be together; he had a wife and two wonderful children at home.

He concentrated on counting his blessings.

54   - Saturday 6:43 a.m.

Mars had woken up at dawn and had lain there relishing the fresh salty air and his warm memories of Angela. All too soon the deep-seeded fear that he had totally destroyed his life crept in. Still he wasn't sorry for a single one of the too few minutes that he had spent with Angela.

His lack of regret tormented him until he was no longer able to lie still.

He got up, threw on his running shorts, grabbed a tee shirt, socks and sneakers and went out on the deck. The sun was half hidden by some low clouds, and was casting a warm yellow glow over a slice of the bay.

He stood letting it warm his face, but his mind was still blue. He wondered where Angela was this morning and if she was missing him like he missed her. With his eyes closed, the heat of the sun and the images flashing through his brain quickly had him in a sweat.

He spun around and studied his house.

Count your blessings, Marshall. Sally, Peter, Beck, this house, this beautiful beach, the bay, your job, your freedom, your moments with Angela... He knew those memories were something he would treasure forever, but he felt a longing that shook him to his soul. He would never wake up beside her – or behind her – again.

He started running remembering how she felt against his body, how she loved him, and he loved her. He ran faster, but he could not escape the simple truth. *I love Sally, but I'm in love with Angela.*

Again he tried to convince himself that he was blessed. In a way he had it all. And in a way he had nothing.

When he got back home, he bent over panting and sweating from the extra vigorous workout, and from the realization that he might never kiss Angela's lips again. He walked wearily into the kitchen.

Sally was there pouring her coffee. "Hey honey, want a cup?" she asked going back to the paper that was open on the counter.

"Thanks, I'll get some in a minute," he answered giving her a peck on the cheek as he went to the fridge to get some cold water.

He leaned against the counter and guzzled. He felt completely spent. "Shew, it's going to be a hot one." He was dripping wet with perspiration.

He had an encouraging thought. If he could just function in a way that kept Sally happy, maybe this could all work out.

"I'm going to run through the shower. What's on the agenda this morning?" he asked trying to engage in his reality.

"I'm going to the park to watch Beck play field hockey at ten. It's the last day of camp and they're having a tournament." She looked up from her paper. "Want to join me?"

"Definitely, I'll go get cleaned up."

After showering, enjoying their coffee-and-newspaper ritual and having a light breakfast, Mars and Sally were sitting in their chairs in the hot morning sun watching Beck. She and her teammates played a great game. Their daughter was in the left wing position, and Mars could see that her game had come a long way. She had always been fast and skilled for her age, but she looked much more confident than she had the previous fall in her school games. She knew where she was supposed to be, and what she was doing. She played hard.

As they watched, Mars told Sally what he had done with the e-mails the day before. "I needed to make a point. Now if they fire me, they should have to fire twenty other people in the department."

"What if they figure out that you sent the mails. Then they would have even more reasons to let you go, wouldn't they?"

Mars was a little worried about that too, but he thought the risk was worth the possible reward. It could save his job. "I don't think they could prove I sent them. As a manager, I have valid reasons to be on all the computers except our CIO's, and I doubt that they will fingerprint his keyboard. Besides I hen-pecked with my pen." He gave her knee a squeeze. Let's try not to worry about it today," he said all too aware of the memories of Angela swirling in his head, vying for air time.

A few minutes later, cheers brought him back to the moment. Beck's team had just scored, tying the game at 1-1 with a minute left. They were going crazy on the field. The other team took advantage of their lack of focus and quickly took the ball into the circle. They scored on a penalty corner in the final seconds.

It was a single elimination tournament so Beck's team was done. She gathered up all of her stuff, and came dragging it over to them. Her face was beet red.

Mars handed her a bottle of water and said, "Great game, Beck, you're looking good. Your stick work has really improved, and you were always in the right place. Great effort."

"Yeah, but we lost." She was despondent.

"Look on the bright side kiddo," he said putting his arm around her shoulders, "it's a scorcher today, and you won't have to run around in the heat for another hour."

Beck tried to smile, but couldn't quite pull it off until her friends yelled to her that they were heading back to the park dorm where some of them were staying. "Can I go?" she asked excitedly.

Sally looked at Mars. He shrugged, indicating it was fine with him. His wife looked at her watch and answered, "Okay, we'll pick you up here at three o'clock."

"How about four, Mom? The final game won't be over until then. Please," she pleaded as she backed away.

"Okay, four o'clock sharp at the Nature Center," Sally called to Beck, who was already running to catch up with her friends.

"Geez, she's really growing up," Mars said putting his arm around his wife. They watched as their daughter walked away with five other girls.

"They both are," Sally replied reaching for his hand. "Soon it will be just the two of us."

A week ago Mars would have relished the thought, but after recent events, he wondered if they could make an empty nest work.

55   - Sunday 7:42 a.m.

Mars woke up spooned against his wife. He was aroused. Remnants of a dream of Angela were stuck in his still groggy mind. He tried to fall back into his nocturnal fantasy, but he could not.

As he lay there trying to get oriented, he realized that it was Sunday - *SOS time*. It now had dual meaning: Sunday Only Sex, and Sally or Sofia. He struggled with the question of whether it was morally right to have sex with his wife when he wanted Sofia Angela Ignazio Pitasi. Before he could reach any conclusions, Sally's rear grazed him eliciting an inadvertent moan.

She rolled onto her back – a silent and familiar invitation. As he kissed her he whispered, "SOS" and tried to push the other meaning out of his mind. It didn't work, but he was grateful that Angela's name did not slip from his mind onto his lips.

"Mars that was," Sally struggled to find the right word, and settled on "wow." She had obviously noticed that he was more inspired than usual and had not minded, but Mars did. He felt like a real shit.

"I missed you," he offered lamely, feeling that he owed her an explanation.

"I'm glad. I missed you too."

Mars heard her declaration through a fog of emotions. He couldn't help but compare the practiced rather sedate love-making with his wife with the steamy version he and Angela had shared. He was sexually satisfied, but was overcome with a deep longing for the woman he could not have. His mind had things all twisted around; he felt like he had betrayed Angela.

He knew how wrong that was. He needed to engage in this world, his real one, if he was going to have a prayer of not totally mucking everything up.

He turned to his wife, gave her a quick peck on the cheek and asked, "How about I cook breakfast?"

He was already rolling out of bed when she moaned in appreciation.

"Coffee will be delivered in ten."

Mars liked to cook a big breakfast once or twice a month. He looked at the bread supply and decided that it was enough to make his grandmother's French toast. He made it just like she had shown him; eggs, milk, a little vanilla, a dash of cinnamon, and a couple of tablespoons of flour to thicken the batter. Peter had already left for work so MARS set the table on the porch for three.

After breakfast, Beck went out on the Sunfish with her girlfriend while he and Sally cleaned up.

"Mars, do you think you did the right thing logging onto all those computers and sending those e-mails? It worries me."

"I think it gives me a much better chance at keeping my job." Mars tried to sound confident, but he knew that it could backfire.

"Well, I'm glad you didn't send confessions of the actual embezzlement. Wouldn't you have been guilty of interfering with a federal investigation or some such crime?"

He was about to say that yes, that they had already discussed that when he realized that the conversation he was remembering had been with Angela.

He answered his wife, "That's what I was afraid of, too. This way the only thing I'm guilty of is a breach of the bank's policies."

He was thinking about how untrue that was; there was also the gigantic breach of his marriage vows.

Sally interrupted his self-flogging. "Have you talked to your father about when she'll turn herself in?"

Mars noticed his wife could not seem to utter Angela's name. "As far as I know, she is meeting with her lawyer tomorrow. Then I guess my father and her attorney will get together and work out the details." That's what Angela had told him, but he, of course, didn't want his wife to know that they had been talking. "I need to call Dad tonight and see if he has any more updates."

They went out to the deck where Mars spotted Beck's blue, yellow and white Sunfish sail way down the beach. They were a quarter of a mile offshore and had caught a good breeze. A couple of kite sailors were out further doing some wild acrobatics.

The whole scene blurred into the background as Mars again thought of Angela. He wondered where she was; maybe at the rehab unit with Tony, or enjoying her own reunion morning sex with Vinny? He perspired at the thought and tried desperately to relax.

Mars gave in and focused on the flashes of his time with her that were running through his mind. It seemed that they were like the ticker tape on the bottom of the CNBC station, always vying for his attention.

It was a constant challenge for him all day long to stay in the moment, but Sally did not seem to notice. She caught him not paying attention once or twice, but she seemed to attribute it to the embezzlement issues. At one point she came over and massaged his shoulders saying, "Don't worry, Mars, it'll all work out. Your dad's a great lawyer. He'll prove that you are innocent."

I wish I was innocent, he thought as his wife attacked the spot where his tension often settled between his shoulder blades. Her mind was clearly on the embezzlement, where his should be until he cleared himself, or rather, until Angela cleared him.

"The more I think about it," she said, "I think you were right to send the e-mails. How could they fire you and not the others?"

Assuming Angela confesses, he thought then felt guilty for doubting that she would. Remembering his wife's question he answered. "I don't think they could."

Her thumbs worked on the tension at the base of his skull. As he relaxed he remembered the sensation of Angela straddling his butt giving him a backrub.

Sally was standing behind his chair and noticed his reaction to those memories. Understandably, she misunderstood and slapped him playfully and almost giggled, "Mars, you better go take a swim or something. I've got some work to do."

With that the backrub was over, and she was gone.

Mars got up and took her advice. He swam for twenty minutes. Reality cured the symptom long before he dove into the cold water, but his mind remained on Angela.

After a shower, he was tempted to call her while his wife was out hanging the sheets on the clothesline. He just wanted to hear her voice. He knew it was crazy, too risky - she could be with Vinny - but he visualized her at the rehab center. He felt bad that she was probably missing this beautiful day.

The afternoon passed slowly. Finally, Peter arrived

home from his lifeguard duties. Mars was glad to be busy with another cookout followed by a nice big bonfire on the beach. At Beck's insistence they roasted marshmallows which even his son enjoyed. It was a nice evening, just the four of them hanging out. Like the old days, before Angela collided with him again.

Under different circumstances it would have seemed like a perfect night. But intermittent thoughts of losing his job and the possibility of jail time mixed with his constant thoughts of Angela made Mars realize how fragile it all was.

He was grateful that his life had not turned on a dime - at least not yet.

56 - Monday 7:45 a.m.

As soon as Mars was on Cedar Avenue on the way to work, he dialed Angela. He hoped that Vinny left for work early, but figured that, worst case, if her husband was still home, he could camouflage it as a business call. She was after all a consultant for his bank.

"Hello." God, he loved the sultry sound of her voice.

"Angela, it's me. Are you alone?"

"Yeah, Vinny leaves for the deli around seven-thirty every day. I was hoping you would call."

"Great minds think alike," he said lightly then added, "I couldn't stop thinking about you all weekend. I almost called you a few times, but decided I shouldn't."

"Ditto. I think you're right, we should limit our calls to business hours – unless there's an emergency."

"I know, but it's hard." There was some dead air time as Mars tried not to think of the double-meaning of his statement. "By the way, how much of this does Vinny know? And Tony?"

"Tony has known all along that I framed you. He had worked for a bank. He and I had talked about how vulnerable dormant accounts were. When we needed money for his surgery he mentioned that he wished that he had embezzled money from his bank while he had a chance. Needless to say, he was rather bitter about losing his job in the merger in spite of his outstanding performance over the years. He had been loyal to them, had even turned down other lucrative positions, but the job market had dried up by the time they severed him."

"Sounds like maybe he planted the embezzlement seed in your mind."

"He did, but he was mostly kidding. To his credit, he was totally against me doing it. When I told him my plan, he wanted to do it himself - on my logon. He figured that - worst case - he would go to jail where he would probably get the operation he needed, compliments of the taxpayers."

Mars had seen on a *20-20* or *Dateline*-type program that showed how true that was. He remembered watching and being infuriated at the fact that a murderer could get healthcare that was not available to needy law-abiding citizens. It occurred to him now that Angela should have let Tony do it. Yet he knew that he would never have let Peter do it. Parents were supposed to take care of their children, not the other way around. He couldn't fault Angela for what she was trying to do even if her plan was misguided.

"How about Vinny, does he know what's going on?"

"I told him right after I did it. He was furious. He's still very upset, but he's also relieved that Tony is doing well and that I haven't been caught."

"Does he know that you framed me?"

"He does," she said evenly.

"What does he think about you confessing?"

Angela did not answer right away. Mars took that as a bad sign. He waited and she soon confirmed his fears.

"Let's just say that Vinny is struggling with that. He's a very religious man – Thou shalt not steal and all. So on the one hand he thinks that I should take responsibility, but since it would probably involve prison for me –"

Mars interrupted. He could hear it in her tone. "He's pressuring you to let me hang."

"Vinny's always had a bit of a problem with rich kids. He thinks guys like you have had it too easy. To him it's another case of the haves and the have-nots."

Mars had arrived at work, parked and shut off his car. He leaned his head back and shut his eyes. He toyed with defending himself - he wasn't rich - but at the moment he wasn't all that concerned with what Vinny thought. He was almost afraid to ask, "Angela, you are still willing to confess aren't you?" He reflexively stopped breathing as he waited for her answer.

"I think so Mars, I definitely don't want you to pay for what I did –"

What happened to *won't* let him pay? He prodded her, "But?"

"*But* they haven't even found my e-mail yet. They might never find it. I may be able to get away with it if-"

"If what, Angela? If I wait to see if they show up to arrest me? Maybe my little girl would get to see her fath-"

"Okay, Mars. I get it. I do. Just please don't do anything rash."

Mars felt nauseous. *She might not confess. Oh my God.*

"Angela, I really think you will have a better chance of staying out of jail if you confess before the Secret Service finds the e-mail. They're scanning backups of our hard drives. They will find it. When they do, they'll come for me, and I'll tell them the truth - or some of it. And you won't be in the same bargaining position. You still have half of the money. Use it as a bargaining chip. "

He had spoken with as much control as he could. He tried not to let panic creep in. He imagined that she was going to say, "And I'll tell the feds the rest of the truth," but she didn't.

Mars thanked his lucky stars when instead she said, "You're probably right. I need to see what my lawyer advises."

"Dad said something about an agitated capacity plea – I think it's a form of temporary insanity. Let's Google it. It sounds like it would be more believable if you showed remorse."

She laughed. "I don't have to Google it to know that it was a form of insanity. We'll see... I hope you don't regret loving me. "

I hope I don't either, Mars thought not knowing if she meant he might regret loving her based on the current predicament, or based on what she was about to do. *Or not do.* It did not sound good.

He tried to appease her. "I don't regret it. I'm just worried about federal agents showing up at my door. Please, Angela. Don't risk traumatizing my family. We've all been through enough. Please just talk to your attorney. Then call me. Leave a message if I don't answer. I want to know what your lawyer says as soon as possible."

"I will. I'm sorry, Mars."

57   - 8:07 a.m.

Mars walked down the long hallway to his department wondering if her lawyer would support her husband's point of view and convince Angela not to confess.   He wasn't sure what the attorney's oath required, but he knew that if he were her lawyer he wouldn't be in any hurry to have her implicate herself.

She may have committed the perfect crime. God help me.

Mary Thompson greeted him soberly as she passed, "Hey, Mars,"

"Morning, Mary," he responded wondering what was up then he remembered the e-mails that he had sent. He was so disturbed by Angela's change of heart that his mind raced back to her.

What the hell will I do if she changes her mind? Mars wished that he had called his father before entering the building. He really didn't want to call him from inside the bank; someone might overhear the conversation since his department and the whole bank was a big cubicle farm – there were no doors to shut except in the conference rooms.

He made it to his desk and was turning his computer on, still deep in thought, when Liz came bursting in. "Mars, did you hear the latest?" she whispered excitedly.

"No what?" He hoped it was about his confession e-mails and not something worse.

"Randal Gregory is coming down this morning to talk to our department. Ten o'clock in the gymnasium." She obviously thought that it was a big deal, and it usually was when the CEO gave a command performance. The gym was about the only place big enough to seat the entire department. The maintenance staff would set up chairs on the basketball court.

Mars was actually relieved that it was going to be a big meeting. That meant Mr. Gregory wasn't coming just to see him.

"How were you notified?"

"It's written on the board, didn't you see it?" He had not. She continued, "Plus we each got an e-mail. Do you think it has something to do with the investigation?"

She sat. So did Mars. He got logged on and went to the e-mail system where he found his copy of the notification. He read it before answering Liz. It was totally ambiguous. It just announced the meeting and stated that attendance was mandatory for the whole department.

"That would be my guess. Hopefully nothing else is going on."

"Maybe they broke the case."

"Maybe." Mars didn't believe that they had. If they had found Angela's mail they would have come straight to him. There would be no reason to hold a big meeting. He was pretty sure that it would be about the confessions which only he knew were related to the case.

"I hope they did solve it. Then we can all get back to

business as usual." Mars tried to sound convincing, even though the last thing he wanted was for them to crack the case today with Angela waffling. "Guess we'll see at ten. Coffee?"

They walked to the cafeteria together, stopping several times to talk to other members of the department who were as keyed up as Liz. Everyone seemed to expect Mars to have an answer.

At nine-forty-five Mars invoked his screen-lock and left for the meeting. Liz and Jason beckoned to him as soon as he walked into the gym indicating that they had saved him a seat. He waved them off and sat with Tim and the other managers in the front row.

Tim was passing the time watching Mr. Gregory's assistant Mitzi Robinson as she prepared the podium for her boss. As always, Tim felt compelled to share his innermost thoughts with his neighbor; Mars had the pleasure this time.

His boss hummed *Coo Coo Coo Choo Mrs. Robinson,* before saying, "I give her a nine today. That top is not very flattering, but love the skirt."

Mars couldn't help but check her out himself. She had on low black heels, a straight beige linen skirt that hit right above her knees but that was slit well up her thigh. Her black blouse was slightly tapered. *I'd give her a ten,* Mars thought then whispered, "You are such a pig, Tim."

"Hey, just cause you're too much of a prude to admit how hot you think she is, don't rag on me, choir boy." Tim ogled her more intently. He even shifted in his seat to get a better view as she moved to a table on the other side of the podium and sat down.

As she crossed her legs, Mars thought that Tim was right in a way - he did think that Mitzi was great looking. You would have to be blind not to notice her. But unlike

Tim, Mars did not think about banging every nice looking woman that he saw. He just appreciated beauty... but he had done much more than appreciate Angela's. A month ago he may have been a prude. Now he was an adulterer – something even worse than his boss who was mostly hot air.

He felt empty. He longed to be with Angela, but the ache was more than tempered by their conversation just two hours ago. The emptiness quickly filled with doubt.

Please, Angela, he pleaded as if they were as cosmically connected as he often felt. *Please follow your heart. Don't let them talk you into turning against me.*

Mars was jerked back to reality by Tim elbowing him. His boss had changed his tune and was now doing his best rendition of the death-march, "Dum dum da dum dum... our MVP has arrived!"

Mars looked up to see Tim's boss, the un-honorable Nick Collins, entering the room with Randal Gregory at his side. Nick went straight to podium, grabbed the microphone, and was apparently getting ready to speak when his boss took him by the elbow, and said something to him in a hushed voice. Nick handed the microphone to their CEO and went over to the table where Mitzi was seated. Unperturbed by his boss's rebuff, he stared at her hint of cleavage as he sat.

What a prick, Mars thought for the thousandth time. Tim had a few traits in common with Nick, like leering at women, but basically Tim was a nice guy masquerading as a jerk. As far as Mars knew, Nick had no redeeming qualities. *A jerk masquerading as a prick.*

Randal Gregory looked at Tim. "Is everyone here?"

"Yes, I think so, Mr. Gregory." Tim sounded

professional, even formal, as he was capable of on a need-to-do basis.

Their CEO scanned the room then began. "First I want to thank all of you that are assisting the Secret Service as we work together to resolve the embezzlement case." He paused giving Mars time to be fearful that maybe it was solved. Maybe they had found Angela's mail. "But that's not why we are gathered here this morning." Mars sighed in relief. "It seems that we have another very serious problem." Again, he seemed to make eye contact with many of the employees in the room including Mars. "As members of our elite Information Technology team you have all been granted authority to the technical resources that your managers have deemed necessary to do your jobs. Many of you have controlled access to the data for our customers and their accounts. As guardians of those resources you have responsibilities."

Mars settled back into his chair, trying to relax, or at least look relaxed, as he waited for the group reprimand that was no doubt coming as a result of his confessions.

"As we speak, I have some of our Systems Security officers checking each of your workstations to see how many of you have logged off, or properly locked your workstations, while you are here."

A group gasp sucked the air out of the room. Mars fought the urge to smile. He managed to furrow his brow in what he hoped passed for genuine concern. Perhaps it was his imagination, but the gymnasium suddenly reeked of sweat.

"It seems that one of you noticed that many employees in this department do not follow our security procedures. This brave, albeit misguided employee, sent me messages late Friday afternoon, from twenty of you, alerting me to this problem."

The room erupted as most everyone whispered to their neighbor in a frenzy trying to figure out who all was in trouble.

"Please raise your hand if you remember signing a security policy regarding your responsibilities in this matter."

Mars did not have to turn around to know that most employees had probably raised their hands; even fewer of them secured their desktops when they left their desks for a meeting than when they left for the day.

Randal Gregory turned to his dumbfounded CIO. "Nick, would you be so kind as to come up here and tell the group what the clearly defined penalty is in the policy that all of us signed?"

Nick, who had turned a paler shade of gray than his bland tie, made his way to the podium where he reluctantly accepted the microphone. He breathed the now fouled air in deeply, and croaked, "Any breach of the security policy is grounds for termination, sir."

Their MVP looked at his boss like a kid looking at his teacher to see if his correct answer would buy him a favor. From the look he got, it was clear there would be no gold star for him.

"Very good, Nick," Randal replied. "Please be seated."

Their CEO stood silently observing the discomfort of the group as the room was again rumbling with whispered concerns. Mars's internal smile was gigantic. He hoped it was not outwardly visible. This was going better than expected. He could hear snippets of what was being said. "Oh my God, are we going to be fired?" and "They can't fire us all."

Randal waited watching the collective squirm. He unscrewed the cap on the water bottle that Mitzi had left for him, took a big swallow then calmly screwed the cap back on. Only then did he pick up a paper that his able-bodied assistant had left for him. Slowly he began to read each and every word of Security Policy that they had all signed the day their employment began.

Mars noticed that Phillip Brooks, Director of IT Security, had entered the room. He stood stiffly by the door. With his buzz-cut hair, broad shoulders and pumped-up body he looked like a well-aged marine. He had an air of authority about him that was amplified by the fact that he may very well hold the fate of many department members in his hand – literally. In his firm grasp was a piece of paper that, no doubt, listed the names of those in the room that had not secured their computers before coming to the gym.

Mr. Gregory gave him a cursory glance as he continued reading the failed policy. When he was done, he nodded to Phillip who strode across the room. When he reached the podium he handed his boss the paper.

Their CEO scanned its length before squaring his shoulders and speaking. "As of this moment there are seventy-eight employees in your department. I hold in my hands a list of forty-one of you who are now eligible for termination."

The room erupted in hushed anguish as Mars glowed with the knowledge that they would never fire over half of the department. *They need us,* he thought.

He glanced around and saw some tears and real fear on the faces of his friends and co-workers. A wave of guilt kicked in. He probably should not have drawn so many people into his mess, but - on a brighter note - it looked like his plan was going to work.

Randal Gregory continued.   "You are all very fortunate that the problem is so pervasive in this department, and most likely in other departments. It is such a common breach that I have no choice but to conclude that management is guilty of a failure to educate and enforce our rules." He eyed Nick first then every manager in the room. "All employees, including all levels of management, will be required to take a Security refresher course. Details will be forthcoming. Any future breaches will result in immediate termination."

On that note their CEO left the podium and the room. Mitzi gathered his belongings from the podium and followed a dozen steps behind him.

59   - 2:01 p.m.

Mars had checked his phone all day for a message from Angela. There were none. He was dying to hear if her lawyer was going to have her confess; he guessed not.

Finally at two o'clock he walked out of the bank to a picnic table that was shaded by a white dogwood.

He called her cell phone. No answer. He checked his watch then hung up without leaving a message. It was too soon to be worried about not hearing from her. She probably hadn't had her meeting yet.

He decided that he should relax and enjoy the success of the morning. He did some deep breathing exercises in the fresh air. He could not relax.

He called his father's office.

His receptionist answered on the second ring. "Stewart Law Firm, how may I help you?"

"Hello, Barbara. It's Mars. Is Dad in?"

"I'm sorry, Mars, but he's not. He's been in court all morning. Can I leave him a message?"

"No thanks, I'll leave one on his cell phone."

They hung up. Mars called his father's cell and left a

message to call him back ASAP. He stood and stretched his shoulders and neck. Then he sat on the top of the table with his feet on the bench. He was in the shade, but it was still hot and humid. The breeze barely helped.

He needed to think. It seemed like he had dodged one ball - he probably wouldn't get fired for leaving his computer on - but two more important ones were still hanging in the wind. The embezzlement and the family balls were still in danger.

He was sitting there with perspiration running down his torso willing Angela to turn herself in when a familiar voice startled him. "Hot enough for you, Marshall?" It was Lance.

Mars stood and shook hands with the agent. "Good to see you again, Agent Williams." The Secret Service agent was dressed much as he had been last Sunday - it seemed like years ago - when Mars had first seen him. He donned a navy suit - with a white shirt and a navy and light blue rep tie - even though the whole building was business casual. He looked important, and to Mars's fate he was.

"Sorry about your loss," he said giving Mars a light punch in the shoulder. "We missed you last week, but you have a good team. Jose and Amanda are very impressed with Liz and Jason."

"I'm very fortunate to have them working for me." They started walking towards the building. Mars wished he had thought to compliment Lance's agents even though Liz and Jason had not been impressed. *Oh, well, too late.*

"I was back at work Friday. They brought me up to speed on the research that they've been doing."

There was a lull in the conversation as they were cleared through the security gates then Lance continued. "So far all of the changes look clean, but I'm still confident that we'll find the evidence."

Mars had a hot-flash on top of his summer-heat-induced sweat as they walked up the long chilled hallway. He did not trust himself to speak. Lance did.

"Randal Gregory called me Friday night about the e-mails he received. Information Technology staff leaving their workstations unattended certainly opens the door for some major problems."

Tell me about it, Mars thought. "Sure does," he replied.

"Randal said he was going to come down here today and meet with all of you."

"He did. While we were in the meeting Phillip Brooks checked all of our computers. They found that over half of our staff had not secured theirs properly."

"Damn... Wow, that's not good. Anyone that walked into your department could have access to all sorts of information, which may be the least of the potential problems."

"True, it's bad. But, keep in mind that we do not have the authority to change production directly. That's a carefully managed process."

They had reached the conference room where the Secret Service was set-up. They stopped and Lance studied Mars a bit too thoroughly for Mar's comfort before he replied. "Yes, but my guess is that the department that does have the keys to the kingdom - Modifications Management - may have similar security problems." A look came over the agent as if he had had an epiphany.

He seemed to switch into a faster gear as he asked, "Mars, do you know if Mr. Gregory has left yet?"

"He has not. I just saw his limo in the front lot."

Lance gave him another friendly, but more powerful punch to the shoulder. "Thanks, Mars." Then almost as an afterthought, "I want some time with you before you leave today."

Oh my God, Mars thought as he calmly said, "No problem, I'll be here until at least five o'clock. Just give me a call."

Lance ducked in the conference room. Mars continued to his department wondering what Lance had just figured out.

Whatever it is, he hasn't found the e-mail yet. Maybe Angela was right; maybe they would never find it. *Why the hell hasn't she reported in?*

He knew he hadn't missed a call, his phone would have vibrated, but he unclipped it from his belt and looked at it again anyway.

Damn.

Mars had an uneventful afternoon. Nothing much got accomplished in the department; everyone was buzzing with excitement from the morning meeting. Over half of them had thought - at least for a few minutes - that they were going to lose their jobs. Some of the rest of them - the ones that had locked down their computers before leaving for the meeting - probably had short-lived dreams of promotions, salary increases and other good stuff that might come their way as a result of the others being fired - in between sympathy pangs for their fallen peers, of course.

Liz, Jason, and Agents Amanda and Jose were a few of the ones back at work. They were researching the remainder of the modifications that had been installed recently. They seemed to have the task well in hand so Mars left them to it. He checked on the status of the other work being done by his team members. The Student Account Enhancements were still a week behind. Mars reassigned some tasks to try and get back on track.

All the while, he stewed about why neither Angela nor

his father had called. His phone vibrated once, but it was just a call from Lance saying that he wasn't going to be able to meet today after all. He said he would catch up with Mars the next day. Mars wondered what that was all about.

The hours passed like days. Finally, at five-fifteen Mars left work. He called Angela as soon as he was out of the building. Again, there was no answer. This time he left a message for her to call as soon as possible.

Come on, Angela, call me, he thought. *Please don't do this to me. Call.*

He got in his car, started it and turned the air on full blast. His phone vibrated in his hand. It startled him. She had heard his cosmic plea.

No such luck. It was his father.

"Hello," he said dismally.

"Hello, Mars," his father answered. "Sorry I didn't call earlier, but I was in court and then I wanted to speak with Abe Bernstein before I retuned your call. He's the attorney that's taking Angela's case."

Mars recognized the name, but he couldn't remember why. "Did you get an update from him? Angela was meeting with him today." Mars was anxious.

"We just got off the phone." Mars could tell by his father's voice that it was not good news. "He didn't come right out and say it, but I gather he's reluctant to have his client confess to the embezzlement when there is absolutely no evidence against her."

Mars shut his eyes and let the cold air blow on his face. *I knew it.*

"Are you okay, son?"

"I was afraid of that. I talked to her this morning. She told me her husband is pressuring her to not confess."

"Well, it seems that her attorney may have jumped on that bandwagon too. Not only is there no evidence against her, but you have not yet been implicated either."

They sat in silence. Mars was crushed at the thought that she might back down on her word. How could she do that to him?

"Honestly, Mars, if I were her lawyer I might be giving her the same advice."

"So what the hell do I do, Dad?" Mars had rarely looked to his father for advice, but he desperately needed it now.

"Is there any chance that the feds can follow the money trail back to her?"

"I don't think so. The LB&T account where she dumped the money was not in her name, but somehow she was able to wire it to a numbered account in the islands. I'm sure it's untraceable." Mars felt powerless. He was totally at Angela's mercy, and she was not even answering his calls.

Suddenly Mars had a migraine. The stale air from the air-conditioning was not helping. He opened the windows and let the hot humid fresh air in. It did not help.

"I gather that they haven't found the e-mail yet."

"Not yet." It was amazing. He started thinking maybe Angela was right; maybe they should just wait and see. But he knew if they found it they would arrest him. He had no trouble imagining how that would traumatize his wife and kids, especially if it happened at home, in front of them. He visualized Beck sobbing as he was taken away in handcuffs.

"Mars, you better talk to Angela. *If* she loves you - as you think she does - you should be able to convince her not to wait until they come for you." Obviously, his father did not believe in Angela. Mars was having doubts too.

"Dad, I've been trying," he whined. "She said that she would call as soon as she left her attorney, but she didn't. I called at noon, and I just left her another message." It was starting to seem that she had set him up then manipulated him into believing that she would come through for him.

His father tried to console him. "Well maybe she'll call soon." He didn't sound convincing. "Mars, I'm sorry, but I'm going to have to run. Call me on my cell as soon as you hear anything."

"Okay, Dad, thanks."

Mars tried again to will Angela to call him. He knew that it was silly. No matter how connected he felt, it was a bunch of crap. There was no way that she could hear him begging for mercy. She knew that he would be waiting anxiously, and he could not come up with any good reasons for her not calling.

There was one bad reason that he could no longer dismiss.

61 - Tuesday 6:15 a.m.

The evening had crept by even slower than the day had. Mars checked his phone frequently - no messages. Finally, around twelve-thirty he had drifted off to sleep. When his clock radio started playing at six-fifteen, his first thought was whether Angela had called. As nonchalantly as he could, he went to his dresser and checked his phone. His pulse quickened when he saw that he had a voice message.

Sally stirred.

Mars knew that he shouldn't listen to it yet. It was killing him, but he needed to stick to his routine. He would listen to it in a few minutes when Sally got up to make the coffee. Reluctantly, he left his cell on his dresser, and went outside to shower.

His heart was telling him it would be good news. She would be his hero after all. Just the fact that she had called was a relief. He was petrified over what would happen if she didn't confess. He prayed that her husband and Bernstein had not convinced her to let him take the rap.

The shower ran on his head long after he was clean. He was anxious to hear what she had to say, but whatever it was it wouldn't change in the next fifteen minutes. The call could have been from his father.

What if Angela still hadn't contacted him? Mars had never felt so vulnerable in his life. He was at Angela's mercy. The water washed away fearful tears. He lingered trying to get his emotions under control, trying to imagine what his grandfather would do.

Play one shot at a time. Don't get ahead of yourself. First he needed to listen to the message, and if it was from her then he would hear what she had to say.

When he returned to the bedroom Sally was still gone. He could hear her moving around in the kitchen. The toaster popped.

Mars accessed his voicemail box.

"Mars, it's me Angela. I am so sorry. I know you must be beside yourself wondering what's going on." The compassion in her voice melted most of his anxiety away. "We had a scare with Tony. I had to rush there directly from my attorney's office. His infection came back with a vengeance. They think it was from the catheter. Anyway..." She sounded exhausted. "They were about to ship him back to Hopkins, but the antibiotics finally kicked in a couple of hours ago. I was going to call you from the rehab center, but my cell phone battery died and that was the only place where I had your number. I planned to call when I got home. Then Vinny picked tonight to stay up to watch the Phillies game which, of course, went to extra innings. Anyway, I'm sorry, Mars. Call me on your way to work. Please."

There was a break in her message and Mars almost hung up before he heard, "And yes, I do love you."

He was grinning. The way she had said it made him believe that they had the kind of spiritual connection that he often imagined. Well, almost. She hadn't said a word about Bernstein's counsel, or whether she would confess, but she had called. As his grandfather had taught him, it was a new day, and anything was possible.

"Well you certainly look chipper this morning," Sally said, interrupting his thoughts. She was carrying a tray with coffee and their usual bagels. The fruit of the day was cantaloupe; it smelled ripe and sweet.

"Umm, thanks I slept better than I should have." He had told Sally that his father had said that Angela might not confess. Under the circumstances his good mood was inexplicable, but his wife seemed content just seeing that he was upbeat. Thankfully, she did not press him.

They enjoyed their breakfast ritual watching *Imus* who was in his not-so-rare form, making them laugh half in disgust, and half in genuine amusement.

To the casual observer it might have seemed like a morning just like the thousands they had shared, but it was not. Mars was not all there. Warm thoughts of Angela were running through his brain colliding with the five-hundred-thousand-dollar question.

He had to fight the urge to wolf his food down so he could get on the road and call her.

He restrained himself with one eye on the clock. The minutes played a slow-motion game of tag. At seven-thirty on the dot he stood up. "Gotta run, babe," he said trying to sound regretful.

Sally held his hand. He pulled her to her feet, hugged her and kissed her cheek. It was another part of their routine.

"Mars, what if they find the mail and she won't confess?" his wife asked still hugging him.

He wanted to get going. "It'll work out, babe. It has to."

"I sure hope so, Mars." She held him tighter. He was

getting antsy. Seven-thirty-two. She spoke into his neck. "I don't know what we would do without you."

"I'm not going anywhere," he said stroking her hair, hoping that he could stay out of jail, and out of Angela's arms. He fought the urge to run to his car.

62   - 7:35 a.m.

As soon as Mars was on Cedar Avenue he called Angela. He felt bad for having questioned whether she loved him. One ring. Two rings. *Not again*, he thought as he heard the third ring and was certain that her voicemail was about to pick up.

"Hello," she said breathlessly.

His mind flew to the one thing he knew of that left her breathless.   "Angela, it's me." Logic told him that she wouldn't have answered his call if she were enjoying a morning tumble with her husband. Still, he wondered.

"Hey Mars, I am so sorry about yesterday." Well that answered that - Vinny was not there.

"No problem." He tried to relax, or at least to sound nonchalant, like it had been no big deal, like he had never doubted that she would call.

"I hate to do this, but can I call you right back, I just got out of the shower."

Ah, that's why she was breathless. She just ran from the shower... naked.

"I promise, I will call right back, just give me five

minutes."

"Okay." They hung up.

He waited visualizing her lithe body. He could almost smell her freshly shampooed hair. He longed to have her in his arms again.

He drove out of Lewes and started up Route 1 without seeing any of the landmarks. His mind was full of Angela still wet from her shower, but he was also wondering how her meeting with her lawyer had gone. Would she confess?

His phone vibrated. He answered.

"Hey, Mars."

He could scarcely remember what they needed to talk about.

"Are you there?" She asked as if the connection had been dropped, apparently oblivious to how much she distracted him.

"I'm here." He focused. "How's Tony doing?"

"I called over there this morning. He's fine. It's so annoying that - with all that he has been through - an infection from the damn catheter is his biggest problem."

"It is ridiculous, but infections run rampant in medical facilities these days. If you're not sick when you go in, you probably will be before you get out."

"It's ridiculous," she said then shifted gears. "I wanted to update you on my meeting with Abe Bernstein."

She sounded so formal. "How did it go?" His gut gurgled.

"I told him everything."

"Everything?"

She continued. "Well everything except the fact that we had those wonderful nights together in Baltimore."

"They were the best part," he remembered.

"But," she sighed, "that's another story. Anyway, he

understands that I do not want you to go to jail for what I did."

"But?" Mars asked afraid to hear what was coming next.

"But he is recommending that I hold off on turning myself in. It may not ever be necessary."

Mars had figured this was probably coming, but still he was speechless. Part of him was desperate to change her mind, but he understood where she was coming from – there was a slim chance that the mail would never be found. He didn't want her to go to jail, but she needed to take responsibility before it impacted his family.

"Mars, you're disappointed aren't you?"

He listened for a con, but all he heard was the affection he craved. He answered. "Honestly, I don't know what to think."

There was a lull in the conversation. Mars had his reoccurring vision of being arrested. Sally and both kids were sobbing as Lance took him away.

"Angela, I'm not sure that I can just sit back and wait to be arrested."

"Let's think about it," she said before changing the topic. "What happened at work yesterday?"

Mars had almost forgotten. He brightened. "My plan worked great. Our CEO came down. He held a meeting about security for our whole department. While he lectured us, our chief of security checked everyone's computers and made a list of who hadn't shut them down properly. Over half the department hadn't followed the policy."

"Sounds good. Your plan worked. What happens now?"

"No one got canned, and we all have to take a security refresher course, but to me it should mean amnesty." Mars was smiling. It had worked even better than he had hoped. One could certainly argue that his breach should be grandfathered in too.

"So that'll help a lot... I mean *if* they find your mail, right?"

Mars noticed that she was no longer taking ownership of the message she had written. He had decided back in Baltimore that even though he felt like he and Angela should have been together all these years, they weren't, and they were never going to be. He had responsibilities; he needed to do whatever was required to save his family.

Hearing her waffle about turning herself in made him think of his other options. Another plan began to surface, but he decided to give her one more chance.

"Angela, having the CEO fully aware that we all leave our computers unsecured at times will help, but only if I'm not in jail. And not being in jail won't even matter if I destroy my family in the process. I don't want to wait until I'm arrested. I need you to turn yourself in. Let Bernstein plea bargain for a short sentence. Use the money you still have to barter. Make a deal."

He tried to sound emphatic even as he envisioned her clad in an orange jumpsuit behind the bars of a cell. It was not what he wanted for her, but part of him was thinking that if Martha Stewart could do it, so could Angela.

She did the crime, now she might have to do the time...

He didn't want to tell her what he was thinking of doing.

"Angela, I've got to go. I'll call you on my way home."

"Okay, Mars... Please don't be mad."

"Angela, I'm not mad I'm..." he stopped. He couldn't find a label to put on his feelings; they were all over the place. "We'll figure something out."

Silence.

"I'll call you later."

"Okay, Mars."

She sounded worried, but Mars didn't have the energy to mollify her.

63   - 5:08 p.m.

Mars had spent his day at work thinking about a new plan; he would turn Angela in before the authorities latched onto him as their suspect. Setting her up for a probable jail sentence was far from ideal, but it was his family's best bet. He remembered the thirteenth rule of golf and his grandfather's lessons - play it as it lies. *I need to get back in position.*

He decided to consult with his father, and figuring that he would have to leave a message with his secretary, he placed a call to him from his desk. He had guessed wrong; his father was available. Mars didn't want to talk to him from inside the bank, so he arranged to call his attorney-dad back from outside the bank.

His father was pleased with his son's change of heart. No doubt he doubted Angela's motivations for not confessing, but he didn't go there. Instead he offered to try to catch up with Abe Bernstein to feel him out then get back to Mars.

Mars was in his office contemplating the risks and possible rewards when Lance stopped by for an impromptu private chat. Once they were settled into a conference room, the agent got right to the point.

"Mars, I'm starting to think that what we are looking for is not on the list."

Mars concentrated on staying calm. He knew Lance was no fool. He focused on his breathing as he waited for the agent to continue. He was so rattled he could barely swallow. His eyes welled up with the effort of choking his saliva down.

Apparently Lance had expected his comment to elicit some sort of response. He locked his probing eyes with Mars's watery ones. "Any ideas?" he prodded.

Mars held his gaze for a few seconds. Then he focused on the wall over Lance's shoulder. "Early on I had mentioned a couple of other options. I'm not sure if you have had a chance to check them out or not." Mars sighed louder than he should have as he wished the agent would go away and give him a chance to invoke his plan.

"Refresh my memory," Lance instructed as he leafed through a file folder looking for something. When Mars didn't respond immediately, the agent glanced up and gave him a curt go-ahead nod.

"Well, it doesn't seem likely, but there could be some latent back door in the Banksall's Deposit Account System code -"

Lance cut him off, "We've contacted Banksall Software as well as each client of the DAS system. So far no other bank has had a similar case," He glanced up from the folder, "What else?"

"Someone that has the authority to change the production system or files could have installed some rogue change that isn't on any list."

"Or," Lance added pulling a sheet from the file, "If a person with that authority left their computer unsecured

- as seems to be S.O.P. around here - *anyone* could have accessed the production system."

"Right," Mars muttered, uncomfortable that Lance had hit on the truth. He caught a glimpse of the paper Lance was reviewing and saw that it was Mars's own notes from that first meeting with his team - where Lance had them all document ideas on how the embezzlement could have happened.

Lance skimmed both sides of the page then placed it back in the folder. He made eye contact again, studying Mars way too intently. "So who all has the authority to change production?" Lance asked his pen tapping a clean sheet of paper.

"George Mumford in Modifications Management. No one on my team can directly change anything. We install all software and file changes through MM." Lance jotted something down. "The DBAs have update authority to the databases."

Lance chewed the end of his pen as he studied Mars. "Is that it?"

"Well... that's all that comes to mind, but I may not even be aware of everyone that could install stuff. You should check with Phillip Brooks. He would have a definitive list."

"I will." Lance said obviously fully aware that Brooks was in charge of IT Security. The agent tapped his pen some more. "George is the one that came up with the list that Amanda and Jose are working with your guys on. So if he..." Lance leaned his elbow on the table, propped his chin up on his hand in a thinking pose. He worked his jaw back and forth as he mulled something over.

Suddenly the agent pushed back from the table and stood, signaling the end of the meeting. Relieved, Mars stood too. Lance extended his hand. "Are you available tomorrow if I need you?"

"Yeah, sure, I'll be here all day. I have a few other projects going on, but I'll be around." Maybe he watched too much television, but Mars found himself wondering if Lance was consulting him as some sort of ploy to gain his trust. On the other hand, his gut told him that the agent was going to be hot on George Mumford's trail for a day or so.

Back in his cubicle, Mars checked his phone. It hadn't vibrated, but anxious to hear back from his father - and hoping Angela would have a change of heart - he looked for a missed call anyway. There were none.

Damn. Mars could feel his window of opportunity was about to slam shut, Lance was getting too close. He needed to act fast.

64   - 5:33 p.m.

Mars was on his way out of the bank with Tim when his phone vibrated. It was Angela. He didn't want to talk to her in front of Tim, but he didn't want to risk her not being there when he called back if he didn't answer.

"Hello."

"Mars?" He must have sounded weird; she didn't seem sure that it was him.

"Hey, Dad," he said, "can I call you right back?"

She played along. "Yeah sure, *son*," she laughed then hung up.

Mars stifled a grin as he made a beeline for his car. "See you, Tim, I have to run."

"Sounds like you and your Dad are getting along better."

"Yeah we are," Mars said realizing it was true. They were getting closer as a result of this ordeal. His pace quickened. He called her back before he reached his car.

"Hello, sonny," she said sounding playful.

"I remember you," he growled, "and you are definitely not my father."

"What was that all about?" she asked interrupting a bastardized silent version of one of his favorite Diana Krall songs.

"No big deal, I was walking with my boss, and didn't want him to know that you were calling me. Stupid I know since you are a LB&T contractor."

"You are a lot of things, Mars, but stupid you are not."

She blurted out, "I did it."

She confessed Mars thought smiling broadly. Then he checked himself, not wanting to be too hopeful. "You did what?" he asked almost holding his breath.

"I wired all of the money back, and gave it to Abe Bernstein. He put it in an escrow account."

"Wow." Mars was disappointed that it was the money and not herself that she had turned in, but his plan would have a better chance of working out well for Angela if she was willing to turn over the money that hadn't already been spent. So it was a good thing.

"Good. How much?"

"Two hundred thousand, plus change. I hope it helps convince them to make a deal if I have to confess."

"Me too," Mars said feeling a bit annoyed that she was still balking at taking responsibility.

"Mars, thank you for not pushing me."

"I love you Angela. I don't want you to go to jail if there is any way around it, but I can't just sit and wait for them to come for me." He was warning her.

"I understand," she said charitably. "Do you know what you're going to do?" She sounded scared. He knew she should be.

"I need to talk to my father, but the Secret Service is closing in. Lance linked the security breaches and the unattended logons with the case today. I don't know if he was fishing or what."

"God, Mars, I'm nervous. Are you?"

"I am." He wondered if they would find the mail today. Lance was probably with Mumford now. They could find the override request at any minute. He wished Lance would leave for the day.

As if he had willed it, the agent came striding out of the door towards his car.

Yes! Mars turned the ignition key and drove out of the lot believing that things might work out after all... except for things with Angela. They were never going to work out the way he had dreamed. He would be testing the strength of their bond with what he was about to do.

65 - 6:04 p.m.

The first thing that Mars saw when he pulled in his driveway was his father's Mercedes. The second was Beck running towards him screaming, "Daddy, Grandpa is here!" She said it as if it were as rare as a whale sighting and as wonderful as a hot-fudge sundae. It was the former, but Mars doubted it was the latter.

As his daughter bear-hugged him, he wondered what was up with his father that he hadn't just called. They walked together into the house where Sally greeted him.

Wonderful aromas were in the air.

"Yum, what's cooking?"

"Pot roast," she said as they exchanged their welcome-home-peck on the lips. "Your dad's gone for a swim," Sally said with a questioning look. His wife obviously wanted to know if something was the matter, something that had caused her husband's attorney father to suddenly show up.

He gave Sally an I-don't-know shrug, and said, "I think I'll go join him." He started towards the bedroom to change with Beck trailing him.

"Can I come too? Please Daddy?" she said with puppy dog eyes.

Sally saved him from having to say no. "Beck, I need you to stay and help me with dinner."

"Mo-om," she pleaded.

"Beck, set the table," Sally commanded in her best no-nonsense voice. Beck stomped back into the kitchen while her mother followed Mars into the bedroom. She shut the door. He was stripping off his work attire.

"Honey, is everything okay?"

"I think so. I called him this morning about my plan. Since Angela hasn't turned herself in, I want to go ahead and turn the e-mail over to the Secret Service. I can't risk that they'll find it first." Mars was buck-naked in the closet hanging up his slacks.

"She isn't coming forward?" she asked as she straightened some hangars oblivious to his nudity.

"No, she's hoping that she won't have to." He pulled on a pair of swim trunks.

"So turning over the mail, is that wise? Will they just take your word for it, that you didn't send it?"

He didn't try to convince her, he wasn't all that sure himself.

His wife gave him a clingy hug. "Mars if they don't believe you, they'll arrest *you*."

He hugged her back. It was a distinct possibility. He wanted to get outside and talk to his father. "Well, I can't just sit around waiting to be arrested for something that I did not do." He hadn't meant to be short with her. He kissed the top of her head. "Sorry," he said as he released her from their hug. "It's just I'm anxious to see why Dad is here."

"Go," she said pushing him lightly away as she started back to the kitchen.

Mars grabbed a beach towel from the pegboard,

walked across the deck to the dune line where he stood and scanned the bay for his father. He saw him a hundred-and-fifty yards south swimming parallel to the beach, heading back towards the house. Mars ran across the hot sand, digging his feet in deep to avoid the burn. He dropped his towel and dove into the cool soothing water. He swam under the small waves until his air was gone. Surfacing, he floated, and waited as his father's strokes drew closer.

When his dad stopped, they both stood, and shook hands. "Son, how are you?"

"You tell me," Mars challenged.

"I spoke with Abe. Angela wired the money back."

"Yeah, she told me."

His father gave him a disapproving look before adding, "It's in an escrow account."

"You wouldn't come just to tell me that," Mars said eying him.

His dad's lips pursed. "Unless something else occurs to change their minds, they are definitely not confessing."

Mars had already figured that out. He said nothing.

"Anything new at work or from your discussions with Angela today?" his father probed.

"No, just that Lance, the agent in charge, seems to be getting close to finding the mail. Angela still wants to wait until they do."

"Then we better do this first thing tomorrow," his father said draping an arm briefly over his son's shoulder before quickly diving and swimming away.

Mars dove and swam beside him thinking that he and his father hadn't had many close moments like this ever - just the two of them, together. It was a shame that it had taken pending criminal charges to make it happen.

As they swam, Mars found himself growing angry again at the man that had kept him from a life with

Angela. But as their cadence synchronized, Mars felt his resentment washing away.

On the second lap, he realized that a third swimmer was matching their strokes. Mars raised his head on his next breath, and saw that Peter had joined them. He could not remember another time when three generations of Stewart men had shared such a moment.

The three of them completed two laps up the beach to the Lewes Yacht Club and back. There was no talking, just long fluid strokes and practiced strong kicks. When they stopped Mars's father embraced Peter saying, "My lord boy, I think you've grown a few more inches since Christmas."

As the three of them walked together back to the house, thoughts of Angela and worries about the embezzlement were overridden by warm thoughts about the undeniable bonds of grandfathers, fathers, and sons.

The extended Stewart family had a nice dinner together – rump roast, mashed potatoes, gravy, carrots and peas. That meal was known as comfort food for good reasons. Mars's father ate heartily. "Your mother doesn't cook much anymore," he commented to Mars. "We mostly eat out or get takeout." He turned to Sally and raised his glass. "This has been a real treat. Thank you, Sally."

She lit up. "I'm glad you like it, Hamilton. Eat up; there's plenty."

He did, and so did Peter. The two of them made a serious dent in what should have been enough for a left-over meal.

"Grandpop, we had the Lifeguard Olympics last Thursday," Peter commented, eager – for a change – to participate in the discussion.

"How did your team do?" His grandfather asked.

"We came in second, which is good for us. Our squad is small compared to Ocean City and Rehoboth."

"What's your specialty?"

"I came in fourth in the Paddle Board rescue, and I

was on our four-by-two-twenty relay team. We came in third."

"That's great. Your dad was always good at the Paddle Board and the Half Mile Swim."

Mars was stunned. He marveled at the fact that his father had ever known, let alone remembered. He had no memory of his father ever saying anything about it at the time. A big smile formed.

"How about you, Miss Rebecca, what have you been up to this summer?"

"I went to field hockey camp at the park," she answered enthusiastically.

"Ah, field hockey. That's a lot of running isn't it?"

"It is. I'm fast." Rebecca glowed with confidence.

Mars sat back and watched in amazement as his father was the perfect gracious grandfather. The kids were gobbling him up. Mars felt a pang of sadness as he realized what he and his father had missed out on. *Why had the man never shown this interest in his own son?* He decided not to dwell on the past. Maybe they were back in position. Maybe they could finish their round well.

After dinner his father took them all downtown for King's ice-cream. They rode to the parking lot at Lewes beach, rolled down the windows and tried to eat their cones before the ice cream melted on his leather seats.

Mars remembered he had not been allowed to eat in his father's car.

Later Peter went out with some friends, and once Beck went to bed, Sally disappeared giving Mars and his dad a chance to discuss their plans for the next day.

Once everything was finalized Mars called Lance and left a message saying that he needed to meet with him – somewhere outside the bank. He asked the agent to call him back on his cell.

When Lance retuned the call a half hour later, Mars

gave him directions to The Rookery North. The clubhouse did not serve breakfast. Mars knew they would be able to find a quiet spot in the dining room.

67   - Wednesday 7:59 a.m.

They drove to the club separately so that Mars's father could continue on to Wilmington when they finished. As was becoming habit, Mars called Angela as soon as he was on the road.

"Mars, thank God, I've hardly slept last night. What's going on?" She was wound up tighter than Mars.

"I'm on my way to the club now to meet Lance, the Agent in Charge. Dad's meeting us there." He tried to sound calm and reassuring, but he was sure he had not pulled it off. His stomach was gurgling and a headache was starting to crawl up from the base of his skull.

"Are you okay? You sound … tense."

He was scared for both of them, but not wanting to rock the boat he simply said, "I'm okay, just anxious."

"Mars," her voice was soft and tentative.

"Yes."

"Do whatever you need to do. Mr. Bernstein told me that you may have to tell them that I am the one that sent the mail." She sounded stronger this time.

"I don't want to, but I feel I have to. I can't wait… but

there won't be any proof until you confess."

"I know. I dragged you into my mess... I'm prepared for whatever happens next." Her voice trailed off. "Except..."

"Except what, Angela?" He feared the worst. She still hadn't said she would confess.

"Except not having you in my life."

He was relieved, and flattered. "I know, but we'll always have our memories, and if you ever need -"

"Bite your tongue," she said managing a laugh.

His mind whirled with the thought of Angela's tongue. He felt grief, like a rogue wave, tumble him. He wasn't prepared for life without her either, but that's the way it was going to have to be, and he didn't want to think about it now. Not when he was about to reserve a cell for her.

It ate at his soul as he tried to regain his focus. "Angela, we'll be okay." He was trying to convince himself as much as her. "Let's just take it one hurdle at a time."

"Okay, Mars. I am so sorry I put you in this position. Can you ever forgive me?"

"I already have." As he said it, he knew that it was true. He knew that what she had done was wrong, but he didn't begrudge her that. She had saved her son. But if she did not confess it would be a whole new ballgame.

"I hope so, but things might get worse."

Unconsciously he analyzed her words, and his conclusion made him weak. *Oh my God, she might not ever confess.* Surely if she left him hanging, surely then he would feel differently about her, wouldn't he? Or would she always own his heart?

He tried to change the subject. "Are you spending the day with Tony?" He knew she was still on family medical leave.

"No. I was going to go back to work today since he's

doing better, but –"

He saw where she was going; there was no sense in her going back today with all that was about to happen. "Are you and Bernstein prepared in case the Secret Service wants to question you later today?"

"Yes. He has to be in court this morning, but he counseled me last night. He'll have his cell phone. He's expecting to hear from me, or maybe from them."

"Okay." Mars was approaching the club. "Angela, don't ever forget that I would have gladly spent my life with you if...."

"I know, Mars. Now, do what you have to do."

Mars and his father arrived at the club just in front of Lance. They parked in three adjacent spots. Mars broke out in a nervous sweat as he got out of his car and greeted Lance.

"Lance, this is my father, Hamilton Stewart. Dad, this is Secret Service Agent Lance Williams."

"Agent Williams, pleased to meet you."

Lance looked perplexed and very interested in what the Stewart men were up to.

The elder Stewart took control. "Lance, why don't we go inside? I'll explain why we asked you to meet us."

As they approached the double doors, Mars noticed four of his retired friends were walking up the fairway of the par three ninth hole. Mars was second guessing his decision, but he knew it was too late for that. He took a deep breath and led them to the help-yourself coffee bar. "Agent Williams? Dad? Coffee?"

They each poured a cup at the self-serve table, and followed Mars into the main dining room. They sat at a table in the furthest corner of the otherwise empty room.

Mars saw that one of the guys had just left his first sand shot in the bunker. He had not completed his swing.

His father began, "Lance, I'm an attorney and I'm representing my son in this matter."

Lance leaned back in his chair. "I wasn't aware that he needed representation."

"In the course of his investigation at LB&T, my son discovered the e-mail that caused the embezzlement."

"Go on," Lance said as his eyes narrowed.

"The mail requested an override to one of the conversion jobs that ran on July Fourth weekend. That override resulted in a test file - that had been manipulated - being read as input to a critical conversion job."

Lance was looking directly at Mars when he asked, "Okay, Mars found the mail, but why does he need a lawyer? Did he play a role in the crime?"

"No. The e-mail was sent by someone else who had manipulated the data. Unfortunately, the message was sent on my son's logon." Hamilton opened his briefcase, extracted a manila file, opened it and handed Lance a copy of the mail.

Lance read it then looked back at Mars. "So I guess I can assume that you are the one that sent the confession e-mails to your CEO alerting him to the fact that many employees were leaving their workstations unsecured."

A nervous grin tugged at Mars's mouth. He had no intention of confirming it, and his father's look reinforced that he should not.

Lance didn't seem to expect him to. He continued. "So you're saying that you left your workstation unsecured, and that someone else used that opportunity to embezzle the funds?"

"Yes, Lance. That is the unfortunate truth. My son is guilty of a breach of the bank's security policy, but he is not guilty of any crime."

"Well, this certainly is an interesting twist." Agent Williams stared at the e-mail, but he was obviously thinking about something else. "Is this override on the list that George Mumford provided to us? The one your folks have been reviewing?"

"No, it's not. George only included the components that were in the package of changes that were approved and installed before the project deadline. He did not include the last minute corrective and emergency changes even though they were all requested through him. He even installed this particular modification."

"Is he my man?" Lance asked. He looked excited at the prospect.

Mars shook his head. "No. George's only crime is that he's unorganized." Mars sat back, and met Lance's accusatory gaze. "Remember Lance, in our first meeting, I told you that emergency changes can be installed as needed and that the requesting e-mail is the only audit trail."

Lance didn't confirm or deny, but Mars knew that he had included that information on the worksheets his team had filled out on the first Monday of the investigation.

"Am I just supposed to take your word for this, that you did not send it?"

"How stupid would I be to embezzle the money under my own logon when I obviously could have borrowed one of the many available unattended ones?" Mars was picking up speed now, "And if I had done it, do you really think I would have told you where to look? And when you didn't find the mail that incriminates me, do you think I would have printed it out and handed it to you?" He took a breath then added, "I did not send that mail."

Lance looked away for one brief second before staring

Mars down again. "You know that you are responsible for everything that is done under your logon."

"I know that's the bank policy, but the reality is that I did not send the mail. I did not embezzle the money." Mars pled his case. "In the interest of justice, you should want to arrest the right person."

Angela was the right person - right for the arrest and for him to have spent a lifetime with. Both meanings were dismal thoughts. He felt like a traitor.

"Do you know who sent it?"

"We do," Hamilton answered. Mars knew he was about to sacrifice Angela. His father wasn't sure his son would actually do it.

The agent studied both men. "Mars, I think I actually believe you - or I want to - but certainly you realize that we can not just take your word for it."

Mars's father again. "There was a very good chance that you would never find this e-mail. If my son had committed the crime he could have just sat back and waited. We brought it to you in good faith that you would want justice to be served."

"We will investigate, but," his eyes bore into Mars's as if they could seek out the truth, "Mars knew that we're starting to focus on the Modifications Management department. Maybe he just realized that we were getting close - too close - that we were about to find his mail."

Lance kept his focus on Mars even as his father spoke.

"My son is innocent, and I expect him to be treated as such." His father spoke with conviction.

Lance's eyes disengaged his and turned to lock on Ham's. Mars had just enough time to breathe a sigh of relief before Lance spoke.

"I'm afraid in this case - since the mail was sent under his logon - Mars will be assumed to be responsible unless or until he is proven innocent."

The agent stood and began to move away from the table. "I need to report this to my superiors and the bank immediately."

69 - 8:46 a.m.

Mars had always known that he would be assumed to be guilty. He had deluded himself into believing that he could handle that reality, but now - as the full weight of the agent's words weighed on him - he knew that he was not emotionally prepared. Visions of himself in a prison jumpsuit being visited by Sally and the kids overcame him.

He rubbed his eyes trying to blot out his negative thoughts. When he opened them again he saw Lance had extracted his cell phone. Mars remained seated as his father spoke in measured words. "Regardless of any bank policies, my son is innocent until proven guilty. I told you we know who did it. Please sit. You can make your calls after we talk – off the record this time."

His father sounded like an older wiser man. Mars was starting to think that he might be.

"Why off the record?" Lance asked suspiciously, but he was interested enough to sit back down.

"This part of this story *is* incriminating to my son." Hamilton paused, searching for the best way to phrase what he had to say. Mars shifted nervously. Lance leaned forward. He was literally on the edge of his seat.

"The facts that I am about to share are incriminating not in a legal sense, but in a deeply personal one. This is information that, as you will soon understand, Mars can not make part of any official record."

Lance's gaze ping-ponged between the two Stewarts. He set his pen down. "Go ahead."

"The e-mail was sent at a time and from a location where there was only one other person that would have had access to my son's logon."

The agent looked again at the printed mail. "July Fourth at ten-twenty-eight p.m." He looked up at Mars. "Weren't you on-site for the conversion that night?"

His father gave Mars a nod letting him know that it was okay to go ahead and answer the question.

"I was there later that night, but at that particular time I was at home." Fragmented frames of Angela's skin moving in the blue glow from his computer screen interrupted his thoughts.

"At home?" Lance asked mulling it over.

"Yes, he was at home. His family was away on vacation, but Mars had stayed behind due to the conversion."

Lance's practiced gaze was back on Mars. "But he was not alone."

It was a statement. Mars hoped maybe that meant that he believed him.

"Again, this is off the record, but he was in the company of a woman."

"And this woman just so happened to know enough -" Lance stopped himself. A light bulb had gone off. "This woman, is she also an employee of LB&T?"

"No, she is not." Mars watched Lance's face as his father answered. The agent's look changed from one of understanding to one of disbelief. His father continued. "She is a consultant at LB&T. Her name is Sofia Angela Ignazio Pitasi."

Lance consulted a list that he had in his folder. "Sofia Pitasi." He circled her name and studied the accompanying information then put the list back in the folder. 'So Sofia had access to your computer long enough to compose and send this e-mail without your knowledge?"

"She did." Mars thought back to that night wanting to disappear into the arms of those wonderful memories. More snapshots of him waking up tangled in the sheets flashed through his mind.

"When did you first learn of the e-mail?" He heard Lance ask somewhere in the distance.

"Huh? Oh, um late last Monday night. I was at home looking for clues about the embezzlement."

The agent's eyebrows went up again. Mars doubted that Lance would make a very good poker player.

"So can I assume then that there was no death in your family?"

Mars's father jumped in again. "There was not. Mars went to confront Sofia. He knew that it would be his word against hers. He tried to get her to come forward on her own."

Lance sat back and looked from father to son. "So, did you convince her? Is she willing to confess?"

"She chooses to believe that you would never find the mail," his father answered bluntly. "Thus far she has refused to confess."

"Then what we have is a classic case of he-said-she-said?" The agent looked at Mars who looked at his father.

"Yes," his father conceded, "at this point that is essentially what we have. We are hoping that she will see her way clear to exonerate my son."

Lance looked at Mars with just a glimmer of pity in his eyes. "So she used you, took the money, and is probably ready to fly off into the sunset, leaving you -"

Mars could not control himself. "She's not flying anywhere. She needed the money -"

His father grabbed his arm and gave him his let-me-handle-this look as he answered for his son. "There are some extenuating circumstances."

Lance had a look on his face that said it really didn't matter what the circumstances were, but he said, "Okay, shoot, counselor."

"Her son had a medical condition requiring cash that she did not have. There is also a long history between her family and ours." Mars's father launched into a condensed version of Mars' early interest in Angela, the pregnancy, the deal he made with Carmen Ignazio, the bastard son's death, her son Tony's illness, and his lack of medical insurance. He also noted that Mars had not even known that the consultant Sofia Pitasi was Angela until after the fact.

"Hard to believe you didn't recognize her, but can I assume then that this was an act of revenge on her part?"

You can, but you'd be wrong, Mars thought.

"My son does not believe that it was, but we should not attempt to speak for Angela," his father said as he opened his file again. "She has hired Abe Bernstein to represent her." He handed Lance Bernstein's business card.

A look of recognition spread across Lance's face. "She'll need most of the bank's money just for this guy."

Lance studied Abe Bernstein's card for a moment then looked up and asked, "Where's the restroom, Mars?"

"I'll show you," his father replied.

Mars had to pee like a race horse too, but he wanted a minute to himself so he did not accompany the other two. Instead, as soon as they were gone, he flipped his phone open and started to give Angela a quick call. He wanted to tell her what was happening; mostly he wanted to hear her voice. He wanted to hear her reassure him that she would confess.

He thought better of it. What if she isn't reassuring?

He shut the phone, clipped it on his waist and started back to the locker room. When he passed Agent Williams and his father he said, "There's more coffee if you're interested. I'll be right back."

As he relieved himself, he wondered if Lance had returned to the table or if he had posted himself outside the locker room door afraid that Mars would attempt a getaway.

Mars felt half drunk, but he wasn't as nervous as he

had been earlier. He was laying all of his cards on the table. It would soon be out of his hands.

Maybe it was the lack of control over what happened next, but he felt like he was in a fog. He splashed cold water on his face and looked at himself in the mirror. He was bummed about what he was doing to Angela, but she had forced his hand. He had to protect his family.

Mars stopped and got coffee on his way back to the dining room. Both of the other men were on their cell phones at opposite corners of the room. Mars had a burning desire to make his call, but again he restrained himself. He set his cup on the table and did a few neck and shoulder stretches while he waited.

"Are you a runner, Mars?" Lance asked startling him. Mars wasn't sure if the agent was asking if he was a flight danger, or if he was a recreational runner. He decided to focus on the second option.

"I used to be serious about it. Now I run a couple of miles three to five times a week, but I need to stretch every day, especially when I'm stressed."

"Well sounds like she certainly put you in a very precarious position," Lance said without sounding particularly sympathetic.

Mars's father joined them. He hadn't hung up yet, but he apparently did not want to leave Mars alone with the Secret Service. He finished his call from a few feet away then asked Lance, "Did you get through?"

Mars looked at him blankly wondering what he had missed. "Agent Williams was calling the field office in Wilmington. He wants you to take a polygraph test."

"Today?" Mars looked at his watch. It was after nine. "I'm due at work - in fact I need to get going."

His father put a hand on his shoulder and gave it a squeeze. "Mars, Lance has agreed that if the test results are favorable, you'll be allowed to return home while they follow up with Angela. You'll just have to call your boss."

The implication was that if he didn't take the test, or if the results were not favorable, he would not be allowed to go home. Mars saw bars. Sweat formed on his torso he heard Lance continuing, "Our technician has agreed to fit you in. I've set the test up for noon."

"Okay, great," Mars said, feeling that it was anything but that. "What's the address?" Mars was mentally prepared to rush out the door as soon as he got his answer, but Lance stopped him in his tracks.

"Mars, you'll be riding with me."

"That won't be necessary," Mars's father stated firmly. "Mars has shown good faith bringing the e-mail to you. He has been more than forthcoming. He'll drive himself."

Mars's father did stern well, but the secret Service had trained their guy not to back down. "Mr. Stewart, as it stands now, Mars is responsible for the theft. The conversion job override that was authorized via his secure logon, his e-mail, is evidence enough to have an arrest warrant issued," Lance countered.

"I beg to differ," Mars jumped in, his voice was shaky, but he was confident. "I request overrides all of the time, so that e-mail in and of itself is meaningless. I believe that you would need evidence that this particular request resulted in the embezzlement before you could obtain a warrant. You do not have that. I believe you will find that the file and the override parameters have long since been deleted by the bank's space management software."

Mars could see they had won before Lance spoke. "Okay. We'll do it your way. The office is at 1865 North King Street. I need you to be there by eleven thirty sharp." Lance glared as they shook hands. "If you are as much as one minute late, an arrest warrant will be issued."

71 - 9:27 a.m.

Lance left the club first. Mars's father wanted to discuss matters further, but Mars was mentally exhausted and hungry. His attorney agreed to continue the conversation over a sausage sandwich at Helen's Sausage House. Once alone in his car, Mars knew that he should call Sally, but Angela was the one that he needed to talk with.

She answered on the first ring. "Mars," she sounded frantic, "what happened?"

He tried to sound calm, but his voice was still unsteady. "I'm on my way to Wilmington to take a polygraph test."

"You sound upset."

"It went as well as can be expected." He stammered, "I'm okay under the circumstances, but..."

"What Mars?"

"I'm worried about you. Has anyone called you yet?"

"No." She was scared, but he could tell she was trying to be brave.

"They will soon. Dad gave Lance your name and

Bernstein's card." Mars was feeling horrible that Angela would soon pay because he was unwilling to wait to see if the authorities would ever find her e-mail. "I'm sorry Angela, but I had to do this."

"I know, Mars… It's not your fault. I'm the one that should be apologizing. I brought this on us both."

"But you did what you thought you had to do at the time. You saved Tony."

"But I never should have framed you."

"Angela, Tony is going to be fine. You have already accomplished what you wanted. Now you need to take your lumps."

"I know, but I don't think I can handle prison."

"Let's just take this one step at a time." He realized how trite his words sounded.

"I'm trying," she said dismally.

Mars drove for a mile or so before he broke the silence. "I wish I was with you now."

"I wish you were too."

More silence.

"It's sad knowing that we'll probably never be together again."

"Depressing," he offered remembering having her in his arms. Angela's skin on his skin; it was a fantasy that he could get lost in, but… not… now. He forced himself back to today's reality. He was on his way to take a lie detector test to eliminate himself as a felony suspect. And he was incriminating Angela.

"Let's just get through today." The plea was as much to him as Angela. He had to do what needed to be done for Sally, and Peter, and for happy little Beck. He couldn't get sidetracked by his feelings for Angela.

Shit. I need to call Sally. "Angela, I've got to go."

"Will you call me after you take the test?"

"Definitely. I should be done by one, or two at the

latest."

"I'll be here - if they haven't come for me."

"Call me if they do."

After they hung up, Mars took a few minutes to regroup before calling Sally. His thoughts kept drifting back to just how much he longed to hold Angela in his arms, to comfort her, to help her.

His wife answered on the first ring. "Mars, thank God you called, I was so worried. What's happening? Where are you?"

Mars's thoughts were elsewhere, but he gave Sally a brief positive update. "I'll be home for dinner."

"They believe you. I knew they would."

"I don't know what Agent Williams believes. *Obviously* that's the point of the polygraph." The words sounded sharp even to his ears. He adjusted his tone. "Sorry babe. I'm stressed. I'll call you as soon as I get done with the test. I'll know more then."

"I love you so much. I don't know what we would do if something..." She sounded pathetic. She was understandably worried he was going to be whisked off to jail.

He was worried about that and the very real possibility that his cheating on their vows was going to get him kicked out of his family.

They can have the beach house.

Mars switched his self-talk back to the positive. So far his plan was working. By the end of the day Angela would be in the crosshairs of the Secret Service. That was good, right?

"It's going to work out, babe. It will. Try not to worry too much."

Mars arrived at the Secret Service office full of Helen's sausage and hope. He assumed that he would pass the lie detector test. Over their late breakfast in the Elvis Room at Helen's, his father had reported that Agent Williams had agreed to keep the personal questions off the test. The interview would be conducted as if the incident had occurred at work. No questions regarding location would be asked in this test. Mars prayed that the Secret Service would adhere to the gentlemen's agreement. Regardless of what they asked, Mars intended to tell the whole truth.

As they entered the building together, Mars's father updated his son on Bernstein's plan for Angela. As of a half an hour ago, her lawyer was not going to let her confess until they had a deal. There was no evidence against her except Mars's statements, and Angela had something that the bank wanted - the money. Mars's dad thought that bargaining chip gave Angela a pretty good chance of avoiding any significant time in jail, but doubted that she could get off completely.

Unless she never confesses, Mars thought.

Mars was foggy headed as they walked down the halls of the Secret Service offices with Lance. It felt surreal. He apologized to his grandfather; he had been such a great student but in the end he had not learned his lessons. He had been risk-adverse his whole life on the important stuff - like family. He never considered that he could possibly cheat on his wife. *But, I always loved Angela. I had no chance.*

And how's that working for you, fool? He was embroiled in a felony investigation and his marriage was hanging in the balance, like a golf ball on the precipice of water hazzard.

I'm an idiot.

Mars was still reprimanding himself when Agent Williams appeared and escorted the Stewarts to a conference room. They were instructed to wait for the technician. Two bottles of water had been left for them. Mars opened one and drank copiously. Helen's sausage was greaseless, but he suspected it had plenty of sodium.

One of the walls had a large mirror on it. Mars figured that they were being watched, and that the walls had ears. His father must have thought so too. He steered the conversation to Peter and Beck. His sudden interest in his grandchildren seemed oddly genuine. Mars became engrossed in bringing his dad up to speed and almost forgot where they were.

A fifty-something guy in charcoal pinstripe suit pants, a white shirt, sleeves rolled two exact rolls, and a boring tie popped his head in the door. "Marshall Stewart?"

Both Mars and his father raised their hands to half mast.

Boring-tie referenced his paperwork and added, "the third."

Mars stood.

"If you'll come with me, we'll get started."

The elder Stewart stood too, introduced himself as Mars's lawyer, and asked to observe.

Agent Boring-tie nodded his assent. As the three of them walked down a long hallway, Mars wondered if his rapid pulse would throw off the results. He wanted to ask his father, but did not get a chance.

The technician hooked him up and started by asking benign questions. Mars tried to relax. It was impossible. He was in a sweat by the time they asked him if he had sent the mail, and by the time it was over he could have rung out his shirt. He had serious doubts about the results even though he had been totally honest.

It was way unnerving.

Agent Williams met them at the door and asked them to wait for him in the conference room while he conferred with the technician. Hamilton gave his son a reassuring squeeze and patted him on the back as they made their way back to the conference room. Mars felt goose bumps pop up on his arms. He wasn't sure if they were a result of the air-conditioning cooling his sweaty body, his fear, or the bond that was developing, albeit late, with his father. He guessed that it was a combination effect.

"I was so nervous, I don't know... I might have messed it up."

"No, son. You told the truth. I'm sure the machine will affirm that."

As they waited, his father chatted about golf, telling his son about a near hole-in-one the day before. He had hit a five iron on the sixteenth hole on the North Course at Wilmington Country Club. He had been playing with Sid again, and said they both about had a stroke as they watched his ball fly directly at the hole. When they got to the green they found that his ball-mark was half in the hole. Unfortunately, the shot had careened off the flagstick, and had ended up in the bunker. Sid had won the hole and the match. His father was pretending to still be upset about it when Williams came through the door.

The agent sat, folded his hands on the table and looked at Mars. "Okay, we're going to let you go home." Mars felt a jolt of relief. "I'll need to see you first thing tomorrow at the bank. We have a meeting scheduled with your CEO, Mr. Gregory, at nine, and I think you and I should talk first. How about eight-thirty in my conference room?"

"I'll be there," Mars said as he pushed himself up onto his wobbly legs.

"Thank you, Agent Williams. We'll see you tomorrow." Hamilton Stewart said shaking hands with him before ushering his son to the nearest exit.

73 - 12:57 p.m.

Standing outside the Agency's offices, he and his father agreed that Mars would go to the bank meeting alone. Mars wanted to operate under the assumption his mass-confession e-mails had worked. He did not want to act like he needed an attorney present. His father warned him not to discuss his current personal relationship with Angela then reluctantly parted company issuing instructions to call as soon as the meeting ended.

Mars walked to Rodney Square. He found a bench in the shade and called Angela.

"Mars," she said anxiously. "Did you pass?" A voice in Mars's head told him he should wonder if she was just concerned for herself, but deep down Mars knew she cared about him too.

"It went fine." He mulled it over some. "I was so nervous, I was afraid that I had blown it, but they seem satisfied; they're letting me go home." Any sense of elation that he might have felt was missing knowing that his good fortune was probably bad for her.

"That's great -"

Mars was distracted by a guy in a suit that had arrived shortly after him. He was sitting on a bench across from him down the Square a bit. He was reading a newspaper. He looked familiar, but Mars couldn't tell with the sunglasses. *Was he the same guy that he saw talking to Lance inside the Secret Service building?* Mars wasn't sure. Maybe he had just been watching too much TV.

"Mars?" Angela asked as if the connection had dropped. He must have missed something that she had said while he was watching Suit Guy.

"Sorry Angela, but I'm in Rodney Square, and a guy seems to be watching me."

"Oh." She said in a hushed tone. "Is he an agent?"

"I don't know, but you don't have to whisper," he whispered. She laughed. He smiled, and tried to ignore the man. "So what were you saying?"

"I said that it's good they're letting you go home. I'm happy for you."

"Umm," Mars agreed as he watched the guy and worried about her. "I'm sure that they'll be calling Bernstein soon if they haven't already. Have you heard anything?"

"No, nothing." There was a lull in conversation. "Are you heading home now?" she asked.

"Yeah, pretty soon. I think I'm going to walk up to Leo and Jimmy's and get some seafood salad. I love that stuff." The man was obviously peeking over the top of the paper. Mars got up and started walking toward the deli.

When he got to the top of the steps on the Square, he looked back to see if the guy was still on his bench. He had disappeared. Caesar Rodney - frozen in time on his horse - was the only other man left in the square. Mars walked towards the Market Street Mall glancing around trying to spot the suit guy without being conspicuous.

"Their seafood salad is good," Angela agreed, "but I can't even think about food. My stomach is a wreck."

"That's the way I felt this morning," Mars said empathetically, "but somehow I managed to eat a Helen's sausage sandwich. Guess I have an iron gut." Mars stopped. He looked in a window at the Hotel DuPont staring at the reflections for any sign of who he imagined was an agent - nothing. He continued down Market to the pedestrian mall.

"I miss that gut of yours," she said.

"And it misses you." That was all that Mars needed to jumpstart the memories of him and Angela together. His stomach lurched like he was freefalling off the top of a roller coaster again.

As he continued walking, he started thinking that maybe he should skip the deli and get Angela to meet him somewhere. A room in The Hotel DuPont would do nicely.

Good sense won out. "Angela, I better go." He didn't want to hang up, but he hadn't called Sally yet. "I'll check in again once I'm on the road."

"Okay, I'll be here… I hope."

74 - 2:10 p.m.

Mars left Leo and Jimmy's with two pounds of seafood salad packed to go in a bag of ice. As he started up the Market Street mall towards his car, he was sure that he saw suit-man disappear around the corner of Eighth Street. It unnerved him, but he decided the hell with it. If they wanted to watch him, there was nothing that he could do about it. He had decided not to try and meet Angela so he had nothing to hide.

Once he was in his car on Delaware Avenue he called home.

"Hello." Rebecca answered.

"Hello, Becky Bear, how are you." Mars asked feeling warm emotions rushing through him.

"I'm fine, Dad," she said sounding all grown up.

"What are you up to today?"

"I've been swimming, and I'm going over to Gracie's for dinner."

"Well have fun, I'll miss you. Is my other girl there?"

"Mom went to the store. Do you want me to leave her a message?" The kid had better phone skills than most of the adults that Mars dealt with.

"Tell her I'll be home around four-thirty and not to make dinner."

"Okay, Dad."

"Bye, hon. Have fun."

When they hung up he started to think about having a quiet dinner with Sally, but before he realized it he was thinking about dinner with Angela at Tio Pep's. God, he wanted her.

He knew that he needed to get past this insanity. He had a wonderful life; he needed to mentally get to a place where he could be content again with Sally and the kids.

No Angela? No Angela!

He wasn't quite convincing himself. In the very core of him he felt he needed to be with her. Yet, he knew it was too late for them. This had to be about saving what he did have. Still. He hoped.

His cell phone was back in its holster. He wanted to wait a while to call Angela; he wanted to give her time to be contacted by her lawyer, or by the Secret Service. The phone was burning a hole in his side.

He held out for all of five minutes then dialed.

It rang once, twice. *Where are you, Angela?* Three rings later her voicemail kicked in. He hung up. She would know he had tried from her Missed Call list. He drove south on Route 1 wondering what had happened. Maybe she was just in the bathroom or something. He waited for her to call back.

Five minutes later his phone vibrated. *Thank God!*

"Hello," he answered grateful that she was okay, and feeling stupid for starting to get concerned.

"Hi Mars, sorry I missed your call."

"Oh, hey Sally," Mars hoped he did not sound as disappointed as he felt. "So you got my message from Miss Rebecca."

"Oh yes, she left a note on the kitchen table. It says that I should not cook, that my date is going to take me out. Does that mean that you have good news?"

Beck had obviously misinterpreted. Oh well, the seafood salad would keep. "So far so good," he answered trying his best to sound upbeat. "I passed the polygraph, and I have a meeting with our CEO tomorrow morning."

"And you're coming home now?"

"Yep, I'm on my way."

"Great. See you soon, honey."

She sounded ecstatic. It made Mars feel like a heel. He started thinking about where they would go for dinner. It had been a while since they had had a night out alone. Too much had happened. He could hardly wrap his mind around his reality.

He checked the phone to see if maybe he had missed a call from Angela while talking with Sally. He hadn't.

He sent out another cosmic plea. *Angela, call me...*

75 - 7:03 p.m.

Mars and Sally were at the outside bar at Gilligan's on the Lewes Rehoboth Canal. Built into the hull of an old boat, it served as a nice perch above the boat slips and below the cooling evening sky. The air was still muggy, but the canopy provided shade from the sun which was sinking low in the sky behind them. A breeze was blowing from the northeast making it a very pleasant evening, except for Mars's angst.

A couple was loading a cooler and a bottle of champagne onto a center cockpit sloop directly in front of them – *Sail Pending*. Mars assumed it was a realtor going out for a sunset cruise with his girl.

He thought how wonderful it would be to be sailing with Angela. He was worried about her. When she didn't call him back he had left a message on his father's cell phone asking him to try to find out what was going on and to call his son back. He hadn't heard anything from either of them. *I wonder if she's already in jail.*

"So Mars, tell me about today," Sally said, sipping her gin and tonic.

Mars forced himself back into the moment. He filled his wife in on the discussions with Lance, the polygraph, and Suit Man at the square. She listened wide-eyed. She was thoroughly engrossed even though he was not.

As they drank their G & T's and ate popcorn, part of his brain was visualizing Angela at the helm. He was behind her with his arms around her teaching her how to sail.

Trying to fend off thoughts of her, he wondered aloud what tomorrow's meeting with LB&T's CEO would bring. The bank had every right to fire him, and Randal Gregory might just do it. But Mars was hopeful that his security breach e-mails may have circumvented that.

"Too bad she didn't frame Nick or someone else that left their computers unattended," his wife stated.

"Yeah, her framing our MVP would have been like divine intervention." Mars replied, forcing a laugh.

He ordered another round. The drinks had just arrived when his phone vibrated on his hip. His heart immediately started racing. He pulled his phone out of its holster.

"Hey Dad, what's up." Mars tried to sound nonchalant, but he was going crazy wondering if Angela was okay.

"Are you alone?"

"Sally and I are at Gilligan's having a little celebration."

"Can you talk?"

"Do you have any news?" Mars asked cryptically.

His father seemed to catch on. "The Secret Service interviewed Angela for about three hours late this afternoon. Apparently they had your cell phone records, and they've questioned her at length about your current relationship. They seem to be of the theory that you two colluded to embezzle the money."

Wow. Mars had never considered they would come to that conclusion. "Interesting theory, but obviously flawed."

"I know that, Marshall, but they don't. *Do not call her again until this is over.*" His father was emphatic, all business. Just like the olden days there was no room for discussion. Mars hated that tone. He didn't want to have this conversation within inches of Sally. "Can I call you later, when I get home?"

"Please do, Mars; just do not call that woman."

As soon as they hung up, Sally pressed for an update. "What's going on, Mars? You look like you've seen a ghost."

Mars felt empty at the thought of not being able to talk to Angela. He tried to filter what his father had said to decide what he could share with his wife. "Apparently the Secret Service questioned Angela about a theory that the two of us conspired to embezzle the money."

Sally's jaw dropped. "What in the world would make them think that?"

"I guess they're trying to make the simple complex." Mars leaned back against the bar and drained his gin and tonic.

Sally watched him set down his empty glass. "Come on Mars, we can go home." She started to get up, but Mars gently pulled her back down on the bar stool.

"No Sally, there's nothing I can do tonight." He made an effort to put on a happy face. "Let's stay and get some dinner."

"Are you sure?" She looked him over carefully. He was deep in thought, wondering how Angela was doing. He felt so isolated from her already.

"You look miserable, Mars. I'll understand if you just want to go home."

"No, I'm starved. Really. Let's stay." He gave her as

good a smile as he could muster. He feared that it looked as insincere as it felt, but they stayed and ate Gilligan's signature crab cakes which were snowball size and made with big lumps of back-fin. They were Mars's favorite, but tonight he hardly noticed what he was eating.

He was tempted to have a third gin and tonic, but he already had a buzz. The last thing he needed to do was get drunk. Lord knows what would come out of his mouth then.

76   - Thursday 6:03 a.m.

Mars slept fitfully. He got up before his alarm, put on his running gear and went out the back door. He was tired and worried. If the Secret Service were trying to make a case that he and Angela had colluded, they were basing it on his confession about having been with Angela that night. That was supposed to be off the record.

Angela - he hadn't spoken to her since yesterday afternoon, and it felt like it had been a week. As he leaned against the house stretching he found himself thinking about her, and him, naked, in her hotel room.

God, I'm a freaking pervert. How can I be thinking about that now?

He set off running at a punishing pace that he had no hope of maintaining. Just as he was about to round the first corner he noticed a dark Ford Crown Victoria further down Bay Avenue. He was tempted to change course and run by it. He decided that he was being paranoid; besides, the feds all drove Suburbans now, right?

He ran to Roosevelt Inlet then instead of retracing his

steps on Cedar Avenue as he would ordinarily do, he ran back on the beach. He slowed to a jog in the sand hardened by the last receding tide. A sense of dread for all that could go wrong squeezed his chest.

Mars could feel tears welling up. He fought to keep them from running down his face. As he approached his house, he still hadn't gotten a handle on his emotions. He sat in the cool sand facing the rising sun and removed his shoes. He shut his eyes, leaned back on his elbows, and tried to relax.

Every time he thought about the bank or the Secret Service or Angela, he tried to push the thoughts away and just focus on each breath that he took.... It didn't work. A myriad of thoughts flooded through his mind, but there was something about having the sun on his face and the bay breeze blowing in his sweaty hair that calmed him.

As he listened to the sound of the waves breaking softly on the beach he realized that no matter what happened today in his meeting with CEO Randal Gregory - or with Angela - there was comfort in knowing that the sun, the wind, and the bay would be here tomorrow.

If I'm lucky so will Sally, and Peter and Becky Bear.

He sat for fifteen minutes before pushing himself up. He walked back to the house where he showered and joined Sally for their morning coffee ritual. As he was finishing his bagel, she looked him over and asked, "Are you okay, Mars? You look exhausted."

"I didn't sleep well." He rolled his head from side to side and heard the familiar popping and crunching of things loosening up in his neck.

Sally turned sideways on the couch, leaned back against the arm, spread her legs, and patted her abs. "Come on, give me your feet."

Mars didn't argue, he positioned himself at the other

end of the couch and put his feet in her lap. She began massaging them, first his arches then one toe at a time as she tried to assure him. "Honey, whatever happens, we'll be okay. I know I've been worried too, but we'll survive no matter what."

No matter what? It seemed like a stretch.

"But I could lose my job and -" Mars considered the true measure of what all was at risk.

"You are not going to prison," she said forcefully. "Don't think that way. You passed the polygraph."

Mars was not sure if polygraphs were admissible in court, but he appreciated her faith. As long as he didn't go to jail, and as long as he had Sally and the kids, he knew he would be okay... even if memories of Angela continued to torment him.

He hoped Sally and Angela would be okay, too.

Sally was still talking. "... okay for a while financially. You could get another job. We've got the kids' college money and our retirement funds -"

"I'm not digging into the college funds." Mars was firm on that. His college had been paid for. He would pay his children's. He and Sally had been investing in their 529 college plans for over a decade.

He knew if he got fired there weren't going to be many opportunities like the bank in the area, but as long as he was free he would find a way to provide for his family. He loved to make furniture, but he had never seriously thought about trying to make a living at it. But now with eBay maybe it would be possible.

In the late seventies, he had made several pieces out of cherry leaving the shapes natural. Later he had been in New Hope, Pennsylvania and had seen George Nakashima's work. He was humbled, and had never mentioned it to anyone, but he had seen lots of similarities in their style and their workmanship.

He felt himself becoming more hopeful. While Sally worked on the arches of his feet he thought maybe he could write for James Patterson. He knew a little something about how quickly lives could be shattered, and - like in Patterson's *Now You See Her* - what a woman would do for her child. Sally was working on his toes. He was overwhelmed by how much his wife doted on him, how much she loved him.

Poor Sally. You deserve someone better than me.

He sat up and reached for her hands. "I hate to go, but I need to face the music at work."

He swung his feet around, slipped into his loafers, and stood.

"Well, I hope they are playing something upbeat," she kidded trying to lighten his mood.

"Yeah, hopefully it won't be the Blues," he replied already drafting lousy country-like lyrics in his head. *Lost my job, never got my girl, but she screwed me into giving jail a whirl.*

Mars half chuckled as he walked out the door. *Note to self, song writing is not an option.*

77   - 8:30 a.m.

Mars was sitting in the Secret Service conference room at the bank. He was eating a glazed donut, balancing two more on a plate. He was indulging in Krispy-Kreme therapy as he waited for Lance to return from the cafeteria. The two had passed in the hall.

Mars glanced around. He was tempted to do some quick snooping, but he had dug a deep enough hole already. He savored the yeasty honey-glazed donut as it melted in his mouth. Its yumminess reminded him of Angela.

He was going nuts not being able to talk to her. Maybe he could call her later from one of the bank's phones. But if the Secret Service was monitoring her phones they would probably assume that a call from the bank was from him even though they couldn't prove it. It would not help his cause.

"Two donuts, wow Mars, you'll have to run a couple extra miles." It was Agent Lance Williams returning with his coffee and a more sensible breakfast; an English muffin and a small yogurt.

"Actually I'm having three. You know what they say bad things always come in threes."

Why the hell did I say that? Idiot.

The agent's eyebrows pinched as he considered what Mars might have meant. He shook his head as if he were trying to rid himself of some strange thought. He peeled the foil lid off his yogurt, gave it a stir, and ate a couple of quick bites.

"So Mars, here's the deal. I want to believe your story." He crunched into his English muffin and chewed as Mars inhaled the last two bites of the second donut. "Actually, at this point I do believe you."

"But?"

"But, it's the stuff that you want kept off the record that make it so believable." He gave Mars a poor-sucker look and shook his head in sympathy. "Who would make that up? But..." He took another bite of his muffin.

Mars controlled himself and did not jump in. Instead, he started on his last donut.

Lance continued, "Unless we share some of the personal stuff with your CEO, I'm afraid you'll get canned today."

A bite of donut wedged in Mars's throat; he gagged slightly then took a swig of his now tepid coffee. He dislodged it, but his eyes were glossed over. "If I have to choose between my job and my marriage," he could hardly speak. He took another swig of coffee then managed to croak, "I'll get another job if I have to."

Lance studied him as he finished his yogurt.

Mars explained, "My wife knows what happened thirty years ago, but she can never be told what happened the night of the embezzlement. She doesn't deserve that."

"Are you having an ongoing affair with Angela?"

Mars took his time responding mainly because he did

not know the answer. "Unfortunately, Angela's and my fate was sealed thirty years ago by our fathers. I have a family; so does she. We have no future together."

Even as he said it, Mars hoped for one more night.

"You've been talking to her several times a day. Some of my fellow agents think that maybe the two of you conspired to take the money and run off together."

"So I heard.... Angela took the money to save her son's life. He's had his surgery, and she still has a big chunk of the money. My understanding is that she is willing to return what is left and confess if you will make a deal with her."

Mars set his donut down, licked his fingertips and began massaging the headache that had started with a pounding in his temples and had spread through much of the space in between. "I know that it could end up her word against mine, so yeah, we've been talking." He continued bitterly, "I like to think that I have some influence. But now I've been advised by my attorney - my father - to cease and desist so that you guys don't misinterpret our ongoing conversations. The upshot is that I no longer know what the hell she is thinking. Her husband and lawyer may get her to turn her back on me."

In spite of all he had consumed, Mars felt hollow. His hope was fading. He needed to talk to Angela. He stuffed in the last sugary bite, licked his fingers again, and then dried them on the napkin. The emptiness was still there. He looked up with pleading eyes, "My only hope is that you guys make her a deal that she can live with. Otherwise, it'll be my word against hers, and I'll lose."

"We're trying," Lance said in an uncertain tone. He devoured the last of his breakfast with gusto. He glanced at his watch. "Eight-forty-five already... Okay, I need to know how much of the personal stuff are you going to share with Mr. Gregory? At this point, we'll make it your call."

Lance crumpled up his trash and hooked it into the can in the corner of the room. *Swish.* Mars followed suit. His shot banked off the wall and missed - not a good sign. He crumpled a page out of his portfolio and shot again. It went in, but he felt no satisfaction. He shifted uncomfortably in his chair.

"I need to protect my family." He brushed some glaze off his slacks, his eyes beginning to well up. "Look Lance," he said in his best man-to-man voice, "I found the e-mail the first day. No one else that was copied on it had thought it suspicious. You may *never* have found it or figured out that it was how the money was stolen. Angela may have committed the perfect crime for the most noble of reasons, and I've turned her in even though I'm probably in love with her. All I'm asking for in return is for the record to show that she and I were in this building when the mail was sent."

Lance studied Mars sympathetically. "There are undoubtedly security records showing that you were not here."

"There *were* records, but have you verified that they still exist? LB&T captures data from our employee badges showing when we enter and leave the building - same for consultants and other guests. Thing is, I don't know how long they keep the records. Most of our non-critical files are only kept for a month."

Lance made a quick note as Mars went on. "But if the records do still exist they would prove that Angela and I weren't here. I need for the public record to show that the crime occurred when we were here - in my conference room. Sofia Pitasi embezzled money on my logon when I left my computer unattended. No one needs to know the rest. What difference does it make? Why can't we just say it happened when we were here?"

"Was anyone else in the conference room?"

"Yes, Liz and Jason were both there." Mars thought back to that night. Jason had left several times to go back to the buffet. Liz also left a few times. "I'm sure there were a couple of occasions when the three of us were out of the room leaving Angela - Sofia - alone."

"Seems fair enough – it really is irrelevant to the case," Lance said reasonably.

Mars still had the feeling that Lance might be playing him, and that the agent didn't believe his story as much as he seemed to. He was too tired to worry about it.

"The only relevancy that I see," Mars offered, "is that the security refresher training needs to emphasize the need to secure your computer at home as well as at work. I'm one of the few that followed the procedure at work, but I never worried about logging off at home, and I seriously doubt that anyone else does either."

"Good point." Lance looked at him like he was just realizing that Mars was a loyal employee. He leaned back and picked at nothing on the leg of his trousers then looked up. "Okay Mars, I think that Randal Gregory is a good guy. You should come clean with him. If you do that, I'll recommend that the official record show a different time. As long as you fully cooperate we will not make public the fact that this occurred in your bedroom."

Mars remembered Angela still semi-comatose with the sheets tangled around her waist, her face was at the foot of the bed, her long legs were stretched out, and her feet sandwiched a pillow at the head of the bed.

"Mars?"

Mars refocused. "Mr. Gregory is a great business man. I'm willing to take my chances with him, but I will not have this conversation with our MV-" he corrected himself, "with our CIO, Nick Collins, in the room. I do not trust that man."

The agent snickered almost imperceptibly, which led Mars to believe that he was aware of the well-earned Most Valuable Prick nickname.

Lance stood and walked to the door.

Mars followed.

He and Lance stopped in the cafeteria for a second cup of coffee then settled into the well appointed executive conference room. Mars had a few minutes to contemplate the fact that the CEO was making a trip from Baltimore to see - and maybe to fire - him.

He knew from Randal Gregory's point of view, he was guilty at a minimum of breaching the bank's security policy. Amnesty aside, that violation alone was grounds for dismissal. Then there was the well-established fact that the bank would need a scapegoat.

Mars was not optimistic about the meeting. He prayed that he would not be fired, but stopped himself. There would be no divine intervention on his behalf. He needed to convince the CEO to let him keep his job, but he knew all bets were probably off if Angela didn't make a deal.

Mr. Gregory arrived almost exactly at nine looking, as usual, perfect for his role. He had on slacks from a navy summer weight flannel suit with the jacket slung over the shoulder. He wore a brilliant white pinpoint oxford shirt.

The ensemble was paired with a great looking club tie in multi-color stripes that reminded Mars of a fishing boat in a picture he had taken in a bay off St. Johns.

The three of them exchanged pleasantries before the CEO took control. "Mars, I've read the e-mail from your logon on July Fourth. If you wrote the e-mail then you are guilty of a felony." He held Mars's gaze. "If you didn't write the e-mail then you are an accomplice - either wittingly, or due to a breach of our security policies." His eyes which had been boring into Mars's suddenly shifted to look over Mars's shoulder where they stayed during the brief time that he paused. Then they were locked on again like heat seeking missiles, but his voice was quiet as he asked, "Tell me, Mars, why shouldn't I fire you on the spot?"

His question took Mars by surprise, but he barely hesitated before answering in a sure, albeit slightly shaky, voice. "I have been a loyal hard-working productive employee for twenty-two years. I did not embezzle the money, nor did I have any knowledge of the crime until your emergency meeting on that Sunday. I know that what I did was a security breach, but failure to secure one's computer is a pandemic at LB&T. It would not be a good business decision to fire all of us that have broken that rule, and it would especially not be good to terminate me."

"Did you send the e-mails that alerted me to the mass security breaches?"

"Yes sir, I did," Mars answered spontaneously knowing that his father would not be pleased with his confession.

Randal Gregory leaned back and seemed to study the wood grain in the table top. His brow furrowed. Without looking up he said, "Tell me how this happened, Mars."

"How much time do you have?" He tried to sound as

sincere as he was, but he was immediately worried that he had sounded flippant.

"I have nothing pressing until my 3:08 tee time at Baywood Greens." The CEO folded his hands over his belt buckle and leaned back. "You have one shot to tell me the whole truth."

"Sir, I need for part of this to be off the record, it's incriminating... um, personally."

"If it's relevant then I need to hear it. We can sort out what needs to be official later."

Mars had always assumed that there was something to Randal Gregory's relationship with his Administrative Assistant Mitzi that broke a few rules on a personal level as well as professionally. It had never really mattered to him, but he found himself hoping that his CEO was having an affair. Maybe that would garner him some sympathy. Maybe Mitzi would be his saving grace.

He had no choice, so Mars gave the CEO the condensed version of what happened in the seventies with Angela, with the pregnancy, and the deal the two fathers had made in the aftermath. Then he told his CEO what he deemed the salient points from the night the e-mail was sent. Mr. Gregory's expression seemed empathetic as Mars told him about finding the e-mail and tracking Angela down. He told him about Tony's medical problems, about convincing her to wire money back in hopes of her making a deal.

Randal Gregory never interrupted Mars. As soon as he was done, the CEO turned to Lance and asked. "Is there anything that you would like to add, Agent Williams?"

"Sir, just that Mars's story has not been totally checked out yet. We are in the process of interviewing Sofia Pitasi – um Mars's Angela. She has not yet confessed to sending the mail."

Thanks a lot, Lance.

The CEO studied his own hands for a full minute before looking up. "Mars, I'm not going to make a decision on this today, but rules are rules Mars. We'll wait and see how this pans out. I am going to place you on administrative leave effective immediately."

"Paid?" he managed to ask as he breathed a sigh of relief that he had not heard the dreaded Trump line, "You're fired."

Mr. Gregory leaned forward his folded hands were on the table. "For now." He studied Mars. "I've been noticing your work for years. I had plans for you. I want to believe you. But rest assured if the facts don't bear out your story, I *will* terminate you."

With that the CEO left the room. It took Mars a minute or two to gather himself and stand. When he left the room he was greeted by Nick Collins smiling smugly and demanding his security badge.

Mars handed it over and was escorted back to his desk to get his briefcase and then he was ushered out of the bank.

Mars couldn't stand not being able to talk to Angela. His whole life hinged on whether she confessed or not. He knew he should not even be considering what he was considering. Nonetheless, as he left LB&T's parking lot Mars took a detour to purchase a prepaid cell phone *just in case* he told himself he decided he needed to talk to her; as if he had not already made that decision.

Back in his car in the Walmart parking lot, phone in hand, he decided that her line would be tapped by now. Then he thought he was probably just being paranoid. What was a half a million in the scheme of things these days? How much federal manpower could be spared for a rinky-dink case like this?

He threw the phone in his briefcase and drove home.

Sally was out watering the flower beds. When she spotted him she turned the hose off and walked towards the car removing her flowered gardening gloves. Concern etched her face.

Mars got out, took a deep breath of the sea air, and mustered up a smile. "I'm on paid administrative leave until further notice."

His wife let out a big sigh. "So far so good? Are you okay?"

"Yeah, I'm relieved. It certainly beats getting canned, and I really couldn't expect them to let me continue working until this is resolved."

"So you think you'll be reinstated when it's over?"

"I do." He hugged his wife tight then released her. "Nothing is definite yet. Everything hinges on her confession. They need to make her a deal."

"Are they going to?"

"I think they will. It's not worth the taxpayers' dollars to pursue this. LB&T should take the money that's left and call it a day."

"I hope that's what happens, but Mars don't you think she deserves some punishment?"

"I do. Otherwise, everyone would do it." Mars replied honestly. He didn't think she should hope for no prison time. That was the reason why he was so desperate to talk to her – or at least it was one of them. She would probably see it the same way as him if he could get to her. He needed to convince her to be reasonable.

Mars realized Sally had asked him something. "What?"

"Did you talk with your father today?"

"No, but I need to call him tonight." His father had left a message on his cell phone while he was in Walmart, but Mars hadn't wanted to talk to him then. He glanced at his watch and figured his Dad would be at lunch now, probably at the club.

"Did you eat?" he asked Sally.

"No, and I'm starved."

"Go ahead and finish with the watering, I'll fix us seafood salad sandwiches." It was over ninety degrees, and they hadn't had rain for weeks. The plants needed her attention.

"Okay, just yell when it's ready."

Mars was glad to have the quiet house to himself for a few minutes. He considered calling Angela. He toasted the bread instead. He was thinking about the case and Angela as he assembled and cut the sandwiches. He took a couple of bites of the leftover salad as he wondered if she was capable of letting him take her punishment.

Sally came in and caught him spaced out, spoon in mouth. She studied him as he put the sandwiches and two glasses of water on a tray. "You okay, Mars?"

"Yeah, why? He smiled weakly.

"Nothing..." she said as she walked over and enveloped him in one of her warm hugs. "I love you, Marshall Hamilton Stewart the third. We'll be fine."

He hated himself for a few seconds before she released him from her arms. ""I'm going to throw some shorts on. I'll meet you on the porch." He walked to their bedroom convinced that he was not worthy of his wife. He never should have broken his marital vows. He could hear his grandfather coaching him when he stewed too long over a bad shot. *That one is gone son, get back in position.*

That was easier in golf than here. No fade or draw, no lob or putt could save him. His life was no longer within his control. Someone else was going to deliver his next shot.

Out on the deck, Mars continued to lament his predicament. No doubt Sally heard the usual sounds of gulls scrapping and motors purring, but for him the sounds of summer were drowned out by the noise of his thoughts.

It was hot and humid, but they were in the shade and there was a breeze. It was comfortable, but Mars was in misery.

What Would Gramps Do?

He knew he had to do something. He had some faith in Angela doing the right thing, but he could not count on it. For the sake of his family, he should not sit idly by.

The breeze shifted and picked up. Sailboats were gliding across white-capped waves. A ferry was coming in past the breakwater. A group of teenagers were hanging out on the sandbar.

"I might go for a sail," Mars said, figuring that would get rid of some cobwebs.

"Why don't you call your father first?" Sally said sounding worried. "You need to tell him how the meeting went. Maybe he'll have an update."

"Good idea," Mars said. He was eating slower than usual mostly because he couldn't keep his mind on what he was doing. He was sure that Sally assumed that he was worried about his job, but he was also worried about Angela and about prison. One of them was going.

When he finished lunch, he excused himself to make the call. He speed-dialed his father's office as he made his way out the wooden walkway towards the beach. By the time he reached the dunes, Barbara - his Dad's secretary - had patched him through to his cell at the club.

"How did it go, Mars?"

"I still have a job, but they put me on administrative leave until they see if Angela confesses."

"If you need any financial help, I -"

"No thanks. Not yet anyway. Thankfully, it's a paid leave, for now."

"Anything new come up?"

"Not really. Our CEO, Randal Gregory, did make it perfectly clear that he would fire me if my story doesn't pan out. If they don't make a deal with Angela, she may not confess; then I'm toast. Either way, Mr. Gregory made no promises."

"If she loves you like you say, she'll confess."

The 'if' pissed Mars off. He drew a deep breath. The air was fouled by a dead fish nearby. He could hardly blame his father for doubting Angela's love. He was right. It was that simple; if she loved him she would confess.

"If she comes clean and they still fire you, maybe we'll sue them. The security breach should no longer be grounds – good move there, son."

Mars smiled.

"And you said they may not have the evidence to link all the pieces, right?"

"I don't know for sure. The files have been deleted, but there is always the chance that Contingency back-ups of them exist off-site – but they may not think of that. Plus, I don't think the test file would have been backed up... But if they do try to fire me, I don't think I want to fight it. Screw them. If they don't want me, it'll be their loss. I've worked my ass off for them. Maybe doing something else wouldn't be so horrible."

"For what it is worth, I think your grandfather had the right idea, Mars. Do whatever you have to do to stay at the beach. You used to be good at carpentry."

Mars grinned. All these years he had thought that his father was oblivious to his likes and dislikes. "Yeah, I would love to make furniture or repair classic wooden boats. But it's doubtful that I could make a good living at it."

"You're probably right. I think we better fight to keep that job of yours. You can piddle with woodworking when you retire."

"I hope she confesses." Mars said contemplating the nightmare of going to trial. "We can't do anything that will force them to make public -"

"Understood," his father interrupted. "Let me call Abe

and see if he has anything to share. I'll call you back if I have any news. Hang in there, son, it'll work out."

Mars desperately wanted to believe it, but he couldn't be sure that Angela was coming to his rescue. Even if she did love him - and he was almost sure she did - she had Vinny to contend with. He was an unknown, and so was her lawyer.

I need a Plan B.

Mars came up with the brainstorm as he tacked back to the beach on his sailboard. He showered and dressed quickly. A half hour later he was sitting on the veranda of Baywood Golf Club drinking a frosty beer, trying to be inconspicuous. Like half the other guys, he had on a golf cap and sunglasses. He hoped it was enough to keep him from being recognized.

He checked out the golfers on the practice green. His eyes moved to the driving range. He scanned each stall then moved over to the railing to get a better look at the guy in the second to last station. He was hitting wedges. It looked like his CEO, but Mars had envisioned him having a much better swing since he was rumored to have a single-digit handicap.

Coo Coo Coo Choo! Mars spotted Mitzi Robinson in the next stall. He had noticed that her left hand was never as tan as her right one, and correctly assumed she was a golfer too. It had occurred to him belatedly that she probably shared the 3:08 tee time with her boss.

Mars relaxed knowing there was no way he was going

to lose his job now. They were definitely an item. Well almost definitely. Time would hopefully tell.

He noticed that her swing looked smoother than Mr. Gregory's. Mars watched her for a while then turned his focus back to his CEO. He had moved directly from his wedge to his driver - that did not bode well, but the results were surprisingly good. In fact, they were very impressive given his over-the-top swing. Somehow he managed to square his club at just the right point.

Randal put his driver in his bag and went over to Mitzi. She hit more smooth iron shots. To Mars's delight, Mr. Gregory moved in close. He said something to his employee then put his arms around her from behind. He placed his hands over hers and guided her through a slow motion swing.

You should let her show you, Mars thought as he got his camera in position. He zoomed in just in time to snap a shot of Lightship Bank and Trust's CEO, Randal Gregory, as he accepted a grateful on-the-lips kiss from his able-bodied Administrative Assistant.

Yes!

Mars got several more incriminating shots before Mitzi resumed her practice. Then there was an even better photo opportunity when they were by their cart. Mars could not believe his good fortune. In a way he felt bad because this was really none of his business, but his CEO's words echoed in his head, *rules are rules,* and fraternization with subordinates was also against them. Then there was the matter of their respective marriages.

One could even argue that the CEO's affair was a security risk; that having this big of a personal secret could set him up to be bribed. Mars preferred to think of this as an insurance policy that he hoped he would never have to use. He liked the man and did not want to disrupt whatever balance his CEO had found in his life.

Mars wasn't proud of what he was doing, but – as Angela had said of him leaving his computer unattended – this seemed like a godsend. It was his best shot at restoring harmony in his own world.

When Mars had all of the pictures he needed, he put the camera away, but he could not stop watching them. They reminded him of what he felt for Angela – the passion that had gotten him in this trouble. Mars would never get enough of her. He longed to have his arms around her one more time... even if it was only to help her with her swing.

When he refocused, Randal and Mitzi were driving out to the first tee. Mars retreated into the shade where he sat remembering the day he and Angela had golfed. He visualized her in that *alluring shade of pink* that his grandfather had warned him about. He had been so attracted to her that whole day. She had his attention from the minute she came into that conference room. Actually she had it the first time she took his Hot Italian sub order decades ago.

He sipped his beer and thought of the prepaid cell phone that was in his briefcase. He was itching to call her, to see what she was going to do. He needed to hear her voice, tell her what he had just done, but he knew that he should not. He worried that maybe her husband would convince her to save *their* family life, by letting Mars hang. He wondered if she would do whatever she needed to do to keep peace with Vinny.

Mars was in a sweat. He went inside and collapsed on one of the couches in the bar. The waitress caught his eye and brought him a second cold beer. He reviewed the digital images and couldn't help but smile. They were sufficiently incriminating: the first kiss, then another where his hands appeared to be precariously close to her breasts. He had several good shots at the cart. One of them clearly showed her hand on his butt as he whispered something in her ear.

Mars felt empowered. He knew that he had exactly what he needed if his CEO was tempted to make an unfavorable decision. As long as Angela did the right thing - and deep in his soul, he believed she would - he was going to be able to keep his job.

He was ready to play hard-ball if need be.

81   - Friday 3:34 p.m.

The untraceable cell phone tugged at Mars the whole way home, but he decided he really didn't want anymore drama today. He just wanted to go home.

Sally noticed the change in him the minute he walked through the door. She gave him a big smooch on the cheek. "It's good to see you smiling again. Where did you go in such a hurry?" She pushed back from his chest and tried to read his face.

"I had to run out to Baywood." He extracted four pictures from a photo envelope and spread them out on the kitchen island. "This is my CEO and his long-term Administrative Assistant."

Sally gave him a blank look.

He explained, "She's his subordinate."

"I don't know, Mars, she looks pretty willing," Sally said unconvinced.

"She is, but they are both pretty married." Mars said knowing that was the trump card.

"Oh," Sally said in a tone filled with disapproval. "So what, you're going to add bribery to the charges?" She obviously did not approve of his actions too.

"I don't want to, but if Angela confesses and Mr. Gregory still wants to fire me just because I broke a rule, then..." He stopped. She had already walked away from the pictures.

Mars realized that, in his exuberance, he may have made a mistake. He really hadn't meant to interject the topic of adultery. He shouldn't have shared the pictures with his wife. He should have left infidelity out of the equation – at least as far as Sally was concerned.

He followed her out to the deck. "Sally I have to do whatever I can to keep my job. I hate to stoop to this level, but I *will* use these if I have to." He put them back in the envelope.

"I agree that what your CEO is doing is morally worse than you guys all leaving your computers on. If anyone should be fired, it should be him, but still..."

Christ, what have I done? He back-peddled, "I'm not here to judge their personal choices, but I need to save this life we all enjoy. I'm no Nakashima. I would have to make a lot of furniture to earn the salary I have now. I am not going to let them fire me without a fight."

She didn't respond. He changed the topic, "Where's Beck?"

"She's down on the beach. I think she's trying the sailboard again." They both remembered Beck getting frustrated the last time and giving up. "Why don't you go ahead down and see if you can help her. I have a few things to do before dinner."

Mars gave his wife a long hug. They really were good together. He remembered how content he had been before he and Angela collided again.

"Go," his wife said patting him firmly on his butt.

As he changed into a pair of surf trunks, he longed to feel settled again. Sally's reaction to the adulterous pictures reinforced what he had always felt. If she ever found out what he had done, she would be gone in a heartbeat – with the kids.

No, she'll stay in the house. I'll go.

That possibility left him feeling nauseated and so did the thought of never being with Angela again. It was torturous not being able to talk to her.

Rebecca saw him as he crested the dunes. She sailed in and sat on her board yelling, "Dad, Dad, you should have seen me. I sailed all the way down to Gram and Gramps's." That was Sally's parent's cottage about five blocks south.

"Wow that's great, Beck."

"Get the other board, Dad. Ple-ase"

Mars assessed the wind. It was a mild breeze. Ordinarily he would hold out for more.

"Please, Dad, please."

His daughter's enthusiasm was impossible to refuse. "Okay, I'll go get the sail." He jogged to the garage, returned with it then dragged the board across the beach into the water. He popped in the mast.

After paddling out, he stood on his board and hoisted the red, white and blue sail. He watched as Beck raised hers. There was more wind than Mars had thought. They sailed all the way to the public beach. Beck looked very comfortable on the board. She was grinning ear to ear.

Her smile was contagious. *Life is good,* Mars thought as the breeze blew his hair back. His board cut easily through the waves. Watching his daughter, he knew that no matter how much passion he felt for Angela, he belonged here with his family on this beautiful bay.

This is home.

"Race you back," she yelled as she came about unexpectedly.

Mars gave her a hundred-yard head start then took

off after her. As he pulled along side of her she was laughing, pleading, "Daddy, please."

Mars did not let her win, but he made sure that he did not beat her by much. He dropped his sail in the water and sat down on the board. "Great job, Beck," he said looking up at her proudly. "You almost had me."

"I've been practicing," she confided before she dove in and starting swimming parallel to the beach. She was a fish - just like he had been as a kid. He slipped into the water, slicked his hair back then pulled himself back onto the cool board.

It occurred to him that he had not thought of the embezzlement or Angela in the last half hour. It was a milestone. He shut his eyes and basked in the sun which soon absorbed into his navy-blue trunks. He shuddered as he remembered her soft warm lips -

Oh, shit!

Beck had flipped him off his sailboard. She was giggling like crazy when he resurfaced. He grabbed her, pinning her arms to her side. "Just for that young lady," he said as he threw her as high as he could. It wasn't very high. His baby girl was growing up too fast.

82 - The Long Weekend

Mars spent a quiet weekend with his family. Peter worked until five each day, but the four of them had dinners and the evenings together before Peter went out with his friends. It was nice.

He and Peter ran together each morning. His son was training for fall soccer which would start in a few weeks. Mars had always made a conscious effort to keep the communications lines open with his son. He had never been able to talk to his own father, but he had a great rapport with his grandfather. It had meant the world to him, and he wanted that closeness with Peter.

As they ran, Mars asked his son about girls. Peter reluctantly confessed that he had had a few short romances over the summer, but - he insisted - there was no one special. Mars embarrassed his son by once again giving him the safe-sex lecture. He toyed with the idea of telling him what had happened with his grandparents, and what happened thirty years ago with Angela. Both stories contained some life lessons, but Mars's emotions were too raw.

Another time, he thought.

During those long days, Mars and Beck spent many hours on the bay. She was really getting into sailboarding and even ventured out in brisk winds on Sunday. She did great. They both loved every minute of it. She bragged to Peter at Sunday dinner, and he surprised his father by suggesting that he go out with his little sister that evening.

Sally and Mars sailed the Sunfish, and the four of them had a blast. In most ways it was an idyllic weekend. The topic of the embezzlement was never discussed.

Monday morning, when Mars got back from his run, the reality of the situation was impossible to ignore; he had no job to go to.

Sally tried to convince him that it was a sweet deal, not working and still getting paid. He tried to play along, but his employment situation was on his mind whenever Angela wasn't.

To occupy himself, and to feel productive, Mars made waffles and sausage for breakfast. Peter must have smelled it because he came downstairs half an hour earlier than usual.

"Awesome, Dad, are you on vacation?"

Mars and Sally had decided not to tell the kids what was going on. They didn't want to worry them. "Yep, we're in between projects so I'm taking some time off."

"Cool."

"Set the table for me, and you can have the first batch." Mars got the maple syrup out, poured it in a measuring cup and microwaved it. While it was heating he got out the OJ and the butter.

Mars put the first whole waffle on his son's plate, started the second then went to get the girls. Sally had showered, and was just coming out of the bathroom. He gave her a good morning peck on the cheek.

"Breakfast is ready, babe."

"I could get used to this." She smiled and walked towards the kitchen. Mars followed her and squeezed past her to check on the next waffle. Once it was ready, he gave half to Sally and half to Peter, poured a third on the griddle, and went to wake his daughter.

Mars muzzled his morning beard against his daughter's cheek, and whispered, "Wake up, Becky Bear," and then in his best Goldilocks tone, "the waffles are just right."

"Daddy, what are you doing here? Isn't it Monday?"

He grabbed a toe that was sticking out of the sheets. "I'm taking some time off. Come on or Peter will eat them all up."

Beck sat up, and rubbed her sleepy eyes. Mars hustled back to the kitchen just in time to rescue waffle number three. Peter's plate was clean again so he gave him half and buttered the other half for Beck just as she stumbled in.

Mars used the rest of the batter and kept the last waffles warm in the oven until he could sit. By then Peter was rushing off to his lifeguard job.

As Mars ate, his wife reminded him that she was otherwise engaged. "I'm going down to the Art League for a watercolor class. It's today and tomorrow, ten to three. I'll stop on the way home and do some grocery shopping. I should be home by four-thirty," Sally informed him.

"And how about you, Rebecca, what do you want to do? You've got me all to yourself."

Now fully awake, Beck almost squealed, "Can we go golfing?"

Mars had expected her to say she wanted to sail, but now that she mentioned it, golf seemed like a great idea. That was the one activity that might keep his mind off his problems. "You should have seen me hit the ball in

Hatteras, Dad. I made it over the water on that long par three." The family always played a scramble when Sally's clan went to the Outer Banks in July. Mars had missed the trip, but he knew which hole she was referring to.

"Wow, that's great!" He got up and looked at the club's calendar on the side of the refrigerator. Becky watched anxiously. "Nothing is scheduled so we'll leave when Mom leaves, around nine-thirty."

"I'll meet you two back here at three-thirty-ish and we'll go to the beach," Sally added as she left to get ready to leave.

"Can I drive the cart?"

Mars didn't want his daughter to be interested in golf for the wrong reasons. "Not today, we'll walk. It'll be good for us."

It didn't deter her. "Cool," she yelled as she ran up the stairs to get ready for their day.

83   - Saturday 7:30 a.m.

The week had passed painfully slow. Whenever Mars's mind was not a hundred percent occupied, which was most of the time, he was thinking of the embezzlement and of Angela. He agonized over whether to call her or not, but each time he decided not to further jeopardize his family, or hers.

Repeated calls to his father provided no insights. It seemed that Abe Bernstein was not at liberty to share any information about his client with them. Mars had no clue what was going on. He assumed that if, or when, Bernstein brokered a deal that it would make the local news. So each morning Mars scanned the papers and checked LB&T's website for a news release.

He came up empty until Saturday morning. On page one of LB&T's website he saw the short blurb:

> Former Banksall Software, Inc. employee Sofia Angela Pitasi pled guilty to felony fraud charges for the dormant account embezzlement at Lightship Bank and Trust. As a result of a plea bargain, Ms.

Pitasi will return portions of the monies and will be making restitution payments until the funds are repaid in full. She will also serve a jail term the duration of which is not yet known.

All customers and stockholders should rest assured that LB&T has conducted a thorough review of their dormant account processing and has procedures to insure that a similar fraud can not be perpetrated in the future.

Oh my God, she confessed. A gigantic wave of relief rushed over him even as it hit him that Angela was going to jail. He reread it. He was relieved that his name was not mentioned. Neither was the Deposit Account System's client manager - Mary Thompson's. He was happy for them both, but his heart raced.

I've got to see Angela.

Mars grabbed his cell phone and hurried outside and down onto the beach. He called his father first. "Mars, I was going to call you at eight. I guess you saw this morning's paper."

"It's on the bank's website."

"So, you're all clear." His father sounded upbeat and relieved, then more sullen he added, "Legally. What about work? Have you heard from them? Anything new with your job?"

"Not yet. When will Angela have to go?"

"Abe called me late last night. The sentencing hearing is in two weeks. He's hoping for thirteen months, with parole after seven."

"Oh God, seven months," Mars muttered.

"It's a great deal. The money she still had helped. And

she's willing to make restitution payments."

"When will she go?" Mars was trying to think how he could get to see her.

"Abe said that she plans to get everything in order and be ready to go the day she's sentenced. She doesn't want to delay the inevitable."

Two weeks.

"Thanks, Dad, for everything. I've got to go." Mars's head was buzzing.

"Son, I hope you aren't planning on calling -" his father started to reason with him.

"I appreciate all of your help, but I'll ... I'll talk to you later."

Mars sat on the sand. Its dampness made only the slightest impression on him as he mulled over his options. Fifteen minutes later he walked back to the house where he found Sally making coffee.

"Sally, I just talked to Dad. Angela made a deal." He kissed her lightly on the forehead. She wrapped her arms tightly around him.

"So it's over?" she asked looking up at him for confirmation, a tentative smile on her lips until she saw his pain. He couldn't believe that he had turned Angela in, and that she was going to jail.

He couldn't tell his wife what was bothering him. "I'm in the clear legally, but I still don't know about my job."

"But your CEO can't fire you, Mars. It's not right, you didn't do anything, plus – thank God – you have those pictures."

Mars agreed, but his mind was on Angela.

84 - 9:31 a.m.

As soon as Sally was out the door to run errands, Mars retrieved the pre-paid cell phone that he had bought and never used. He carried it outside and stretched out in the hammock. It was another hazy, hot and humid day. The wind was picking up. Mars assumed that the incoming weather was the outer-bands of Hallie blowing past Bermuda.

He watched the wind-whipped bay, and thought about the deal Angela had made. It seemed about as good as she could have reasonably hoped for - she did commit a felony - but somehow Mars had deluded himself into believing that she might not have to do any time. Knowing that she would was a shock.

He counted the months and figured that - best case - she would be out by spring. *Oh God, she'll be in prison for Thanksgiving and Christmas. Good Lord...*The realization bummed him out. He didn't want to depress her any more than she probably was already so he resisted calling. Five minutes later, he entered the number that was emblazoned in his brain.

"Hello?" her voice sounded tentative.

Mars knew that she didn't recognize the new cell phone number. "Angela, it's me, can you talk?"

"Mars?" She still wasn't sure.

"Yes. Are you okay?"

"I think so. In a way I feel more relaxed than I have for a long time. Tony's doing great, that's what really matters. I guess I am relieved to know my fate. I just won't know how long I have to serve until the hearing."

"Dad said that Bernstein thinks you'll be out in seven months."

"That's what we're hoping for, but nothing is definite yet."

"So where are you now?" Mars asked.

"I'm at the Rehab center waiting for Tony to finish his physical therapy."

"Angela, I hate that you have to go... that I can't see you -"

"I know. I wish we could..." she said quietly. Then with more vehemence than he had ever heard from her, she added, "but unfortunately our fathers made sure that *we* are not an option."

It seemed that some of the bitterness that had left him had found her. "I guess we have to focus on all that we would have missed if they hadn't intervened. You have Vinny and Tony. I have Sally, Peter and Beck."

She didn't comment. Mars continued with an inane cliché. "We can't have everything." He regretted it before it left his mouth. Right now, it seemed that she was everything and that he would be nothing with her gone from his life again. They were meant to be together. He was sure of it.

"I know we can't," she agreed, sounding resigned.

Mars couldn't bear talking about it. He changed the topic. "Has anyone said where you will go? Which facility?"

"A woman's prison in Kentucky, I think. I just hope that wherever I end up I'll have access to books and stuff."

Mars had no idea if all prisons had libraries, but he imagined that they did. Plenty of criminals got college degrees, so surely Angela could get a steady stream of books, maybe even take some classes.

"Have you considered pursuing your poetry?"

"No..." Mars could hear her wheels turning, "but maybe I will. Or maybe some song lyrics"

"Better you than me," he laughed. "Maybe you could write a novel. Our truth is definitely stranger than most fiction."

"Now you're pressing it," she laughed. "I'll be okay. How about you and your job?"

"I don't know for sure, but I seriously doubt they'll fire me." He didn't feel like wasting their precious time talking about the photos that should provide job security.

"I hope you're right," she sounded unsure.

"I'll be thinking of you," Mars said thinking it was a huge understatement.

"And remembering," Angela added.

He could feel her smiling as he recalled their night together. It was supposed to be enough for a lifetime. Maybe it would be, but he knew that he would never entirely let go of his dream for more.

"Mars, Tony's ready, I better go..."

Mars's heart sank.

She added, "I want you to be happy."

"I'll be okay," Mars replied then tried out his Bogart impression, "We'll always have Baltimore."

She laughed and they hung up without declaring their love. Mars regretted it immediately. He lay in the hammock breathing in the sea air, trying to soothe his soul as he contemplated life without Angela.

He hoped he would find contentment in the life he had always cherished. He still had everything that he had before they collided again. The only possible exception was his job, but he knew he still had the photo-card to play with his CEO.

As Mars swung back and forth in the hammock he thought about how he had loved teenage Angela, and consultant Sofia, and the whole package - Sofia Angela Ignazio Pitasi.   He was finally a believer in the all-consuming love of fairy tales.

A moot point.

He realized he was being given some sort of cosmic mulligan. It wasn't exactly a do-over, but he was getting a second chance.

"Dad, I'm ready." Beck called from the deck. She had a cute little golf outfit on complete with a visor.

He needed to get moving if he was going to make their tee time. He walked toward his daughter thinking this was as good of a life as anyone deserved.

Back-abrading passion aside, he could not help but note.

He had just hit an awesome Bubba-Watson-like shot from deep in the woods, and he was back in an almost-perfect position. He could hear his grandfather warning him not to visualize the trophy in his hands until the last stroke had been made; there was still time to screw this up.

Focus on the next shot.

Reader Feedback

Thanks for reading my novel. If you enjoyed it, I would appreciate your assistance in spreading the word. Please consider recommending *ON A DIME - Senseless in Lewes* to your friends and family.

Amazon rankings help sell books. If you have an Amazon account, please take the time to sign in, and then search for my novel by title or author name. Once you navigate to *ON A DIME's* page, click / touch the LIKE icon to change it to LIKED. You can also add your comments as a CUSTOMER REVIEW.

If you found typos or other errors that you would like to report, feel free to send them, along with any other feedback, to RevereReed@aol.com. I will try to respond to all e-mails.

To stay abreast of any news related to my book, please LIKE and follow me on Facebook.com/RevereReed.

Made in the USA
Las Vegas, NV
12 December 2022

61995510R00215